I0535468

Heresy

Arianna Swain

Copyright © 2014 Arianna Swain

Cover Art courtesy of Cornado and protected by copyright

No part of this book may be reproduced or transmitted in any form or by any means, electronic or mechanical, including photocopying, recording, or by any information storage and retrieval system, without permission in writing from the publisher. For information address: Merope Press, Los Angeles, California 90068.

This book is a work of fiction. Any resemblance to people, alive or dead, is purely coincidental. All characters, situations and places are fictional and the product of the author's imagination.

All rights reserved.

ISBN: 069226549X
ISBN-13: 9780692265499

DEDICATION

I would like to dedicate this book to my family, friends and all of the people who have supported me through the years. I know it's sometimes been a tough road but I never would have realized my dreams without you. I love you all and thank you for always being there for me.

ACKNOWLEDGMENTS

First and foremost I have to thank God for getting me through the last few years and helping me to finally make this book a reality. For those of you who were fans of the first book, thank you for sticking it out with me and making sure that this book saw the light of day. A very special thank you to my wonderful parents and my grandparents who have always supported and encouraged me, even when I know I made it hard for them to do so. I would also like to thank my very best friends, you know who you are, for always being there to bounce ideas off of, talk character stories in the middle of the night and providing unwavering dedication and support. To my readers, I sincerely thank you because without you my stories would languish in a dusty notebook unread. I sincerely hope that you all enjoy the book.

The goddess glided across the desolate desert landscape, foliage springing from the barren ground at her every step. Danalia stood in the middle of all of this new life her presence was creating, watching her half-brother curiously. A vine reached up from the ground seeking the hand of its maker. It snaked up her arm to wind in her golden hair, adorning her with its red and white blossoms. Her grass green eyes finally met his and she smiled at the anxiety evident in his expression. The very traits that he used in his attempt to show confidence in her presence only served to reinforce the knowledge that he was half-human in her mind. Danalia's bell-like laughter echoed across the sand dunes as she watched Traegar's dark blonde eyebrows push together, forming unflattering creases in the suntanned skin across his normally handsome face.

"Why so scared, brother? Are you afraid of me or what you have to ask of me?" When he didn't respond immediately her smile grew as she caressed the vine around her delicate pale hand like a beloved pet. "Is it possible that you've been too long among the humans, Traegar?"

His green gaze met her own defiantly. "I'm not afraid of you or my request."

"Then you must be afraid of the cost. For whatever the mighty Traegar has to ask it must indeed be a great favor to warrant an audience with me."

"Do not mock me because I sought you out. I remember which of us is the half-breed without your special brand of sarcasm. Drop the act. I need your help as a creator. I want to know how to bring someone back from the dead."

"How did she die?"

"I didn't say that it was a woman."

Danalia laughed brightly, her long curled hair falling back over the shoulder left bare by the long silk dress that did nothing to mask the tall column of her body. "Unless your preferences have changed since last we met it must be a woman. Otherwise it would be Anayasis. And I know he lives."

"She gave her life to a succubus," he admitted.

One eyebrow raised in question as she regarded him curiously. "The white witch? Surely you do not ask this for a mortal. Would Anayasis not assist you?"

"He doesn't know how to do what I'm asking for. I want her brought back as an adult, the same age that she was when she died."

"She is many months gone. Her body has been destroyed."

He stared at her impatiently as she toyed with her flowers. "Don't act like you can't do it, Danalia. We both know better than that."

"Would you have me infuse her with lust as well, to ensure that she runs willingly into your arms?" she shot back, her anger turning the blooms around her a deep crimson.

"No! I just, I want her to live. She shouldn't have died like that. Not for me."

"Do you do this for guilt or for love?"

"Does it matter?"

She heard the change in his tone and the flower at her fingertips wilted and died from the sadness of it. "I am sorry for you that she is gone."

"Can you bring her back," he requested quietly.

"What would you give for me to do this?"

"Anything."

She stepped up, close enough that their bodies almost touched. The life in her eyes met the pain in his and she turned away from the despair there. "Be careful what you wish for, my brother." Danalia stepped past him, continuing to bring life to the desolation surrounding them. Traegar closed his eyes and returned to his own world.

"I cannot bring back what has already been born."

1

Tyler stared across the empty expanse of the living room in the house that he shared with his brother and sister-in-law. His blank, unseeing eyes did not notice the earth-tone wood and linen furnishings, the walnut floors or the crème colored walls that stared back at him. Instead, he sat in his worn, brown leather chair, holding a shot glass full of vodka and wishing that the hazel eyes he imagined were staring back at his green ones. He knew that Karina was gone, but deep in his soul, he didn't feel it.

Is that your soul or your heart you're feeling? The disembodied, annoying voice whispered in his ear, taunting him, making him wonder if he was truly going mad.

"Fuck you," Tyler whispered, taking his shot before reaching across the table to take the one that he had poured for his absent guest. Next month Karina would have been dead for a year and Tyler still couldn't truthfully answer the question of whether he really loved her or he just felt guilty that he couldn't save her. The car crash replayed in his head like a horror movie he was watching in slow motion. He saw her step into the road, the Hummer hit her and then several other cars crashed into each other, trapping her body into a coffin made of twisted steel, broken glass and crushed plastic. He remembered running to her, giving her his Greek god blood, trying to save her in the only way he knew how. And she died anyway. And it was his fault. He should've known what she'd done, that she'd made a deal exchanging her life for the succubus Sabina to kill Zane on that lonely desert road. Tyler poured another shot, placed the glass in front of Karina's usual place on the beige sofa and poured himself another drink. He saluted his missing best friend and stared morosely into her drink as he took his shot.

Before she died, Tyler hadn't realized how much they had bonded, how much he relied on her to be there. It's not like they'd ever really done anything. There was that one time in Las Vegas when they had almost…what had they almost done? Tyler wasn't even sure. It could've been a kiss. It could've been a lot more. Maybe. He still had the feeling that there was some opportunity he had missed that night, one that had forever changed the course of his life. During the year after that night he remembered doing foolish things to see her smile, hearing her laugh while he attempted to teach her yoga and they drank wine to forget their missteps. Drunken yoga. It was their personal joke. It was one of many of their personal jokes. One of many things that Tyler had attempted to forget in the months that had passed since he lost her. Not that he had any right. He had been her friend. His sister-in-law, Jane, had been Karina's twin sister.

Jane had been crushed by Karina's demise. She had spent weeks trying everything that she could think of to beg, bargain and plead for her sister's life to be returned to this plane. After a while, when there was no response, when there was nothing left for her to do, when nothing had been left but for Jane to accept her sister's death, she had. She had given up. She stopped trying. She went on with her life, with her marriage to his brother, Jared. She's scheduled to leave in three days for a book tour and to visit the set of a movie based on her book series in Vancouver and she didn't even care. Tyler couldn't stop. He couldn't stop thinking about Karina, wondering what she should be doing, feeling like someone was missing every time he entered the room or walked into her old room at the house which didn't even show signs that she had ever lived in it anymore. The slate had been wiped clean. The world had forgotten. And he would never forgive her sister for accepting that she was gone.

Danalia had been his last hope and she had failed him miserably. His half-sister, a full-blooded Greek goddess, the last born to his family in several centuries, was a creator. She built things out of nothing. She created life in places where absolutely nothing should have been able to grow. And she couldn't do anything to help him. If anyone was able to breathe life into Karina's long buried body, it would've been her. And she wasn't willing to help him. She said she couldn't. And without that, he knew that there was no hope of finding her, no way to bring her back. Yet he couldn't stop. He couldn't back down. He couldn't forget her, let her slip further away from him. Every day Tyler could feel Karina moving further and further away from him. And he refused let her go. As he drank both of the poured drinks, he realized that in all of his years on earth, Karina really had become his best friend. He wasn't sure how it had happened. One day they didn't know each other, the next they were drinking together and laughing about their past experiences. Shortly after that they were watching every season of *True Blood* together like it was a contact sport, cheering for their favorite characters to survive the episode, relaxing together on the couch, slapping each other playfully when they argued and collapsing together exhausted when the hour was over. That was what had really bonded them. A stupid, melodramatic television show. And now Tyler couldn't imagine his life without her. He couldn't let her go. And after over thirty years, he finally understood why Jane's death in her previous life had driven his brother crazy. He just wished Jared would fully answer his questions and tell him how he'd managed to bring her back to life. Even if Karina came back as a child, he could wait on her. It's not like he didn't know he'd live long enough. His birthdays had already stopped meaning anything, even in his early thirties. Tyler wouldn't start aging again for over one hundred years. Even then, the aging would be a slow process. With an average lifespan of one hundred and seventy-nine years, time was the one commodity he knew he had plenty of. His life was as guaranteed as he could make it. As one of the two golden princes, demi-god sons of Apollo who had made a deal to die and be reborn on the mortal plane every two centuries rather than live on Olympus, Tyler knew that he could die, he just knew it wasn't a permanent state. The deal that he and his brother had made many centuries ago allowed them the freedom to live as humans without the consequences that the mortals lived with such as illness, a short lifespan and death. They just had to reinvent themselves every few decades so that the humans didn't notice that they didn't change.

But Jared refused to part with his secret, no matter how much Tyler begged. Then one day during the last several months he had stopped asking, stopped begging and had started searching for his own answers. He didn't want to believe that there was no answer to be found, that he had lost Karina forever before they'd even had a chance to see what was between them. Before he'd had the chance to tell her all of the things he'd realized since she'd been gone. He still wasn't sure that he was in love with her. The thing was he'd realized it didn't matter. Tyler didn't care if he loved her or if she loved him. Somehow, in the middle of all of the drama and the distractions that permeated their lives, she had become his partner, even if there'd never been anything romantic between them. And then Karina had backed away during the last few months of her life. She'd taken a job in Beverly Hills, moved from their house in the hills above the Palisades to a small studio in Hollywood and suddenly he never saw her anymore. She stopped coming over, quit returning his calls and even only spoke to her sister rarely. Tyler knew now that she had known she was getting close to the end of her life, closer to the moment when the agreement she'd made with the succubus Sabina had necessitated her death. He hadn't known then of the agreement. None of them had. He and Jared had been tasked with killing Zane, Jane's former soul-mate and a supernatural soul that had misbehaved so badly that the gods had determined he needed to be destroyed. Fearing that Jane wouldn't forgive the two of them for the transgression, Karina had arranged in secret with Sabina to have her take Zane's soul for Alecto, the Fury, rather than having one of them do it. Karina had been right; Jane might have never forgiven Jared. But that one act hadn't been worth Karina's life. Tyler could admit to himself that he wanted to find her, probably for selfish reasons, but he also wanted to make sure that she was all right, wherever she was. If such a thing as Heaven existed, Karina Jamison definitely deserved to be there.

Tyler pushed off the dark thoughts that plagued his mind and continued drinking for both of them. Being in the house alone, he was almost tempted to carry on a conversation with the sofa like Karina was there, listening to him and swallowing her own alcohol. If he gave into the temptation, he feared that one of two things would happen. One, he would truly lose what little potentially remained of his sanity. Or two, he would just realize that he was lonelier than he ever wanted to admit.

After a few more moments he heard the front door open followed by the sound of his brother Jared and Jane entering the house. Jane giggled at something that Jared said, whispering a response before they both stopped short, catching sight of Tyler sitting in his chair, both glasses in front of him in their usual places, the half-empty bottle of vodka resting on the coffee table between them. Tyler didn't acknowledge their entrance, he simply continued to stare straight ahead, lost in his own thoughts as he continued drinking first from his glass and then from the one he laid out for Karina. He did notice that his telepathy where his brother and sister-in-law were concerned wasn't working again. He should've known as soon as they made the decision to return to the house. This time he didn't even hear them before they were in the driveway. One of Tyler's superpowers, or his curse as he sometimes thought of it, was that he could hear a pin drop from nearly a mile away. Jane drove either a vintage Mustang or restored Corvette

Stingray, depending on her mood that day. Both have very distinctive engine sounds and they live at the end of a nearly five mile private road. No one came up here unless they were known or expected. Regardless of his enhanced sensory ability, Jane had to stop shielding between the two of them and Tyler. It was beginning to get annoying, at least for Tyler who'd always had his brother's voice in his head.

Sensing his discomfort, Jane stepped away from Jared and slipped quietly down the hall. He heard the door to the bedroom close and his brother's footsteps as he hesitantly crossed from the stairs at the entryway to the chair that Tyler was perched on. "Ty, we've talked about this. This kind of stuff isn't healthy. It really upsets Jane." Jared took a seat on the couch across from his brother, moving directly into his line of sight.

Tyler slowly allowed his eyes to focus on his brother. "That's not your seat."

Jared leaned back on the sofa, his dark hair sliding over his closed blue eyes as he contemplated what words he could offer his brother to help ease his suffering. It had been nearly a year and things had just gotten worse for Tyler. Jared didn't know how he could've missed it, not seen the signs, particularly since he himself had experienced the same kind of loss that had driven him to the brink of insanity when he'd lost Jane in her previous life. "You have to figure out a way to let this go before it destroys you. You can't bring her back."

"I could if you would tell me how." Tyler heard the anger in his voice and didn't care if he was projecting or justified.

Jared shook his head sadly. "We're not having this conversation again. It's not the same situation. What I did for Jane won't help you." He stared down at his long, thin pale hands and noted the small amount of pink color that had been deposited there from the day spent in the Malibu summer sun.

"Out of everyone we know on every plane of existence, you were the one I really thought wouldn't give me shit for this, Jared." Tyler downed both drinks and poured two more. Jared grabbed the second glass before Tyler could claim them both.

"I understand what you're going through. I get that what happened to Karina was wrong and it wasn't just your fault. It was my fault too and there's nothing I can do to take that back. Out of everything that I can give to my wife, the one thing that I can't give her that she wants is her sister back. If I wouldn't do it for you, don't you think that I would do it for Jane if I could? How do you know that Karina is unhappy wherever she is or that she wants to come back from wherever that is to this life? She'd be a mortal in a house of immortals again. Do you think that this is something that she wants to come back to?"

Tyler turned his angry green gaze on his brother, running his fingers through his short dark blonde hair so viciously that he thought he might actually pull some of it out. "I'm sorry, did I miss something? Did you contact Jane's soul in the great beyond or wherever she was hanging out and ask her permission? Did you give her a choice when you yanked her back to this plane so that she could be with you and you could turn her into a goddess?"

"No, Ty, I didn't," Jared snapped, feeling himself beginning to lose his patience. "And I should have. I should've asked, I should've not been selfish but I can't find it in myself to regret what I did because I love my wife so much that I would do anything for her. I made a choice and I've stuck by it. But I loved her. I knew I loved her. I knew that there was something special about her and I couldn't let her die like that. Can you say the same about Karina? Do you love her that much? Do you need her to keep breathing? Because if you do I won't stand in your way anymore. I'll tell you whatever you want to know so that you can know that you tried everything to get her back. But that's all it's going to be is you knowing that you tried everything because you know as well as I do that once a soul is sacrificed to a succubus, it's lost. There's no second chance, no coming back, no regaining the life that was lost. Souls are food to them and they do not return their sacrifices to the land of the living and there's absolutely nothing that you can do to change over two thousand years of history."

Tyler knew that his brother's questions were fair and he couldn't help the anger and helplessness that they provoked. "I don't know. I just know that she shouldn't have died like that. She deserved so much better than the mess that we subjected her to."

"No, Karina did not deserve what happened to her. But how many people die every day that don't deserve what happened to them? We can't change them all. Even if we could, we don't have that power." Jared leaned forward earnestly, trying to get his brother to see reason before Jane gave into the anger he could feel her trying to control and stormed into the room. "Karina made her choice and cannot be saved. There is nothing left to save. Even if there was, how do you know that wherever she is, she wants to be saved?"

"I don't know if she wants to be saved but I do know that she's still out there somewhere. I have to find her. I have to do everything that I can to make sure that she has a choice and even if this isn't the life she wants, if I'm not the life she chooses, she at least has a choice. You gave Jane a choice. She didn't have to choose to be with you but she did. How can you deny me the same thing that you fought so hard for?"

"Because it's not your fucking decision!" Jane burst angrily into the room, electricity visibly pulsing around her fingertips. "You cannot take her life away from her again!" A fire bolt shot out of her hands, catching Tyler squarely in the chest and throwing him backwards across the hardwood floor and into the large stone fireplace separating the living room from the dining room and kitchen.

"I didn't take it away from her the first time! If you hadn't gotten kidnapped, if you had just given up that piece of Zane's soul she would be safe! She would be here, with us. Yeah, I helped but you did this just as much as I did. Take some responsibility and for once in your immortal life get the hell out of my way."

Tears fell from Jane's multi-colored eyes as steam began rising from the tanned skin visible around her swimsuit and sundress. Her long, straight black hair flew around her head in an otherworldly wind and Tyler watched her eyes turn black. "You cannot speak to me that way," her oddly detached voice whispered.

Tyler took several steps to the left until he was standing directly in front of her but still across the wide room. "You cannot tell me what I can and cannot do. You are a fledgling on a good day and I am a demi-god. Kiss my ass, bitch."

Though her eyes looked directly at him, Tyler found himself wondering if she could really see him. "As you wish." One arm flung out to the side sending a lightning bolt across the room and straight toward Tyler. He took the shot in the abdomen, grunted and stood, turning her own power against her as her next shot slipped out of her fingers and slid around her body to nip her in the butt. Rather than laughing or losing some of her irritation as Tyler had expected, Jane grew more furious with him, using fire this time instead of lightning. "You will pay for your transgression, prince."

Tyler rolled out of the way of the fire bolt, his gaze catching his brother's. "What the hell did she just say?"

"I believe she called you a prince and why did you have to provoke her?" Jared sighed, standing to step between the two of them.

"I've never gotten this kind of reaction out of her!" Tyler dodged another fire bolt and used his power to smother it before Jane caught the house on fire. He reached out and attempted to infiltrate her mind. It wasn't the most ethical of things to do but if he could just slip by her shields he knew he could make her feel any way that he wanted her to with very little effort. The next shot he flipped back on her before it reached him, causing her to stumble backwards. She recovered quickly, advancing on him like a predator seeking out its prey. "You need to learn a little control, Jane."

"You are of no consequence to me. I am the fire that burns at the core of the earth. When all else disappears, I will be the one who remains and you will remember that I was the one who caused your destruction." That odd voice she was using grew deeper and her black pupils bled across the whites of her eyes, causing her to look like some kind of demon. Jane gathered her power to her and shoved it out, screaming her anger, pain and frustration.

Jared stepped in between them, flinging his hands up to stop them from continuing to fight and causing damage to the house. "Enough!" he roared. "The two of you cannot continue this. Either work it out or pretend to like a normal family."

Jane threw a fireball at her husband that sent him sprawling across the floor like a ragdoll. Tyler stepped in front of her and held out his hands, power pulsing from them to wrap around Jane and contain her. Jared stood up cautiously, glancing over at his brother who he could suddenly hear in his mind as clear as a bell. "*I don't think that's entirely Jane.*"

Jared grimaced as he noticed his wife's black eyes as she struggled vainly against Tyler's energy binding. "I don't entirely disagree with you there, brother. You really shouldn't have provoked her. You know her powers are unbalanced on a good day right now." He crossed the room carefully, trying to maintain eye contact with the thing currently inhabiting his wife's body. "Who are you?"

Jane's eyes bled back to the blue-green that they normally were when she looked at her husband. "What do you mean who am I? I'm your very pissed off wife."

Tyler's eyes widened. "You weren't five seconds ago."

"What happened to the two of you?"

"You don't remember?" Jared approached her, reaching out but stopping just short of touching her. "You and Tyler got into a fight. You started throwing fire and lightning."

Jane rolled her eyes and slumped into the invisible bands binding her arms at her sides. "It happened again, didn't it? Damnit."

"This happened before? And no one thought that it might be a good idea to tell me about it, just to give me fair warning?" Tyler turned his head to look back and forth between Jane and Jared.

"It's nothing to worry about. She's just coming into her powers. I've never seen anyone turn into an immortal after being a supernatural mortal so I'm just guessing that a little fluctuation is normal." Jared shrugged, visibly unconcerned with how his wife had reacted to Tyler's taunting.

"And I ended up bound by air how exactly?"

Tyler cleared his throat. "You were levitating a little bit and your eyes were black. There was fire coming out of your pores. I thought this would be a bit safer."

"I told you not to piss her off." Jared grinned and leaned against the wall, crossing his arms over his chest as he watched them.

"Yeah, because this is totally my fault," Tyler snarled. "I was minding my own business which was no concern of either of you. You should've let me drink." He released Jane from the binding and grabbed the remainder of the bottle of vodka and his glass, taking them with him as he walked toward his bedroom in the back of the house, slamming the door behind him.

Jane looked up from where she had fallen in the floor. "You really should've let him drink. I shouldn't get so upset about how he chooses to grieve. It's not my place."

Jared reached a hand down to pull her from the floor. "She was your sister. I'm sorry that I said those things so harshly about her. I shouldn't remind you about what happened." He pulled his wife's petite body tightly against his tall, thin frame in a hug.

"It's nothing that I've not thought myself. What happened to her, it was all of our faults." Jane wrapped her arms tightly around Jared, leaning into his warmth. "I'm sorry that I lost my temper and tried to flambé you and the house."

"It'll happen. Trying to keep it under control may just make it worse. Just don't let it take over you. Please, stay with me, Jane." Jared's voice was soft, worried and the words were whispered in her ear, his nose nuzzling her hair as he inhaled her scent. "I'm worried about you. You shouldn't go on this book tour."

"It's two weeks. And it's very tame. I feel sure I'll be perfectly fine. Besides, I need to appear at set so that it's at least assumed that I have a passing interest in the potential travesty that the film industry is making of my books. They bought the rights to the first book for a freaking fortune. Our kids can live off of the money from the franchise for most of their lives. I don't care what they do with it as long as their checks clear."

"Why aren't they filming on location here in Los Angeles?"

"Because the book's not set in Los Angeles, it's set in Norway. So obviously they're filming it on location in Vancouver." She pulled back and rose up on her toes to kiss him quickly on the lips before pulling away. "We have three days before I have to leave." She took him by the hand and began to teasingly pull him toward their bedroom. "Let's not waste them."

Jared looked at her longingly, his heated gaze sliding from her toes to the top of her dark head and back again. "You have no idea how tempted I am. But I need to spend some time with Tyler. I can't leave him like that." He gestured helplessly toward his brother's closed bedroom door.

Jane smiled knowingly and let go of his hand, making his heart ache for just a second with how much he loved her. "Go. I'm going to take a shower and work. I've still got a deadline on a book and you know this one is the first one where I've had to make up everything."

"What's it about?" He smiled, watching her slowly back away toward their room.

"It's a love story. We'll have to try out some of the sex scenes later. Just to see if my description is realistic." She grinned and disappeared down the hallway.

Jared sighed when he heard the shower starting and shook his head, attempting to clear the erotic thoughts his wife had conjured up from his brain. He walked down the hallway in the opposite direction toward Tyler's room knowing full well that his brother could hear him approaching. "Get up and toss the bottle! We're going out!"

2

"Blind devotion en-mass is always entertaining," Tyler commented drily, dropping back against the far wall of the concert venue. He slumped down, crossing his arms over his chest as he watched the enraptured crowd scream maniacally for the band onstage, oblivious to his disgust.

Jared sighed deeply, propping against the wall beside his brother. He didn't bother leaning closer even though Tyler was wearing earplugs in an effort to quiet the roar surrounding the rock concert. "You know that's a little hypocritical coming from a guy who makes a living off of the adoration of others."

"I didn't ask to be celebrities. That was your dream, not mine. I just went along with it." Tyler attempted to shove himself further into the wall, presumably to make himself disappear. The music wasn't bad; it was the screaming crowd that was starting to grate on his nerves. Crowds of people tended to set him on edge. When he was playing guitar with their band Metamorphosis, he rather enjoyed the line of the press pit that kept the crowds from storming the stage. Not that he disliked the band's fans. He appreciated their patronage like any good artist but he also appreciated the distance that his lifestyle afforded him. Privacy became a very valuable commodity when you were never sure who wanted you dead or who wanted to out you as something not quite human.

"You do realize that this is how people look at us, right?"

A devious grin spread across Tyler's face and he extended one hand lazily toward the crowd. "You want to find out?"

"Tyler, don't…"

"Too late."

The audience stopped cheering, their attention slowly turning from the band onstage to the brothers standing in the back of the room. The wave of the effect moved through the room, all the way to the band whose singer smiled in recognition when the house lights came on, illuminating Jared and Tyler.

"Well if it isn't our good friends Jared and Tyler Stateton. Does Metamorphosis need a remake, boys?"

Jared waved and leaned in closer to his brother. "Will you stop that now, please?"

"Oh, fine. Take the fun out of my evening." Tyler released the spell with an impatient flick of his fingers, the house lights going down, the show resuming and the brothers returning to their previously unnoticed status.

"Was that truly necessary? Those people onstage used to be our friends, if you can remember that far back."

"I don't, not anymore. So, are you going to tell me why we're here or let me rot in ignorance?"

"They have a great stage show. I thought ours could use some changes."

"They have fireworks. If you want pyro, get Jane to light something on fire." Tyler laughed at his own joke.

"Very funny."

Tyler shrugged. "I liked it."
"I heard you visited Danalia."

"So what? She's our sister."

"She's one of dad's many other children, not my sister."

"Then why do you care?"

"How is she?" Jared's voice was grudging at best. Tyler understood his brother's stance. The two of them were not raised with Danalia or any of their father's other children and so, to him, they weren't family. To Tyler it meant a lot to have people outside of his brother who understood the kind of life he had chosen to lead and who he could speak freely around. Out of his half-siblings and extended family, Danalia was his favorite. Everything around her was always happy, in the moment and full of life. She lived fully in the present, something that Tyler envied.

"She's good. When I saw her she was building an oasis in the middle of a desert."

"This plane?"

"You know how she despises spending time on this plane. She was on the edge of Purgatory when I found her."

"She's the only person I know who goes to that pit willingly."

"I think she feels sorry for them, the souls that are trapped between worlds. She can't make their circumstances better but at least she's improving the landscape." Tyler shrugged, taking up a perch against the back wall of the concert hall. Even though the venue was standing room only, all of the ticketed attendees were cramming themselves as close to the other end of the room and the band onstage as possible.

"Assuming it wasn't for nostalgia, why did you go to see her?" Jared's curiosity got the better of him and when he saw his brother's facial expression he almost wished he had bitten back the words.

"I thought she might have some answers."

"Well?"

"She didn't tell me anything different. She did say that what you did for Jane won't help me in this situation so I guess you're in the clear. I just don't get why you won't tell me. It's not like we haven't done crazy shit together over the years. Do you really think that I can't handle it?"

"No, I think that you'll run off and do something stupid that you can't take back. If I can stop you from doing something you'll regret later, it's better to keep my secret." Jared paused, watching their friends play on stage for a moment, grateful that Tyler's spell had no lingering effects on the thousands of humans milling around them.

Tyler turned to him angrily. "What makes you think you have the right to make that kind of decision for me?"

"Keep your voice down," Jared ground out through clenched teeth, crossing his arms over his chest and staring straight ahead as if he could actually view the show through the crowd.

"It's not like they can hear me!" Tyler stepped away from the wall and threw his hands open wide in challenge to his brother. "I can control their emotions, their awareness. What makes you think that I can't accomplish something as simple as preventing them from hearing me? You won't even bite back your pride long enough to ask Danalia for help for Jane! She's about to explode. Her mood swings are getting worse all the time. You know it, I know it and for whatever reason you seem to want to keep her in the dark about it when you know that we have someone on our side who can help her learn to control her powers and get through this. Are you really that stubborn?"

"I really want to keep what's going on with Jane from as much of our extended family as possible until she has a handle on it. We've no idea who's really on our side and who would take advantage of her lack of knowledge and make her do something she wouldn't normally even consider. Jane is my business, let me deal with it."

"Jane became my business, brother, when you brought her into our lives before I was even born to this life. Whatever happens to her, you did it. She's spiraling out of control and you're doing nothing to help or stop it or even give her clarity. Is she really aware of what's going on? Do you plan on clueing her in any time soon or do you want us to just explode before you're willing to admit that something's wrong with her?"

"There's nothing wrong with her. She's just coming into her powers. Everything will be fine, we just have to ride out this little bit of fluctuation."

"She nearly barbequed both of us today. That's not a fluctuation. You're in denial." Tyler pretended to turn his attention back to the concert, effectively ignoring his brother's irritated glare.

"I'm in denial. You're the one trying to bring someone back from the dead a year after the fact." Jared knew his words cut but he refused to allow his demeanor to soften enough to regret them.

"Why won't you just tell me what you did for Jane?" Tyler demanded angrily, his jaw clenched as he stared straight ahead blankly.

"Because I don't want you to have to do what I did. Some actions give you hard crosses to bear. I don't want that for you."

"Again, I'll note that it's not your choice."

Jared observed his brother's misplaced anger sadly, knowing that he was doing damage to their relationship that couldn't be undone by keeping the only secret that had ever existed between them. And still, knowing what he knew, he couldn't bring himself to risk allowing Tyler to walk through the same hell he'd seen. "This is my choice, Ty. Not telling you is my choice. I'm sorry." Not knowing what else to say, he pushed away from the wall and walked toward the exit, knowing he was taking the coward's way out and that the discussion wasn't over.

Tyler let him walk away and get almost to the door before muttering a curse under his breath, freezing the whole room in a slow-motion time warp. He pushed through the crowd, stepping up next to Jared who was moving just as slowly as the rest of them. He leaned over to speak directly in his ear, ensuring that Jared would hear the words when he pulled out of the trance. "Fuck you, big brother," Tyler snarled, stalking to the double doors and shoving them open with a bang, signaling his departure.

Jane looked up from the schedule and book edits on her desk when the front door slammed shut. She disregarded the angry footsteps stomping to the bedrooms, returning her attention to the laptop screen and stacks of papers in front of her. She jumped in surprise when Tyler banged into her office, frantically searching for something. "Can I help you?"

"Have you seen my motherfucking athame?" he snarled, digging through a cupboard.

Jane watched her brother-in-law with faint amusement at his obvious frustration. "No, I haven't seen it. Try your motherfucking bedroom," she remarked drily.

"You're funny, you know that?" He left the room nonetheless to check his bedroom.

"What did you do with the other one?" Jane called after him knowing full well that he could hear her even across the house.

Tyler laughed maniacally. "He got held up."

"You left him alone? That's just great, Ty. He'll probably get mobbed." Jane sighed, rubbing her eyes tiredly as she contemplated going to her husband's aide. She mentally reached down the golden strands that bound them and felt Jared's anger at his brother wash over her. She inwardly groaned, deciding to stay and deal with the more immediate problem that was currently trashing their house rather than seek out her husband who was in the process of freeing himself from Tyler's spell. Jane rose and followed the noise to where Tyler was pulling apart the living room.

"Serves him right, the bastard." He pulled the cushions on the couch out as he searched behind them blindly with his hands.

Jane leaned against the doorframe watching but not willing to help him just yet. "What are you doing?"

"I thought I already explained that."

"Use mine."

"Can't, not for what I need it for." Tyler continued his search.

"Not to sound redundant, but what are you doing?" Jane walked behind him, quickly straightening up the majority of the mess that he was making of their house.

"Ah-ha!" Tyler stepped back from the disheveled couch brandishing the bright silver knife. He turned to face his sister-in-law, the blade of the athame gleaming in the lamp light as he stood looking like a maniac in the ransacked room. Jane was unimpressed with the uncharacteristic tantrum. Tyler held the athame out to her blade first. "I need your blood."

"You need my what?" Jane asked, not quite certain she'd heard right.

"Your blood. Your life blood, to be exact."

"Since you're asking me to inflict a possibly life-threatening wound, may I ask what it's for?"

"I need to know how you were brought back. If Jared won't tell me, I'll figure it out on my own. Do you want me to do this or can you do it yourself?"

"Um, I haven't agreed to do it at all," Jane countered, suddenly a bit concerned by the dark gleam in his eyes. "Where's Jared?"

"He's not here. Will you help me or not, Jane?" A note of desperation crept into his voice.

Jane took the knife from him. "This won't bring her back." She allowed her fingers to rest on his for just a moment before withdrawing.

"You don't know that. You're here. Whatever place she's in you came back from. Do you know how he did it?" Jane shook her head silently. "Then do this for me. Please, help me."

"Do you know what you're doing, Tyler?" Jane forced her voice to be soft so that she wouldn't make him feel defensive.

"I can't think of anything else, Jane. I've tried it all and I'm not too proud to say that I'm desperate. I need to try this. Unless Jared

26

will get off his damn high horse and help me, this is my only shot. Please, Jane. For Karina." He let go of the knife leaving it totally in her grasp.

Looking at the shiny knife blade extending six inches from the hilt in her hand, Jane hesitated. "Can't it come from somewhere else? Blood travels all over your body, you know."

Tyler shook his head, his eyes closing as he sighed. "It's this or nothing, Jane. I wouldn't ask if there was another way that I hadn't tried already."

Jane reaffirmed her grip on the hilt of the knife nervously as she turned the point to face her. "You'd better make damn sure Jared's here in time to heal me or so help me I'll haunt you for eternity."

Tyler felt the spell on the concert release in his head and his brother's nearly overwhelming irritation as he drove toward their home. He nodded to Jane that it was okay and watched as she took a deep breath and plunged the knife into her chest for him. He eased her to the floor, settling her against the couch to slow the blood flow, giving his brother enough time to find her before she bled out on their hardwood floors. "One more thing." She looked up at him, her blue eyes turning gold from shock. Tyler braced an arm on the couch and yanked the knife from her chest. Jane made a gurgling sound as she tried to gasp. He felt his brother scream and looked down to see the same wound bleeding slower over his own heart. He kissed Jane on the forehead, holding the bloody knife carefully. "Thank you." He disappeared just as Jane heard the front door bang open. Jared stumbled in, ripping off the bloody mess that had become his shirt. He rushed over when he saw Jane on the floor vainly trying to staunch the blood flowing from her chest. He shoved her hands aside, leaning over her to use the last of his waning energy to heal the self-inflicted hole in her chest. "Jane, talk to me! Are you okay?" He grabbed her face with his free hand, turning her glazed over eyes to meet his. He watched as they lightened from black to gold and finally back to the blue-green that they turned when she looked at him. "Can you see me?"

Jane took a deep, gasping breath, her hand closing over the one that he still held over her heart. "Yes. Damn, that hurt more than I thought it would."

"What the hell did you do?" Jared collapsed in the floor next to her, the relief showing on his worried face.

"Tyler. He needed my blood." Jane held her hand over her heart still gasping for breath.

"That dumb…why did you let him do this? He could've killed you!"

"We were both counting on you to heal me. Though that one might've cut it a little close." She smiled.

"You're both insane. I can't believe he'd do this to you, risk you like this."

"I didn't know how else to help him."

"Help him what?" Understanding dawned and Jared pushed to his feet, his anger pushing outward like a storm cloud rolling through the room. "I'm gonna kill him." Before Jane could blink and try to stop him, he too vanished, leaving her alone and grimacing at her ruined t-shirt. She stood, pulling her shirt off and picking Jared's up off the floor on the way to her and Jared's bedroom. "Boys." She tossed the shirts in to the wastebasket and continued to the back of the house to clean up.

Jared crashed through Danalia's newly created garden, ignoring the goddess as he tackled his brother, pinning the other man to the ground. "You narcissistic son of a bitch! You could've killed her!"

Jared landed two well-placed blows to his brother's face before sitting back, allowing some of the fight to seep out of him before he gave in to the impulse to beat his brother into the dirt along with the dying plants around him. "What if I hadn't gotten there in time?"

"Obviously you did, but you're right, I deserved that." Tyler sat up, gingerly touching the gash in his bottom lip where his brother's new wedding ring had pushed the soft flesh into his teeth.

"You want to know what you deserve?" Jared rushed at his brother again.

Danalia stepped in between them holding the bloody athame that she had been examining. "Boys! Will you please not destroy any more of my lovely garden?" She watched the wilting plants that had shrank back from the violence, encouraging them with her presence to return and bloom. She held the dagger out between them before passing it back to Tyler. "I can tell you his secret but it will not help you find what you seek, Traegar."

"Why not?" Tyler watched his brother as he carefully wiped the blade clean on his already bloody white shirt, brushing some of the dirt from his ripped jeans.

Danalia turned her attention from one brother to the other as she spoke. "Because what you seek has already been reborn. So stop killing my plants." She turned away from them and began using her touch to heal the plants that had been trampled under her half-brothers' fight.

Tyler's gaze remained locked with his brother's as he spoke. "So what now?"

3

Anna saw the car coming toward her faster and faster, but it felt as if she were a bystander, watching the whole scene in slow motion. Frame by frame the speeding car came toward her. A scream welled up in her throat and died on her eerily calm resolve. *This is what's right, what will fix everything.* In the last second her eyes looked to the right, selfishly to capture one last glimpse...

"Honey! Bring me another beer!"

Anna shook herself out of the daydream which lingered like some half-forgotten fantasy in her mind. She quickly shut off the steaming water scalding her hands and dropped the dish that she had been holding into the sink. She dried off her hands and reached into the refrigerator retrieving the bottle for her husband. Anna paused for a moment, cooling her still-burning hands on the cold bottle before carrying it into the den with a sigh.

Her husband turned his dark brown eyes to her, running a hand through his white blonde hair as he took the drink from her outstretched hand. He smiled, returning his attention to the paparazzi infested entertainment news show that he had been watching. He laughed at the retelling of a female pop star's antics as Anna turned to walk back into the kitchen. "These people are fucking nuts. Anything to get attention."

"Yeah, I guess so."

"Hey, what happened to your hand?"

"The water's hot. New water-heater works great," she replied absently, returning to her dishes.

Andrew sat back in his worn recliner with his beer and smiled as his wife retreated. He couldn't wait for everything to come back to her, for Anna to remember who they really were to each other, who they had been and then to watch the horror enter her eyes when she realized exactly what the actions of the last year have meant. As it was right now, he couldn't have planned things out better if he'd done all of it himself. And Andrew was planning to take advantage of every moment of it.

Tyler stomped through the living room, his green eyes flashing as he paced, angrily rubbing the back of his neck. Jane watched him from her position on the couch while she waited for Jared to return. The brothers had come back from whatever plane Danalia had been planting a garden on about thirty minutes earlier dirty, angry and refusing to talk about whatever had happened. As soon as they got back Jared had held up a finger to keep either of them from commenting and then disappeared. Tyler had explained briefly that this was something they could do, travel between planes, something she would be able to do when she gained her full goddess powers rather than the overly violent fluctuations that had been occurring more frequently lately. That had been about fifteen minutes ago and neither of them had spoken since, allowing the silence to grow until it felt almost like a tangible, suffocating thing.

This afternoon's occurrence had been the worst so far. She'd been experiencing power bursts but nothing that had made her eyes turn black like that. What frightened Jane was that she had no reaction to the incident. She didn't feel bad, guilty or afraid of how bad things could have turned out if Jared hadn't been there to diffuse the situation. When the fight ended she was frustrated, like something inside of her wanted the violence, wanted to get out. When she hadn't been able to extinguish whatever battle was raging inside of her through violence, it had turned sexual. Now, since her husband had abandoned her, it was just good old fashioned frustration. And it was starting to make her feel a little crazy. Watching Tyler pace for the last twenty minutes hadn't helped. She wasn't sure if her brother-in-law was waiting on Jared to come back with a solution to whatever problem they were having now or if he was waiting to find out if he should fear an execution. Jane fought the urge to flick her wrist and send him flying across the room so that he would stop wearing a groove in the wood floors.

A few more moments passed before her husband re-entered the room carrying what looked like an ancient, dusty tome. Tyler immediately stopped pacing when he saw the book, his green eyes widening. "Where did you get that?"

"Where do you think?" Jared sighed, placing the book gingerly on the coffee table as he took a seat next to his wife. His arm slid around her shoulders and he twitched involuntarily at the spark of heat that slid from her body to his at the slight contact.

"You went there for me?" Jared nodded carefully in answer. "Why?"

"You need answers. I don't know how else to give them to you. I know what it feels like to be where you are and I wish you didn't have to feel it. I don't want you to ever think that I didn't do everything in my power to help you work through this. I agreed with Jane, that there were no answers out there to find other than the ones you already have. Until today. What Danalia said, that changes things."

"Why do I feel like I need a translator near the two of you?" Jane threw up her hands in the air as the powers warring inside of her fought for some type of release. "What did Danalia say?"

Tyler stopped pacing and leaned back against a console table, crossing his legs and his arms. He had heard Jane's question but he ignored it. The way he saw it, she's Jared's problem to deal with. If someone was going to answer her queries, he wasn't under any obligation for it to be him. His focus was on his brother and his self-righteous attitude. Now that someone else had finally confirmed what Tyler had known for nearly a year, now Jared was willing to accept that he might have possibly been wrong. It made Tyler sick to think of how many times he had taken his brother's words on faith and now Jared was requiring more proof than a legal court to trust him. "I appreciate how candid you're being and that I now finally have your support with this. I appreciate you going to get that book for me. I would appreciate it more if you could trust something because I said it, because I believe it or hell, just humor me and at least pretend. The one time, this one thing I asked for and you're willing to give it to me, but not until someone else, someone you don't even like very much, tells you that it's ok." He raised one eyebrow, waiting on his brother's response.

"You're my brother, Ty. I trust you. But you've got to realize that this is not just about you. I have to consider Jane's feelings as well. And I didn't honestly think that there was anything to this. I admit it, I thought you were wrong." Jared held up his hands in front of him in mock surrender. "Are you happy? I was wrong. Do you want me to tattoo it on my forehead for you?"

"Bite me, you bastard," Tyler snarled. "I didn't believe you when you said that you were bringing Jane back. I didn't think you'd ever find her if you did and yet here she sits, looking at both of us like we've grown three heads because for whatever stupid fucking reason she's not reading our collective minds to figure out that we're talking about her damn sister and how you're ignoring what I need, what I want, because you're so concerned that she might freak out and start blowing shit up and then you'll have to face the fact that there is something seriously wrong. No, there are two things wrong. One, you're completely in denial about the fact that we need help to keep Jane from losing her damn mind over the next however long it takes to turn a mortal into an immortal. Second, she's shielding so hard that you've got no idea what I'm thinking right now, do you?"

Jared's anger propelled him to his feet before he even thought about completing the action. "You have no right! When Karina died we all lost someone, not just you. We've all had our grief and our guilt to deal with. I am done humoring you while you belittle everyone else. Jane does not need this right now. I do not need this right now."

Jane gave into her violent impulses and stood between them, flinging her hands out to the sides and throwing them both into the far walls of the room as she felt her eyes turning black. "Enough!" She turned her furious gaze on her husband. "Jane does not need to sit here and listen to you talking about her like she's not right here. I can speak for myself and I don't need you to protect me or remind me of what I've lost. And you," her black eyes turned to Tyler as he pushed to his feet. "I've been shielding so hard because I know what's going on with me and I wanted to protect you and Jared from it. Neither of you needs to see the madness inside of my head right now and you know what, yeah, it leaks out sometimes. Not like you've been trying to hold anything back for the last eleven months. Karina was my sister! My blood! What exactly was she to you?" Jane gave Tyler a moment to answer, noting his open-mouthed stare. "No answer? That's what I thought. You don't know. Was she your friend? I know she wasn't your lover. Whatever it is that you feel guilty about, stop putting it on us. Right now, I have to deal with my career. I want to enjoy being happily married to my husband. I'm turning into a goddess, whatever that means. I do not have the time or patience to keep feeling guilty about what happened to Karina. I will carry that for my entire life, however long and however many of them I have. It does not have to be my whole life. There's no one to hunt, nothing to break, no way to get revenge because whether you accept it or not, it was her choice." She took a deep breath and pulled the wave of power that had rolled out into the room back inside of herself. It made her feel like she was boiling alive from the inside out and she checked her mental shields to confirm that they were still in place. "I've never had a family so I'm not really sure how this works but I think we're all handling it wrong. We've all been grieving separately, trying to deal with things on our own and we can't do it anymore. It's not working. We're family, not roommates living under the same roof. This is our home. *Our* home. So drop the measuring tape, put your dicks up and deal with your shit, both of you. You're both pretty." Jane took a deep breath, feeling her eyes change back to normal and her energy wane as the power of her goddess mingled with her fire element, feeling like it was festering inside of her. She spun away from them both and walked into the kitchen. "I need a damn drink." Jane reemerged a few moments later carrying a newly opened bottle of malbec, an oversized wineglass and a clean shirt for her husband from the laundry room. She noted them both staring at her as she dropped back down onto the couch, tossed the shirt to her half-naked husband and filled her glass to the brim. "What? Are you both surprised that I've got half an idea of what's going on and I don't need you to protect me like I'm some fragile thing that will break at the mention of stress?" She rolled her eyes in disgust and took a large gulp of her wine. "If you're eying my bottle you're both out of luck. Go get your own drink. This one's mine. The two of you sitting here playing Tarzan's making my goddess want to rip both your heads off so that I can enjoy the peace and quiet for five minutes before I have to put you back together again." Jane propped her bare feet on the edge of the glass coffee table and leaned back into the soft cushions to enjoy her drink. "Now, who's going to answer my question? What did Danalia say?"

Tyler dropped into his chair, his lips pressed together so tightly that they appeared almost nonexistent. Even though his mental connection to his brother was currently cut off, he knew that Jared was waiting on him to answer the question. After a long moment, Tyler sighed, finally relenting to the silence that was growing like a cancer in the room. "Danalia said that Karina's alive. She's been brought back somehow. We don't know by whom, where she is or what she is. She could be a cockroach for all we know. The only thing that Danalia said for certain is that she can't be brought back because she's already alive."

"Well that's good news," Jane took a deep breath to calm herself and try to keep her excitement at bay. Once the words were out there, Jane felt in her gut that she had always known them to be true. She hadn't wanted confirmation, hadn't wanted to search for her sister because she sincerely hoped the life she was living was better than the one she had left. With this new revelation she didn't know what was going to happen but she hoped the only thing that would come out of it would that they'd see Karina living happily and all finally find some peace. "So now that you have the answer that you wanted, Tyler, what do the two of you propose that we do about it?" Jane drained her glass and poured another. All of the conflicting emotions inside of her needed some way to release before they turned into something dark that she couldn't control. Since expelling them from her body wasn't something that she could readily do and keep the momentum of the moment going, Jane elected to try and temporarily numb them with alcohol.

"I want to find her," Tyler admitted finally, his voice tight with strain and defensive.

"I'll pretend to be surprised," Jared commented drily.

"Boys, shut it." Jane's words were less of a request and more of a command. Their constant bickering was starting to give her a headache. As she rubbed her temples, she remembered the book that Jared had returned with from whatever plane he had visited. "What does the book do? I'm just going to jump two steps ahead and assume that it will help."

"It's a spell book. There's one in there that supposedly will locate a soul on any plane. I borrowed it from our father's personal library. If anyone's going to use it, it should be done quickly so that I can return it before anyone realizes that it's gone. Or that I was even there."

"If this spell can find anyone on any plane, why didn't you use it to find me?"

"Good luck getting him to answer anything about that," Tyler scoffed, slumping further into his chair.

Jared took the seat beside Jane, turning sideways so that he could rest his head on her lap. He sighed happily when his wife reached down, absently combing her fingers through his shaggy dark hair. "I couldn't. That was part of the challenge for me. You were blocked from me and from every other immortal. I had to find you using good old human channels."

Jane reached out for the book. "Well the good news now is that if that's the case with Karina, I'm not fully immortal yet."

Jared caught her hand in his. "Don't. Let Tyler do it."

"You are kidding me, right? She's my sister. If anyone gets to decide what we do with the information we gather, it should be me."

"I'm not arguing your point, Jane." Jared rubbed the pulse point on her wrist to try and calm her down when he felt her body temperature rising. "How many times have you been reincarnated? Dozens? Hundreds? You could have relatives, descendants of siblings all over the world. With you, it could go awry or it could lead us in the wrong direction. For Tyler there's only one of Karina. He can find her."

Jane slumped back into the cushions, withdrawing her hand. "Fine." She looked up to pull Tyler's gaze to meet hers. "You try first. If your connection to her isn't as strong as you think it is I'll give it a shot and we'll just have to see where it leads us. If you find anything, you'll let me know? We can't keep hiding things from each other."

"I agree." Tyler launched himself out of the leather chair and grabbed the book from the table, clutching it to his chest as if it were something precious. "I'll go work out on the patio because that's where she spent the most time while she was here. If you need me, let me know." He cut his eyes to Jane and raked a hand through his short bronze blonde hair. "Keep the shields up."

Jane nodded to Tyler as he left the room before placing her glass on the end table and shoving her husband into a sitting position. "We need to talk."

Jared groaned. "Ah, damnit."

"You're going to tell me what's going on. All of it. I'll decide if I share this conversation with Tyler or not. I know there's something about what happened when I was reborn that you don't want him to know. I don't know why you don't want him to know it, but I'm your wife and he's outside of a soundproof house. I'll keep your secret as long as it won't cause him or us physical harm to do so."

"It won't."

"Then I'll do everything I can to make sure that he never knows what you tell me. But you have to tell me what's going on, Jared, and why what happened over thirty years ago is important now." Jane turned to face him, perching with her back against the arm rest. "You made some kind of deal. What was it?"

Jared hesitated, trying to determine what the best answer was to her question and whether or not it was worth the risk to even have the discussion. It disturbed him that he was even considering distrusting his wife with the only secret that had ever existed between him and his brother. "I made a deal with my father to bring you back to life for me. In exchange for his services I had to make a binding agreement in blood. If I try to get out of it in any way, I die. And not the way that lets me spend a few years floating around in the ether and pop back in as a fetus. I'll cease to exist in a corporeal form and what's left over will be my father's to do with as he wishes. And Apollo can be very creative."

"What was the deal?" Jane's voice was guarded and almost so quiet that Jared had to strain to hear her.

"Two lives. I promised him two lives in order for you to live. I also promised that whether you loved me or not that I would find someone to mate with in this life. You were blocked from me because Apollo was still hoping that I would choose another immortal to mate with rather than attempt to make one out of you."

"What lives did he want? What did you do, Jared?" Jane felt her powers mingling, rising and her hands started trembling slightly from the strain of trying to contain it while her emotions raged within her.

"You have to know that I would do it again. I would've promised him anything to bring you back to me." Jared's bright blue eyes pleaded for her understanding. When she said nothing, just stared, he took a deep breath and continued. "I had to take one life, the life of another immortal, and promise to create an immortal child during this lifetime."

"Who was the life you took? Did you know the person?"

"He was my uncle. He was one of my favorite people. He did something to displease my father, I never knew what, but it was serious enough that Apollo ordered his execution."

"Jared, at that time you were a child. How could he expect you to do something like that?" Jane's expression reflected her horror and her blue-green eyes turned a stormy dark gray.

"He expected it of me because I am his son, one who has not acted like his child in several centuries. He did it to teach me a lesson that the price of one life is that if something lives, something else must die in its place. For you to live I was willing to pay that price. My uncle understood why I did what I did."

"What happens when an immortal dies?"

"Like a human, the soul is reborn, repurposed or destroyed. He was reborn as a human. I've seen him, but he doesn't remember me. He doesn't remember anything from his time as an immortal." Jared felt a weight press down on his chest, as if he were suffocating from the lack of response from his wife. With her mentally cut-off from him the only way that he could read her was through what she told him or through her emotions. She was barely talking other than to ask more questions and her emotions were being kept tightly reined. He wasn't sure if it was to keep him from knowing what her true response to his revelation was or to keep her blossoming powers under control. He waited for a few moments in the silence before it became so loud it was deafening. "Jane, tell me what you're thinking, please."

"Tell me about the second life."

"Danalia is the last immortal child to be born to our line and when she was born people thought the world was flat. We need another immortal child to continue the line. I promised my father that no matter what happened, if you wanted to be with me or not, that I would find someone to mate with in this lifetime and that I would be the one to give our line that child."

Jane was silent for a few moments. She picked up her glass, took a large swallow of the dark red wine and returned the glass to the side table before speaking. To Jared, it seemed like the quick movement took an eternity. "So we have to have a child. How much time do we have?"

Jared hesitated before answering knowing that she wasn't going to like what he had to say. "I don't know. Everything's different now. The blood that bound us together, the goddess that you're turning into, I'm not sure how it all works, how long it takes or how long we'll live after it's done. Tyler and I have always lived for a little under two centuries before we're reborn. Sabina was right when she said that we're soul-mated to each other but it's so that we could never be separated."

"Wait, wait, wait," Jane interrupted, holding a hand up to stop him from speaking. "If you're soul-mated to Tyler, does that mean that we're not soul-mated to each other? I thought that happened before we did the binding ceremony."

"I don't know," Jared replied honestly, his face pained. "Everything happened so fast. I don't know if it's possible for someone to have two soul-mates and even if it is, it doesn't have to be someone that you're in a relationship with, even if that relationship is as committed as marriage is in my family."

"So someone I don't know could just swoop in and take me away from you again because we're bound but we're not necessarily soul-mated to each other."

"Well I would hope that neither of us would let someone just swoop in and claim you again. The marital binding overrides the soul-mate bond but it could potentially put another person in your head. You can't shake your soul-mate, as you found out with Zane. Regardless, it doesn't work for an immortal unless you complete a blood ritual spell asking to be bound to your soul-mate and I'm just guessing that you've not done that because I would know about it so you've got nothing to worry about."

"Oh, shit." Jane's face paled and her eyes turned nearly translucent. "I did that spell. Right before we were bound. Do you remember seeing the cut on my palm when I told you I chose you? That's what it was from." She held her hand out palm up so that he could clearly see the thin white scar traversing the skin. "I did that spell years ago."

"Obviously the other person hasn't done it so until they do you've got nothing to worry about." Jared wished his voice sounded more certain to make her feel better. He knew that she had done the spell for him, thinking that because they're meant to be together he must be her soul-mate. He sighed because it was just another indicator that they really needed to get better at communication before all hell broke loose and forced them to talk. "Do you want me to do it? Will it make you feel better?"

"No. What if you get another soul-mate and it ends up being some blonde bimbo that we're stuck with forever? No, I think I'd rather live in ignorance and just assume that you're my soul-mate." She withdrew her hand and sank back into the couch cushions. "What does all of this have to do with our child? What if I don't want a child?"

"We don't have a choice. We may have a few decades or a few centuries for all I know to get used to the idea of being parents but at some point we're going to have to make that decision and go through with it. Otherwise my life is forfeit. Is being mother to our child worse than me dying?"

"That's unfair! You just dropped this on me without warning and I'm suddenly supposed to be all warm and fuzzy about having a kid? How many will we have to have to get one out that's a full immortal? Do you know that?" Jane snapped back, her eyes darkening and her skin heating. "I don't want to live forever just so I can watch our children die as mortals."

"I don't know! I'm a full immortal. You will be once the transformation is complete. We may continue the life and death cycle or we may live forever. Regardless, as long as the child is conceived once you're fully immortal the child will be immortal. So probably only one."

"Since when are you a full immortal? What happened to all of that half human half god crap?"

"We've really got to talk more about things a little more important than current events and sex." Jared sighed and reached across Jane's rigid body to take her wineglass. "I've always been a full immortal. On this plane I've been living as a half mortal to facilitate the life cycle. You broke that when we mated so now, yeah, full immortal."

"What about Tyler?"

"No, he's not."

"So we may live and he might die in a hundred years?"

Jared nodded slowly. "I don't know that our bond is strong enough for him to live past our normal expiration date, for lack of a better word. I've been trying to find a way to fix it. I don't want to lose him."

"I don't want you to." Jane reached out and took her husband's free hand in hers. "We'll figure this out. And we'll deal with the baby thing when we have to. I won't let anyone take you from us just because I didn't want to have a kid. I've never really had a family. Karina was the closest I've ever gotten. Our parents died when we were children in a car accident. We were sent to foster care. As soon as I turned seventeen I left to find Zane. Karina came with me. In all of my other lives it's just been Zane and me. Now Zane's gone, his soul's destroyed, Karina's gone and alive again and we don't know if she has any memory of me. You and Tyler are all I've got left. I'm not losing either of you."

"Why didn't you ever tell me any of that?" Jared squeezed her hand comfortingly.

"You didn't ask and it never came up." Jane shrugged, taking the glass back from him as she returned to her lounging position.

Jared swung his legs up on to the sofa and placed his head back in her lap, closing his eyes as her fingers resumed their idle exploration of his scalp. "I'm sorry I never asked. We had agreed that our pasts weren't important. It seems to keep coming back to bite us in the ass."

"The past usually does." Jane sipped her wine, willing the powers he couldn't sense to slide down somewhere deep inside of her and go to sleep before they exploded all over her husband.

Jared felt the hesitation in her touch and sat up again, examining her face carefully. "How much are you holding back right now?"

Jane sighed tiredly. "Enough that it's giving me a headache. It'll be fine. I can handle it." She glanced up and caught his worried look, annoyed that it only increased the frustration waging a war inside of her. "When I can't handle it, I'll let you know. Right now it's just about becoming acclimated to the thing growing inside of me. I'm not fighting it. It's just an adjustment period. Distract me." She curled up against his side. "Your turn. Tell me about your family."

Jared rested his chin on his wife's head, smiling at her little sigh of contentment as his arms wrapped around her and she settled in to listen to his story. "When my father, Apollo, was a young man he fell deeply in love with Daphne, the beautiful daughter of Peneus, the river god. Daphne was afraid of Apollo's amorous advances so she fled from him and he chased her. When she was finally so overcome with exhaustion that she could run no further Apollo overtook her and she submitted to him twice hoping to quench his lust and stop his relentless pursuit. Before he awoke the next day she escaped into the forest. As she ran from him, Cupid appeared to her and confessed what he'd done, shooting Apollo with an arrow of love and Daphne with one of hate to torture Apollo. Cupid begged her forgiveness as she was now pregnant with the twin sons of the god she hated. She pleaded with him for assistance but he could give her none and left her presence. Daphne ran until she reached the edge of a river where she stopped to give birth. She fell in love with her two sons who she named Anyasis and Traegar but she feared for their safety. To save herself and her sons she pleaded with her father to take away her incredible beauty so that she may raise her sons in peace. Her father, the river god, was delighted that she had given him two grandsons but furious that she had spurned the advances of the great god Apollo, son of Zeus. In his rage Peneus flooded the riverbanks, lifting his infant grandsons above the water and covering their mother. When the waters receded, the beautiful Daphne was transformed into a tree, all of her gone except for her remarkable beauty. When Apollo arrived he was saddened by the loss of Daphne, vowing to forever adorn the heads of himself, their children and his warriors with her laurels. Apollo then took the children and returned to the home of his father Zeus on Mount Olympus. It was there that he brought one mortal woman after another to the realm of the gods to raise the two boys. When he realized that the mortals could not survive the atmosphere on Olympus he sent the children down to earth to be raised until they were old enough to return. They returned to Olympus several years later to take their place beside their father. After many years on Olympus they learned what had happened to their mother. The young men were so angered that they sought an audience with Zeus to request her return. When Zeus would not release Daphne from the tree the brothers asked to be allowed to return to earth to live on the same plane as their mother. Zeus was angered that his grandsons would choose the realm of mortals over that of the gods. As punishment for their insolence he offered them a choice, to remain on Olympus and remain truly immortal or to go to earth with the curse of dying and being reborn every two centuries, give or take a few years. The brothers chose to return to earth, even when it meant facing many deaths. In the hopes that his grandsons would one day change their minds and return to Olympus, Zeus granted them the ability to return at will though they might only stay for a short time before being expelled back to earth unless they brought their bonded mates with them. Zeus gave each man the ability to use his blood to turn one mortal into a god or goddess who could survive on Olympus so that the brothers could return home and raise their families as Olympians. As soon as they mastered the spell the brothers were cast out of the heavens and reborn on earth as half mortal and half god, demi-gods, only being able to return to a full god when they returned to their Olympian destiny and bound themselves to another."

"If your mother is a tree how do you have a sister?"

"That's all you got out of that story?" Jared shook his head and laughed.

"Sorry, I don't know how to tactfully say "I'm sorry your mom's a tree and I hope that she's not been a victim of deforestation." It doesn't sound like the nicest way to grow up."

Jared laughed harder at her candor. "Okay. To answer your question, we have a lot of half-siblings. Danalia is one of them. She's a goddess of creation born from the union of our father and a wood nymph."

"Is that why you hate your father, because his actions denied you your mother and caused you to want to leave your home?"

"I don't hate him, I just don't particularly like him. He essentially made me and my brother the products of rape and then my grandfather turned our mother into a tree, like it was her fault. It took her two millennia to get out of that damn tree. She's now a goddess of spring on another plane and shrouded from Apollo's gaze. I'm pretty sure he still thinks she's a tree. Serves the bastard right."

"Do you want to ever go back to Olympus?"

"I don't have a choice. Eventually we'll have to go back and take our children to raise them as Olympians. Otherwise it might be considered a breach of either deal and my life, and potentially yours and Tyler's, would be forfeit. If I go back and Tyler stays here, I'm not sure what would happen. The plan was always if we went back, we'd go back together. But Tyler has to find a mate to take back with him. His mortal half won't allow him to stay in Olympus without a mate. That's why we have to wait until you're an immortal to have children. If any of them were born mortal they'd never be able to cross the divide into Olympus."

"Does Tyler know all of this?"

Jared nodded, clutching her tighter to his chest. "I think he hoped that he would be unbound from me and allowed to stay here once you and I were married."

"Have you always known that he wouldn't be?" Jane pulled back enough to glance up at his face curiously. She couldn't help but appreciate her husband's strong jaw line and the way that his muscles flexed underneath his thin gray t-shirt as he held her protectively.

"I don't know anything for certain," Jared mused, burying his nose in her hair and inhaling her scent. Vanilla, jasmine and one other thing that he hadn't yet been able to identify. He loved that there were still things about her that he didn't know, despite their close connection. Pushing away romantic thoughts of the woman in his arms, he forced himself to focus on the problems at hand. "He might be allowed to stay if you and I go. But I selfishly hope he won't be. I don't want to lose my brother. I didn't consider all of the possible ramifications when I made the decision for myself to agree to the deal that brought you back. I thought that I would be the only one that it would affect. He's right when he says that I made the decision for him too, even if I didn't know it. It wasn't fair and I should've asked him but I was so concerned with finding you that I didn't think about the long-term consequences of my actions. I was willing to do anything to get you back. If I was given the same options I would make the same choice again."

"Jared, you can't sacrifice one of us for the other. What if one day Tyler needs something and he's asked to sacrifice you. Would you be able to forgive him for that? Would you accept it?"

"I don't know. But I didn't sacrifice him."

"You took away his free will, potentially," Jane reminded him softly. She glanced toward the glassed in patio and sincerely hoped that Tyler couldn't hear what they were talking about. His feelings would be hurt if he found out they were talking about him behind his back but she wouldn't break her husband's confidence either just to give him answers, even if they might bring him some measure of peace. Jared was right in this instance. Knowing might cause him to do something dangerous and now it was a moot point because Karina was already alive. At some point though, her husband was going to have to really face what he had done when he bargained for others' lives behind Tyler's back. Telling her was a step in the right direction. Telling Tyler and dealing with the fallout from that conversation would be something completely different, something she sincerely hoped they were strong enough as a unit to face. "I understand why you did what you did. I'm very grateful for it because otherwise you'd still be miserable and I'd still be dead. But I see too why Tyler's angry. You took away his choice, you ripped away whatever future he may have wanted for himself because you decided that what you wanted was more important than him. Can you blame him for being mad, for wanting out? You have to figure out how to make this right with him."

"Guys aren't really good at talking about their feelings, even those who've been around for a few hundred years. We generally just look into each other's heads, see how we're really feeling and go forward. Tyler and I don't hold grudges or hug it out or whatever it is that women romanticize that men do. We just deal with it. It's what we've always done and it works for us."

"Well right now if you want me to drop my shields we risk frying both of your manly brains with my stunning burgeoning pyrotechnic goddess so I suggest that the two of you figure out a way to communicate verbally. Or if it has to be nonverbal, write it down." Jane pushed him away as she sat back upright, pulling away from his embrace. "Tyler's coming back. I want to see what he has to say."

"What do you want to do if we can find Karina?"

"I want to see if she's okay, if she's happy. And if she is, I want to leave her alone and let her have her normal human life. The life she would've had if it hadn't been for me." Jane quieted her voice when she heard the French doors open and Tyler re-enter the house.

"Just a guess, but you didn't find anything," Jared commented, noting his brother's tired, dejected expression as he entered the room and sat back down in his favorite chair. Jane pushed the wine bottle over to him.

"Nothing but a lot of static. There are some jumbled images but I can't make any kind of sense out of them. I'll keep trying." Tyler took Jane's peace offering and took a swig directly from the bottle.

"Do you want me to try?" Jane asked gently.

"Not yet. I may have pushed myself too hard to try tonight." Tyler pushed the ancient book across the table to Jared. "I made a copy of the spell. I don't want you to face anyone's wrath because I couldn't do a simple spell correctly."

Jared took the book and stood. "Don't beat yourself up for two seconds, Ty. You know she's alive. Let that be enough for today." He vanished, leaving Jane and Tyler alone with the remnants of the wine and a lot of things left unsaid between them.

"I'll keep trying," Tyler repeated to reassure himself and his sister-in-law.

"I know you will." Jane hesitated, massaging her temples. "Are you sure that this is a good idea? I don't want to ruin whatever life that my sister has made for herself because we we're being selfish or feeling guilty and want her back. As long as she's okay, I'd really just like to get some closure so that we can all move on with our lives."

"I want to give her a choice. I don't want to try and force her in any one direction, but I feel that she at least deserves a choice about what kind of life she wants to lead."

"What if we find her and she does remember us, Tyler? Can you handle it if she's already made her choice and it's not us?"

Tyler took another swallow from the bottle. "I guess I won't have a choice."

4

Anna stepped outside, greedily breathing in the warm, humid air. It didn't seem to matter what time of year it was, in Louisiana the air always smelled of green plants, earth and rain. Despite her tepid relationship with her husband, she really liked it here, away from the noise of town and the prying eyes of their neighbors where she could just be herself, take a walk and relax without worrying about an interruption. It had been Andrew's idea to move from New Orleans back out to their childhood home in Terrebonne parish. At the time she hadn't wanted to be that far away from the city but now, now it was nice, peaceful even when Drew wasn't trying to get her to do something for him. Anna set out along the gravel driveway leading to the cracked paved road that ran in front of their modest turn of the century house. She heard nothing but birds chirping, insects humming and the crunch of her worn sneakers on the path as she walked, her tanned skin almost instantly turning clammy beneath her shorts and tank top. She reached behind her head, pulling her long dark curls up into a hasty ponytail, letting her sunglasses fall forward slightly so that she could capture the shorter pieces of hair that framed her oval face. After she was done, she pushed her glasses back up to cover her large hazel eyes against the intrusion of the sun and kept walking. Something inside of her wanted to put as much distance as possible between her and Drew. The urge had become almost like an itch, overwhelming her until she'd finally given in and told him that she was going for a run. Not like he cared. Anna increased her pace and smiled as she felt her muscles starting to warm up.

Drew had been unemployed for as long as Anna could remember. She knew that at some point he'd had a job, she just couldn't picture him as anything other than the guy sitting in a worn recliner watching reality television on their old tube set and drinking enough cheap beer that he was starting to form a gut. Gently reminding him that the unemployment compensation he was receiving would run out eventually didn't do anything but make him angry. Sometimes she secretly thought that he might be bi-polar. Some days nothing she did was right. Other days it was like he couldn't stand to be separated from her. On those days, the look in his eyes did more to disturb her than to make her feel loved and appreciated. Since he'd made her quit her job several months ago so that they could spend more time together, her only time away from him was her daily runs. Anna took every opportunity possible to get out of the house, so she was constantly pushing herself to go longer distances and would run even in the middle of the hot summer's rainy season. She figured the worst that could happen was that she'd be struck by lightning or the levees would break again and she'd be swept out to sea. At least then she'd be away from Drew and the nightmares that robbed her of her sleep and sanity.

The worse the dreams became, the more she struggled in her sleep and Drew belittled her for it the next day. His lack of concern was weighing heavily on their relationship, so she'd sought out a doctor to try and help her overcome whatever was causing them. That doctor had sent her to a psychiatrist and Drew had started telling the whole town from his perch on a barstool at the local watering hole exactly what he thought of his kook wife who had to go to a head shrink. Now she'd become the town joke, pushing her father away from society and further into the small house that she shared with Drew and all of the things that made up their strange relationship.

Anna knew that at some point she had loved her husband. She must have since she married him. Looking at him now, at the sad, angry little man that he had become, she couldn't remember even one reason why. Just like she couldn't come up with one good reason to leave. He didn't really hurt her, didn't cheat on her that she knew of, he just didn't make her happy. Apathy didn't seem like a good enough of an excuse to get a divorce and even if she did leave, she didn't have a job, money or a place to go. She had no life, no friends, nothing outside of her relationship with Drew. And so she picked up the pace, breaking into a slow jog and decided that her goal for the day would be ten miles. That should keep her away from her husband who expected her to clean house and wait on him hand and foot for at least three good hours.

As her mind began to clear, letting go of all of the things holding her back, Anna's thoughts drifted back to the dreams that disturbed her sleep and haunted her waking hours. The most persistent one was the car crash. She kept seeing the same scene replay over and over again. Nothing ever changed and it always broke off right before she could see whatever it is her dream self was trying to look at. It felt like if she could just catch a glimpse of whatever or whoever it was that all of the pieces would fall into place and everything would make sense. The more she struggled to see what existed just outside of her dream's vision, the more the answer seemed to slip away from her. There were other dreams too. In some she was in some sort of clearing on top of a mountain bordered by a forest of dense trees. She was laughing at something that she couldn't quite hear. The vision would turn dark and she would be in the trees watching something black torture a woman lying on the ground, feeling helpless to stop it. The creature would look straight at her and she would feel fear rise in her throat just before the woman on the ground looked back and Anna lost her grip on the dream before she could see her face.

Anna broke into a run, trying vainly to burn off the frustration that she felt as images from her dreams flitted through her mind, confusing her with how real they seemed and how limited her perspective was when viewing them. There was always something in the corner of her mind that told her she was missing something, that the answers were just out of her reach. Unfortunately the nagging little voice did nothing to give her any direction on how to extend her grasp to reach the answers she sought. The most confusing dreams were the ones with Drew in them. She recognized his white blonde hair and dark skin, but in her dreams he was thinner with tattoos and a little younger. His appearance made her wonder if the dreams were trying to tell her something, or if they were somehow really memories, an idea which frustrated her all the more.

Tyler slid into a back corner booth at his favorite Hollywood hole-in-the-wall bar and sat down to wait for his friend Cam to arrive. He ordered a double shot of tequila and sat back, trying to draw as little attention to himself as possible. Cam stepped through the doorway as soon as Tyler's drink arrived. He quickly downed the alcohol and ordered another glass and the bottle of Patron. "Thanks for coming."

"No problem." Tyler's friend and bandmate sat down on the bench seat across from him. "You're here without Jared. What's going on?" The smile didn't leave Cam's handsome dark face or his bright copper eyes.

"Karina's alive. Danalia confirmed it. Now I don't know what to do." Tyler nodded his thanks to the waiter and poured another drink for himself and one for Cam. "Drink up. I am."

Cam shook his head smiling and turned his glass up. "It's a damn good thing that it takes a lot more to get us drunk than it does for everyone else."

"Sometimes that's more of a curse than a blessing." Tyler poured himself a third drink. "I'm really not turning into an alcoholic. I just don't know, Cam. I want to find her. You know I want to find her. Jane's still going through her transition though and she's decided that whatever she says should be what we do because Karina was her sister. But Karina didn't leave her a message, Karina didn't say the things to her that she said to me…" he allowed his voice to trail off.

"I never thought you were an alcoholic. Like I said, it takes more for us. Start drinking this stuff by the case and I'll start worrying." Cam looked down at the clear liquid curiously for a moment before he started sipping on the drink. "You've told me what everyone else wants. What do you want? And does Jared support you or are you on your own?"

Tyler glared at him like he was dumb. "What kind of question is that? Of course Jared supports Jane's perspective. He's so terrified that anything that angers her will blow up Los Angeles that he won't even contemplate going against her. I can't count high enough to record all of the times over the last few months that he's told me to stop doing something or not do something because it might upset Jane or it might cause Jane distress. I'm sick of fucking Jane. Not that I have anything against her but damn, I'm so tired of her life and my brother's adorable little relationship being the center of my whole fucking life. Before he got married, Jared made all of the decisions and I was okay with that for a while. I didn't mind just going with it and seeing where we ended up. It's not like we didn't know we had time to screw around for a bit. Now, when I thought that I was finally getting some space, being able to do my own thing, Jane's making all of the decisions because she's transitioning into a goddess and Karina freaking died on me. Why didn't she tell me what was going on? It's not like she couldn't trust me. What did she think I was going to do, blab to Jared? I would've helped her! I would've found a way out of this! This whole thing is insane! And I can't believe that it got here." Tyler banged his empty glass on the scarred wooden table.

"And now we're getting somewhere." Cam smiled and continued to sip his drink. "At least you order good alcohol even when you're pissed. So you're angry. And you want to hunt down Karina, bash her over the head with a club and drag her back to your man cave, right?"

Tyler laughed in spite of himself. "No! I do want to find her though and give her a choice. If she doesn't have her memories then I want to give them back to her so she at least has all of the information."

Cam propped his elbows on the table, his glass dangling from his fingers. "So let me get this straight. You want to find this woman and if she doesn't have her memories you want to tell a woman with amnesia, who probably has other memories stuck in her head, that everything she knows is wrong and you're the guy she sacrificed herself for in a previous life, wouldn't she like to give a relationship a shot? Unless I'm wrong and you don't want a relationship." Cam downed the rest of his drink and reached for the bottle. "Clubbing her over the head might be kinder."

"You think I'm wrong?"

"I think that you don't know what you want and it scares the hell out of you. You've got too many voices in your head and not enough of yours. What do you want?"

"I want to know what's going on. I want to see what's going to happen. I want to know that she's okay but I really want her to be with me and I don't know what that means," Tyler finished, rubbing his eyes tiredly. "Do you think I'm crazy? Because I feel like I'm losing it. I don't know that I love her, not the way that she deserves. I don't know if I want to find her, if I feel like it would be helping her, because I feel guilty or because I really do feel some sort of connection that I have to explore. And I don't know how much time I have left. I know that Jared's situation has changed, but I don't know what that means for me. It was one of the questions we never asked because it didn't seem like something that would ever happen to us. I never thought that one of us would find someone that would be more important than the other one. Now when I feel like I'm finally free I'm spending what could possibly be the last lifetime I'll ever live bowing to the needs of my brother and his immortal wife, both of whom will live forever while I'll probably be left alone to rot. I don't know if I'll be immortal by extension, I would guess not since I'm not mated, even though it's not like I didn't try, and I don't know if I be reincarnated by myself."

Cam held up a hand. "Wait, you tried to mate? When was this and how do I not know about it?"

Tyler grimaced. "Apollo's hounds don't know everything. When Karina was dying, I tried to save her by binding us together. It didn't work."

"What happened after that?" Cam leaned back in his seat, fascinated by the new information.

"She died."

"I'm sorry. That sucks."

Tyler shook his blonde head sadly, his gaze falling from his friend's. "I should've known. Before it happened, I should've known what was wrong. I should've found a way to stop her."

"Has it ever occurred to you that maybe Karina didn't want to be saved?" Cam raised one golden eyebrow in question.

"She did in that last minute. I know she did."

"Then what are you sitting here talking to me for? Go find your girl."

"Well, there's this one little problem that we could use your help with. You might want to call Jason," Tyler advised, referring to Cam's counterpart and the fourth member of Metamorphosis.

"So shit, this is going to be a night." He turned up the bottle, allowing the last few drops to fall out into his cup. "We're going to need another bottle." Cam held up the empty bottle, signaling the waiter. "You're paying."

Tyler smiled, finally feeling a little bit of relief knowing that he finally had someone on his side in this whole mess. "Yeah, I was expecting that."

5

Jared couldn't help but smile as he stood in the doorway of their bedroom watching his wife who seemed oblivious to his presence. It didn't happen very often that he was able to sneak up on her without her notice anymore. He waited for a few minutes, enjoying watching her, finally obviously comfortable in their home. Before she turned around, he pushed off of the doorframe he was leaning on and crossed the room silently. Jared slipped his arms around Jane's waist and kissed the top of her head. "What are you thinking about?"

Jane leaned back against his hard chest, snuggling deeper into his strong arms. "I was just looking at this, thinking about us when we started." She indicated the framed piece of paper on the wall above their sitting area in front of the floor to ceiling windows overlooking the backyard.

"Your "Things I Want to Do Before I Die" list." He chuckled. "You know, I don't think we ever finished that list."

"Seems that we have plenty of time to do it." Jane turned away from her contemplation of the framed piece of paper and looped her arms around her husband's neck. "You know, I just realized something."

"What's that?" He smiled, lowering his mouth to hover less than an inch above hers.

"No one's asked you what you think of all of this."

Jared bent down to kiss her quickly before pulling her over to the bed to sit beside him. "I just don't want this to be harder on either of you than it has to be. I can't deny Tyler the opportunity to go after what he wants, especially now that we know that she's alive. I just don't want to give him false hope that she'll want to come back here with him and resume life as Karina Jamison. Or whatever version of her that we cook up for a new identity."

Jane pulled him back on the bed and curled up beside him, her head over his heart to listen to it beat. "What if she does want to come back with him? He could be right. It's possible."

"If she can be found, Tyler will find her," Jared attempted to reassure her, pulling her closer.

"How can you be so certain that he can find her?" Jane pushed back from her perch enough that she could meet the bright blue eyes that she loved so much. Every time she looked at him she felt her heart flutter and she knew that if her sister, wherever she was, felt anything like this about Tyler, Jane couldn't stand in her way. She just didn't understand why, if Karina felt that way, she didn't tell anyone, not even her sister who had shared a telepathic connection with her. Karina's interest had been obvious. Her final decisions and her reasons for them had been much less clear.

"He's a man on a mission. I'd do the same."

"If that's how he felt, why didn't he ever say anything to her?"

Jared snuggled her tighter in his arms, nuzzling the side of her neck to breathe her in. "He didn't know how she felt until it was too late. He always thought he'd have more time."

"We should've known."

"I should've known when Sabina helped us get you back. She never does anything without an ulterior motive. I was so concerned with finding you that I didn't ask questions. I didn't care at the time."

"What happened to Karina wasn't your fault." Jane curled in as close to him as she could get, resting her head on his chest to listen to the steady thrum of his heartbeat.

"What happened to you was. I had no idea they'd take you from me, especially not like that. If I had stopped it, none of the rest of it would've happened. Zane would still be gone, but otherwise, nothing would be the same."

 "You shouldn't have been afraid that what you were asked to do would've changed how I see you." She turned in his arms, sliding her hands underneath his t-shirt, meeting his gaze as she felt him sigh. Jane brought her mouth against the steady pulse in his throat and smiled when his short fingernails dug sharply into her lower back, urging her to move tighter against him. Her hands moved lower, pulling his body more intimately against hers as she brought her violet gaze up to meet his hazy blue one. "Jared, there is nothing that you could do to change this, to make me not love you."

"I took away the one thing that I can't give you back." His eyes dared her to contradict him or challenge his words.

Jane watched his eyes carefully to gauge his reaction as she spoke since it was dangerous for her to delve into his mind without risking exposing him to her new powers. "You took nothing away that I didn't help lose. It's not solely your responsibility to make me happy. It's not on you to solve every problem. We're unusual and our lives are always going to be more dramatic than most. It just comes with the territory. We will face problems, maybe not always ones that directly affect the course of someone's life, but there will be problems. It's not up to you to make it okay for everyone. Right now you're pushing your brother away because you're trying to make this whole mess easier on me. You wouldn't take Tyler's side earlier because you were afraid of pushing me away. You can't keep doing this to yourself, Jared. I'm worried about you." Jane licked the column of his throat and sighed as his fingers lightly grazed her spine.

"Don't worry about me. I'm still hanging in here with you just fine." Jared chuckled, pulling her across his body so that her legs straddled his waist. "See," he smiled, pulling her down harder against him, "I am just fine."

Jane slid against him. "I see that physically, you're fine."

He sighed, dropping his upper body back on the bed. "You're not going to let this go, are you? Jane, we've got people rising from the dead, you're turning into some sort of violent fire goddess with black eyes and Tyler's depressed. We can't all fall apart at the same time. Don't worry, when it's my time you'll know it. Right now, if I say I'm fine, take it at face value and stop trying to find something wrong where there's nothing to find. You're leaving in three days for two weeks. Let's not spend it fighting or talking about all of the things that could go wrong and whose fault they are. Please."

Jane sighed, slumping against him with her head on his chest, her long dark hair forming a curtain around her face. "I should cancel the book tour. And the trip to Vancouver. It's too much right now."

"No." Jared pushed her hair back with one hand, forcing her to look at him. "This is your career. It's important. You have to go. I promise that we won't run off and I won't let Tyler do anything stupid while you're gone. We'll let you know if we find out anything new, I promise."

"Why don't you and Tyler come with me? You and Tyler can write for the new album while I'm working and we can search each city for signs of Karina. All expenses paid needle in a haystack search trip," she quipped, bracing her hands on his chest so that he would take her seriously and stop his on top of the clothes exploration of her lower half. It was damn distracting.

"I'll ask him when he gets back. If he's interested we'll go. If he can't get a read on her location from here, maybe a trip around the country will help." Jared glanced past her to the bedroom door and wished that he had closed it coming in, just in case.

Jane followed his line of sight. "I don't think he's coming back for a while."

A large, impish grin crossed her husband's handsome face as he redirected his attentions more toward the present and the woman nestled snugly in his embrace. "How did you know that's exactly what I was thinking?" He held her tightly while he flipped them on the bed so that she was lying trapped underneath him.

"I have a direct link to your brain and it happens that I know you that well. So you'd like to use the time constructively?" Her hands slid inside his tight black jeans, moving around to the front. "Where are the whips and chains when you need them?"

"In our closet, though I don't want to wait long enough to get them." He pulled her tank top over her head and tossed it to the floor. "Mmm, black lace. You know that's my favorite."

"Only on top," she teased.

He looked genuinely surprised. "Since when do you not match?"

She giggled, sliding suggestively against him. "Who says that I'm wearing anything?"

Jared reached up under her skirt and grinned. "Oh, I love you, woman."

A startled screech from the hall interrupted the intimate moment. "Guys! A little warning, please, while our telepathy is on the fritz! Put the naughty bits away, we have guests!" Tyler called, walking back down the hallway. "Start making some damn noise or something. Otherwise I'm getting Jared's dick a freaking bell."

Jane smiled down at her husband, kissing him deeply before sighing as she pulled away. "We will finish this later."

"We could finish it now," he remarked, straightening his clothes as he watched her get dressed.

Jane caught him staring and reached out with her hand, playfully turning his face away. "There are some things that have to come before sex." At his sullen expression she relented, climbing on to his lap and kissing him soundly on the lips. "Once Tyler's got Karina back we'll have plenty of time to play." She nuzzled his head to the side and placed soft kisses down his throat.

"Do you think they'll be like us?" Jared voiced the concern softly, keenly aware of his brother's proximity. "I mean, what if she doesn't remember or want to be Karina Jamison?" He grew very still, waiting for his wife's answer.

"I hope for the best," Jane answered softly, staring into her husband's bright blue eyes. "Didn't hurt us, did it?"

"No." Jared hugged her to him tightly, still slightly unwilling to let her out of his sight for longer than necessary, Karina's unexpected death still haunting him.

"Even if nothing comes of it but that he sees, her, maybe Tyler can get some peace just by seeing her or knowing she's out there. He left so much unfinished with her. He needs an ending, whatever that may be. We all do." Jane climbed off of the bed and her husband's body, walking to the front of the house. "Who did you bring home with you, Tyler?"

"Cam and Jason." Tyler was flopped across the couch when she entered the living room, one forearm covering his eyes from the glare of the overhead lights.

Jane heard clanging and continued into the kitchen. Cam, tall, blonde, tan and the embodiment of the perfect grown up surfer boy, stood in front of the stove attempting to heat water in the tea kettle. Jason, the exact opposite of Cam with brown hair, brown eyes and a compact muscular build, was rooting through the cabinets with a bottle of vodka from the freezer in his hand. "What are the two of you doing to Tyler's kitchen?"

"Tyler's kitchen?" Jason raised an eyebrow. "Aren't you the little lady of the house? Ty! Have we been wrong about you this whole time?"

Tyler groaned in response and Jane laughed lightly. "Hey, every man needs his man cave and Tyler's threatened bodily harm if I try to oust him from the kitchen." She walked over to Jason and snatched the bottle from his hand, returning it to the freezer despite his protests. "No more alcohol is being consumed in this house tonight."

"Just trying to procure a bit of the hair of the dog for my boy." Jason slid around her and reclaimed the bottle. "No worries, mom, I'll drink outside." He slipped past Jane and out into the living room.

"You know better than to try and take things away from Jason." Cam gave her a one armed hug and resumed his struggle with the tea kettle. "Why don't you just use the microwave like normal people?"

"Because we're not normal people." Jane reached around him and heated the kettle with two fingers.

"Nifty trick," Cam commented, removing the kettle from the stove and setting it on a trivet.

"I'm sure you've seen weirder with these two," Jane commented calmly, attempting to study his reaction while lowering her shields enough to try and slip into his mind.

Cam banged the tea cup he was holding on the counter, his face contorted in pain. "Do NOT do that. Ever." He leaned over with his elbows on the butcher block counter, his head cradled in his hands. "I know this is the first time you've displayed any of your special talents in front of me but trust me, I'm okay with it. I'm not okay with that raging inferno you just deposited in my brain." He groaned in relief as she withdrew, slumping to his knees for a moment before straightening. "Is that what you're living with? God, that hurt."

"Sorry, that doesn't normally happen."

"Tyler told me you've been shielding like a son of a bitch. Keep it up. The rest of us won't survive it." He patted her on the back reassuringly. "It's okay, it'll get better. Jason and I've seen this before. I've no doubt that you'll survive." Cam winked and took Tyler his cup of tea.

Jane took a moment to make a cup for herself and one for Jared before joining the men in the living room. "Exactly how long have you all known each other?"

Cam looked to Tyler who nodded from underneath the hands covering his face. "Since they were babies. The first time."

Jane dropped down onto the arm of the chair Jared was currently occupying and he shied as far away as the chair arms would allow to keep from being scalded by the hot water that slid over the sides of the cups she was holding. "Explain, please."

"Jason and I are their protectors. Sort of like the watchdogs of Apollo. Before these two came along we were warriors. When they were sent down to earth to be raised by a mortal, Zeus gave us immortality in return for vowing to guard them for eternity."

"So you're Jared and Tyler's bodyguards?" Jane gripped the tea cups tighter, causing the water to begin to overheat. Jared stood, prying them from her grasp before the tea began boiling.

"We prefer friends until we have to be their caretakers," Cam amended, taking Tyler's usual seat.

"Do you remember the family that I told you kept this house for us until we were old enough to take it back?" Jared sat back down, watching his wife carefully. Jane nodded mutely in response. "That was Cam and Jason. When we're not here causing trouble for them, they prepare for our return."

"Yeah, you two are a full time job. The only time we get a vacation is when you kick the bucket." Cam crossed one leg over the other and settled back to enjoy the tea that Tyler, in his hangover state, was ignoring.

"You conveniently forget all the times you almost got us killed," Tyler remarked snidely from behind his hands. "Could someone please find my sunglasses? The really dark ones? Please?"

Cam calmly reached behind him and retrieved the requested pair of Fendi shield glasses from the jacket dangling from the back of the chair, tossing them on Tyler's stomach. "There, glasses. You just have to remove your hands long enough to put them on. See, still saving your life."

"You would be saving my life if you'd come over here and put them on so I don't have to look at the light," he grumped, squeezing his eyes shut, using one hand to cover his eyes and the other to grope around on top of his stomach until he found the glasses. He fumbled to cover his eyes with the dark lenses, sighing in relief when they were finally in place. "You're forgiven for 1478."

"Will you please get over that? It's been a few centuries. Besides, you made it. Nothing to worry about." Cam brushed it off.

"We almost got burned at the stake!" Tyler's outrage pulled up into a sitting position for a second before he realized how quickly he'd moved and dropped back down, groaning at the movement.

"Almost doesn't count," Cam countered. "It was just a little inquisition. It's not our fault that the two of you gave the wrong answers."

"It's not our fault that you guys picked a woman to give birth to us that thought she was making a deal with a very different God." Jared turned sideways so that he could tell Jane his side of the story. For her part, Jane shook off her unease at Cam's revelation and took a deep breath, trying to make herself more comfortable. "These geniuses were travelling Europe when the time came for them to find someone to give birth to me and Tyler. So they found a very religious woman who made the deal, thinking that she was giving birth to the second coming of Christ. When she gave birth to twins, she freaked out and finally figured out that her God and our dad weren't the same people. She was convinced that one of us would grow up to be the anti-Christ. When we slipped up and showed her our powers one day when we were younger she turned us over to the Inquisition. Genius one and two were hanging out with some not quite so conservative women.

The villagers were practically lighting the torches when they finally showed up and got us out of there."

Jane couldn't help but laugh. "I'm sorry, but that's the most insane thing I've ever heard. We weren't that far from each other though. I was in England around that time. The food has definitely improved since then."

"Yeah, it didn't have a very high bar set for it." Cam wrinkled his nose in distaste.

"Where is Jason?" Jane looked around the room as she reached for her tea cup, noticing the man's absence for the first time.

Tyler pointed to the glass doors leading to the backyard without even glancing up to see if he was right. Jane looked over and saw Jason happily bouncing around in the flower beds in front of the wall of windows, drinking directly out of the vodka bottle. "You told him not to drink in the house. He took it outside."

"The man always finds a loophole." Jared adjusted his sitting position and motioned for Jason to join them.

Jason came in carrying his bottle and dropped down to sit on Tyler's legs. "Feeling better?"

Tyler groaned in pain and rolled over on to his side, pulling his legs up as he assumed the fetal position. "I was. What the fuck was that for?"

"There wasn't anywhere else to sit. You're taking up too much real estate." Jason settled into his commandeered corner of the couch. "So what are we discussing?"

"I was just explaining our roles to Jane and was about to tell her why we've invaded her house this fine evening," Cam volunteered.

"Other than to bring this guy's drunk ass home?" Jason grinned, reaching out to thump the underside of Tyler's foot and earning a swift kick to the arm for his efforts. "Just don't hit the bottle."

"Like I didn't pay for enough bottles for you tonight."

"You were saying why you're here tonight?"

"We're here to help you. Like I said before, we've seen this kind of thing happen over the centuries. How long have you been transitioning?"

"For a little over a year."

"Well I've got good news and bad news for you. The good news is that you're about halfway through and the bad news is that you're about halfway through. For regular mortals it can take a good decade to change fully. You started out as an elemental so it cuts down your time."

Jane clutched Jared's hand nervously as she asked her next question. "How bad is this going to get?"

"How bad is it now? I mean, I know what Tyler's told me but you've probably got more to add to it."

"Black eyes, weird creepy voice, throwing fire and electricity. At one point I was told I levitated a little bit. Oh and then there's the raging inferno going on in my body. What you felt in my head? Multiply it by a thousand and picture that everywhere. The only way to get rid of it is to let it out and I'm a little afraid that if I do that we'll suddenly have beach front property." She paused, regarding him seriously. "Do you know what kind of goddess I'm becoming?" Jane whispered fearfully.

Cam thought for a moment then shook his head negatively. "No, sorry. I don't have that kind of power. I know someone who does though." He sat back in his seat so that he could better address the room. "I'm going to wager a guess that no one has thought to ask Danalia about this?"

Tyler raised one limp hand. "I suggested that earlier. My idea was vetoed."

"On what basis?"

"Jared doesn't want the whole family to know what Jane's shiny new powers are." Tyler smirked. "When she goes nuclear I'm pretty sure they'll figure it out."

"The drunk guy makes an excellent point," Jason offered, finishing off his bottle like it was water and wiping his mouth on his sleeve, grinning. "What are you going to do when they figure it out and you've been hiding it from them?"

"We'll cross that bridge when we get to it." Jared wrapped an arm around Jane's waist and tugged her closer to him. Jane pulled away from him and stood. "Where are you going?"

"To find my phone. I need to postpone my book tour. There's no way that I can go with all of this hanging over my head. Stuffing me in a store full of flammable objects after being ensconced on a plane is probably not the best idea right now," she mumbled, placing her tea cup back on the coffee table and walking toward the door.

Jason extended an arm that caught her at the waist, momentarily halting her retreat. "There's another option."

Jane sighed, her shoulders slumping. "What would that be?"

"If Danalia knows what you are, she might be able to help you deal with it a little better."

"In two days?"

"It's worth a shot, isn't it?"

Jane looked over her shoulder to Jared who shrugged. "Call her."

Anna sat down on the sofa with a cold beer and smiled. It had been a long day, one of the ones where Drew belittled her and blamed her for all of their problems. Now he was out, probably at the bar spending the federal aid check that had been deposited into their account today, and she didn't care. For her part, she was just glad he was out of the house and that she could have some peace and quiet for a few minutes. Anna leaned back into the overstuffed yellow cushions and tucked her feet underneath her, spreading her long cotton vintage skirt over her toes. Not that they'd get cold in the warm evening air, especially with the windows open, it was just a comfort thing. She took a few sips of her drink, closed her eyes and began her meditation. Before she could really relax, she had to take a few deep breaths and focus on pushing all of the negative thoughts, everything that was weighing her down, out of her head. When her mind was clear, she opened her eyes and reached for the book she had left on the coffee table. It was the final entry in a series by an author she had been obsessed with over the last year. The fantastical web she weaved, two characters that flowed through eternity together, gave Anna some sort of hope, no matter how unlikely, that there was more for her, more to her life than sitting at home with Drew forever. Anna sighed happily and opened the book by author Jane Jamison that she had purchased several months ago. As she opened the pages of the paperback novel, she noticed a half-page sized flyer that drifted to the floor. Assuming that the bookseller had placed it there, she leaned over, retrieving the page from the floor. After reading it, she decided that she would have to make sure Drew slept late a week from Wednesday. Anna decided that she really did want to meet the woman who had given her any kind of hope, however small, in her dull, monochromatic life. And Jane

Jamison was scheduled for a book signing in New Orleans. Anna sighed happily, cuddling into a corner of the couch with her book on her lap and a beer in her hand. Now all she hoped for was that Drew stayed out for a long, long time tonight.

"I'm a what?" Jane's voice was loud enough that it caused Tyler to wince in pain.

"You're a destroyer. Take a deep, cleansing breath, center yourself and move forward. There's nothing to do about it. None of us know what our powers will develop into. Your fire and lightning ability comes from the males of our line and those that hold the most power. You will grow to be very powerful. As a destroyer, you will be the one of our line that is called upon in the hours of our most dire need. When fully developed, you will have the ability to decide the fates of worlds. You will be able to destroy and rebuild as necessary. I knew that at some point one would be born who would be the dark to the light of my creator powers. I never dreamed that you would become the destroyer for our line. It is a grave responsibility but one that those higher than us must believe you can handle. Otherwise they would not have placed something as precious as the balance of the human realm in your hands." Danalia smoothed the long pleats of her dress over her legs, her hands practically shaking with excitement. "I've waited so very long to have my counterpart so that we could meld our powers. Our abilities are designed for each other's. I will be able to teach you up until a certain point. After that, you will be on your own to discover what you are truly capable of."

"Did you hear that, baby? The fate of the human realm is in my hands. No big deal." Jane's voice was on the verge of panic.

"You're the destroyer," Jared echoed, his voice hollow as he stared straight ahead, unblinking.

Tyler blew out a noisy breath and crossed the sun filled living room to whack both of them on the back of the head. "Wake up! Yes, you're the destroyer. Yes, she can handle it, Jared. No, we're not all going to die today. Now that that's settled, can we please move on to how we deal with this before our flight leaves for New York?" Tyler consulted his watch impatiently.

"We have to wait for Cam and Jason to get here anyway," Jane responded absently and in a monotone voice.

"I can't believe you are allowing those dogs to accompany you." Danalia's delicate nose wrinkled in distaste.

"They're not dogs, they're our friends." Jared shook himself out of his stupor to defend the two men that had defended him and his brother for centuries.

"They are the hounds of Apollo. They are dogs and they smell like it."

"Look, don't stick your nose up at our friends because they're not gods like you." Tyler grumped, sitting on an ottoman, his feet bouncing in frustration.

"You asked for my help. This was my first chance to be here," Danalia shot back angrily. "I am here to assist you at your request. There are other things on other planes that demand my attention besides you and your melodrama, Traegar."

"Yes, gardening is such an ambitious occupation," he muttered.

"I do more than that as you well know. For her training it's me, our father or one of Athena's feminist warrior daughters. Which would you prefer?"

"I know, I know. You're the goddess and we're the halflings. You dain to be in our presence, on our plane. I've heard all of this before. What is the solution?"

"Do not be short with me, prince. You are the only halfling in this room. Jane and Anyasis are immortals. You will be but it is not your time yet. I understand that there is a timeline, but a few hours is not sufficient time to assist Jane with coming into her full powers. When they surface, it will be extremely painful for her and it will be difficult, if not impossible, for her to control her urges. It is much better that she learn now. I would like to take her with me back to Olympus where she can be surrounded by her magic rather than attempt to complete training her where she is vulnerable. No matter what you think of our family, in this instance they can help. We all can. How you treat that depends on how hard you want to resist the fact that Anyasis has momentarily surpassed you."

"Why am I an immortal and he's not?" Jared leaned forward, truly interested for the first time in his half-sister's words.

"You are mated. You can both cross to Olympus and live safely. You can go home, Anyasis. Traegar is not. His fate is undetermined and I cannot see into the future to see what will happen for the remainder of this lifetime, little less afterwards. All I know is that he should be immortal and he will be, but he is not there quite yet and this is not something that you can remedy." Danalia's voice was strained and she rubbed her eyes tiredly in an uncharacteristically human manner. "I will help all of you, because you are my family, in any way that I can but I cannot go against the decrees of the gods. In this instance it may be better for you if you must stay on this plane that you stay off of their radar, so to speak. That means that Jane must learn to do more than shield her powers from the two of you. She shines like a beacon of power. Others will come to her and they will not be as understanding of human proclivities as I am. So tell me what you need so that I may leave this god forsaken place and get back to my creations. Obviously you do not intend to give Jane the amount of time that she needs to train properly at this juncture."

"We're getting on a plane in a few hours. We're all going to travel for two weeks on my book tour so that we can attempt to locate Karina's soul. I'm more worried about containment than I am learning control right now. Is there a way to shut it down, or at least lessen the effects until we figure out what to do with these powers? I promise that as soon as we return, I will come to you for training. If you show me how to travel between them the way that the three of you do, I will join you on any plane with gratitude for helping me to adjust to being the destroyer." Jane nearly choked on the word.

"Ignoring your powers will not make them go away," Danalia warned. "I can help you but what I do for you, it will come at a cost. You will be human for a time. You will not get sick or die, but you will be blocked from your powers. I cannot block one piece of you without blocking the rest of it as well. You will have no powers, no telepathy. Your element will be dormant until the spell is released. Once in place, I will be able to remove the block and you will only if you strain your powers. Without them, you will be helpless. Is this agreeable to you?"

"Will my powers stop growing?"

"No, they will simply remain dormant for a time. Once they are restored, you will feel a tremendous surge in strength. If this happens in an environment that we can control, such as on Olympus, I will be able to help you contain them. I do not recommend doing this for an extended period of time or the fallout may be exponentially worse."

"Do it." Jane squared her shoulders, facing Danalia bravely. "I understand everything that you say and, for my family, I am willing to take the risk."

Danalia gave a small nod, smiling sadly. "I understand." She placed two fingertips to the other woman's forehead and closed her eyes. Her brow furrowed in concentration as a silver mist slid down her arms and spiraled around her hand until finally gliding into Jane's head. Jane's eyes opened wide, the irises moving through colors in a dizzying array until they finally stopped, turning a color that they rarely were, brown. "How do you feel?"

Jane took a couple of deep, gasping breaths, stepping backwards and almost stumbling into her husband's arms. "I feel like I just lost ten I.Q. points. What did you do to me?"

"I took your powers and contained them with my magic inside of your brain. Do not test my container, don't try to use your powers in anyway. Those that are reflex actions, such as your shields and your telepathy, keep them at bay. Any attempt to use magic will weaken the barrier that holds it. If you attempt to use it too much, it will break and everything you've been feeling will rush back into your body. Your mental shields will not be enough to keep it at bay. You would be better to let me slowly pull pieces back out. I cannot differentiate between what is yours naturally and what belongs to the destroyer, but I can lessen the potential for injury to you, Anyasis and Traegar if I bring you back into your power gradually." Danalia extended one graceful hand to cup Jane's chin, lifting her face so that the taller woman could see her eyes. "It appears to be working."

"I can't feel the destroyer anymore. Or my element." Jane pulled away from Danalia and turned to look at her husband. "I can barely feel you. I just know that you're there. I can't see the strands anymore."

"Stop trying!" Danalia admonished, grabbing the other woman by the arm and turning her so that they faced once more. "Did you not pay attention to my words? Jane, you cannot try to use your magic in anyway. If you do you will break the powers free from their bonds. This is the only way that your safety can be guaranteed while you travel." Danalia released her and took a step backwards. "You have always wanted to be a regular, normal human, correct? This is perhaps the only chance you will ever get. Embrace it and have Traegar or

Anyasis call to me when you return and are ready to have the block removed. I will come as quickly as I can." With that, Danalia vanished, leaving Jane blinking at the place where the other woman had stood.

Jared glared at his brother who was inching toward the door as he stood to hug Jane. "Keep your phone on you and stay close. You don't go anywhere without one of us with you. I can't risk anything happening to you while you have nothing to defend yourself with."

"Remember our conversation the other day? I'm not glass, Jared. I won't break," Jane gently reminded him before pulling away to join Tyler and their suitcases at the door. "We should go."

"That's all you're going to say?" Jared scooped up the small duffle bag that was serving as his carry-on and followed her to the door.

"I have to remain calm or I risk releasing my powers from whatever block Danalia put on them. That means going to the airport early, possibly having a drink before the flight, reading a book, sticking to my schedule and possibly even taking a bubble bath at the hotel tonight. I am going to avoid stress and anything else that might make me tap into that part of myself. Are you okay with that?"

"Fine." Jared held up his hands in mock surrender. "I'm just surprised you're taking this so well."

"Be surprised in the car, Romeo." Tyler grabbed Jared by the shoulder and pushed him out the door into the mid-morning Los Angeles sunlight.

6

"Your nose sucks," Tyler commented, annoyed as he flipped through a book that he wasn't the least bit interested in, sitting in the café of the sixth chain bookstore he had visited that week as a part of Jane's publicity book tour. These things were taking longer and longer to get through and he was tired of wasting time when he could be out there trying to make progress toward finding Karina. Over two weeks had passed and they were no closer for having travelled half of the United States than they were at home in Los Angeles.

Jason grinned, dropping into the chair beside Tyler and placing a cup of coffee in front of him. "I don't actually sniff people out, a fact which you well know. I sense people's energies. With any luck I'll be able to sense your girl's if she comes close enough. If you want someone to sniff her out, go talk to Cam," he joked, leaning back in the straight wooden chair. "So what's the plan after Jane finishes meeting her adoring fans?" Jason tilted his head to the side, his gaze directing Tyler's attention to the table near the front of the store where Jane sat signing books for fans who snaked a line around two shelves of books. Jared attempted unsuccessfully to unobtrusively lurk over her left shoulder while Cam stood at the opposite end of the table next to Jane's publicist talking in hushed tones.

"The plan's the same as it always is," Tyler commented, not looking up from his book. "Jane finishes, we go back to the hotel, I try the spell for the five thousandth time and we start wandering around to see if we can find any trace of her. While we do that Jane will do research to try and find anything on local news that could potentially indicate a supernatural occurrence."

"Supernatural? In New Orleans, home of witchcraft and fictional vampires." Jason chuckled as he sipped his coffee. "I don't envy Jane's job. I'd rather get to wander around the French Quarter all night."

"Slow down, party boy. You're going out to the bayou. We know better than to let you at the clubs. Besides, Karina's not that kind of girl."

"Karina wasn't that kind of girl," Jason corrected. "You've got no idea what she's like now."

"Don't remind me." Tyler glared at his friend over the top of the book he was holding. He stood, looking across the café to the rows of bookshelves that filled the rest of the store. "I'm going to go see if I can find something else to read or burn off some frustration or do something to pass the next couple of hours. Let me know if anything interesting happens." Tyler crossed to the classic literature section, replacing the book that he had been basically pretending to read. He wandered through the stacks until he noticed that he had arrived in the fantasy section. It took him only a moment to locate the shelf that contained his sister-in-law's books. He flipped through the titles idly, not noticing the pretty brunette doing the same until he almost walked into her. "I'm sorry." Tyler took a stumbling step back.

The woman smiled shyly, tucking one long lock of curly dark brown hair behind her ear that had fallen into her face. Tyler took her in from head to toe, noting her black cotton sundress and delicate gold sandals. He estimated her to be about twenty-six, her lean frame resembling that of an athlete with more generous curves in all of the appropriate places. Her darkly tanned skin spoke of many hours spent in the hot southern sun. "It's my fault. I wasn't looking," she mumbled, barely meeting his gaze through the fringe of her long dark lashes.

"I'm Tyler." He held out his hand to her.

"Anna." She shook his hand and turned back to the bookshelf, quickly plucking the novel she had been seeking from its resting place. She smiled at him and his heart almost stopped, catching Tyler off guard. "I should go." Anna clutched the book to her chest as she turned to leave.

"Wait!" Tyler reached out and touched her shoulder. He didn't know what it was about the woman but he really didn't want her to leave just yet.

"What?" She turned back around, her hazel eyes meeting his green gaze for the first time. Her breath caught as she felt a twinge of memory, something lurking just at the edges of her awareness that she couldn't quite grasp. The more she stared at him, the more it bothered her. Anna shook her head slightly to help rid herself of her frustration and the fuzzy images that had developed a nasty habit of appearing at the most inopportune times without lending any clarity to their purpose or meaning.

"I – I don't know." Tyler withdrew his hand and felt a small spark of fire slide from her bare skin to his fingertips. He jumped slightly, rubbing his fingers together. "Did you feel that?"

"Feel what?" Anna peered up at him curiously.

"Nothing, I guess. Do you want to get a cup of coffee or something?"

"I can't." She slid backwards just out of his reach. "I have to go."

"Maybe later then?" Tyler couldn't believe the words that were falling out of his mouth without his consent. His vocal chords seem to have totally bypassed his brain.

"I can't. I wish I could, and thank you, but I really can't." Anna bit back a grin as her grip shifted nervously on the book. "I have to go. I'd really like to meet the author before she leaves. It was nice to meet you, Tyler." She gripped the book in her left hand, extending her right to him.

Tyler shook her hand and it was then that he noticed the thin gold band on her left hand. Mentally cursing himself for his idiocy, he released her hand and smiled. "It was nice to meet you too, Anna. Enjoy the book." He watched her walk toward the front of the store curiously, wondering what on earth it was about her that could have possessed those words to come out, especially while he was taking a temporary involuntary break from searching for Karina. That's where his focus needed to be, on finding the woman he cared about, not flirting with some random married woman in a bookstore. Flirting badly. He laughed at himself, turning in the opposite direction and continuing his exploration of the bookstore, hoping that Jane would finish her signing quickly.

7

"That was a complete waste of time." Tyler entered the house, throwing his jacket in the general direction of the sofa before walking off with his suitcase to his room. "I should've stayed here. At least then I wouldn't have had to eat prepared food for nearly three weeks." His footsteps echoed down the hallway followed by the sound of a door slamming.

"He's taking that well," Jane commented, following her husband into their home with her laptop bag.

"Don't worry about it," Jared attempted to reassure her, taking her bags from her and placing them gently on the floor. "It was a shot. We needed to see if it would go anywhere. Anything we try right now is a long shot. He knows that."

"Why, Mr. Stateton, aren't you being practical about this whole situation," Jane teased, sliding her hands up her husband's back and using her fingernails to chart a course back down to his waistband.

Jared grinned, wrapping his fingers in his wife's long hair and dragging her mouth to meet his in a kiss that ended far too soon for either of them. "Why don't we forget about everything that's going on and focus on us for a little bit?" He pulled away from her slowly, his fingertips lingering on hers until the last possible second. "You get the wine and I'll take the luggage to the back and start a nice hot bubble bath."

Jane laughed, unable to resist the little boy grin that reminded her of all of the reasons she fell in love with Jared in the first place. "Mmm, twist my arm." She turned to enter the kitchen.

"Hey, tomorrow we should call for Danalia. I miss seeing your real eyes," he called after her. The comment stuck in Jane's head, troubling her for some reason that she couldn't quite identify.

Tyler sat in an Adirondack chair in the backyard, sipping his coffee and barely noticing the spectacular colors that the early morning sun was displaying across the horizon. His eyes were busy focusing on the small plastic casino chip that had been Karina's gift to him as she died. "Another time, another place," he mused. Something about the words tried to force him to recall some long forgotten detail. He'd gone over and over them in his mind, vainly hoping that Karina had been trying to tell him something more than a final goodbye. His fist tightened angrily around the piece of plastic when it refused to relinquish any secrets. Tyler's head jerked up as he heard his brother's door open and Jane walk down the hallway. Through his hearing, he followed her progress through the house to the kitchen. He heard her halt in front of the window and closed his eyes tightly, sincerely hoping that she would leave him alone. The breath that he didn't know he had been holding whooshed out of his lungs when he heard the door open and Tyler spent his remaining precious moments of solitude adjusting his posture and facial expression to what he hoped was neutral so that she wouldn't ask how he was or what he'd been doing. It wasn't that he didn't appreciate the sentiment, but unfortunately at the moment the very last thing he wanted was to sit there and listen to yet another person pity him while offering what he could only assume they thought was helpful advice. It was starting to annoy him to such a degree that it was becoming increasingly more difficult to withstand without punching the speaker in the face just so they'd take a breath and quit talking.

"Don't worry, I won't ask how you are." Jane took the chair next to him, drinking her coffee and contemplating the horizon.

"Good." The silence stretched between them for many long moments before Tyler sighed, deciding to break it. "I miss her."

"I know. So do I." Jane said nothing else, continuing to drink her coffee without looking at him.

"I felt like she was close in every city that we visited, every airport we walked into. I can't find her because I keep wishing so hard that I will. Hope is literally keeping me from finding her."

"We'll think of something else." Jane paused for a moment. "Why didn't you tell her how you felt?"

"I didn't want to rush her after everything that happened with her divorce. I thought I had more time." His laugh was harsh enough that she could almost feel shards of his tone breaking across her skin. "How ridiculously human is that, to think you have more time than the present."

"Karina planned this for months without telling anyone, without giving any kind of hint that something was wrong. You had no idea that you wouldn't have time to give her some space and let her figure things out for herself. You can't blame yourself for what happened."

"You trusted me to find her and I failed." Tyler finally faced her, his eyes hidden from her sight by his dark sunglasses.

"You haven't failed. You just haven't succeeded yet. We'll find her."

"How do you know?"

Jane stood, turning to walk back to the house, her empty coffee cup dangling from the fingers of one hand. The other hand she placed on top of the fingers he had clenched around the casino chip. "She wanted you to find her. I think it was a part of her plan."

Something occurred to Tyler and he seriously thought about the physics of punching himself for having not thought of it earlier. "Have you spoken to Sabina since that day?"

Jane watched him carefully, withdrawing her hand. "Why would I have talked to Sabina?"

"The day that Karina," Tyler stumbled over his words, nearly dropping his neglected coffee cup in his haste to stand, "The day of the accident Sabina said something to me about another deal that Karina made for me. I think it's time that we find out what the deal was."

"You forgot about something that important? We've spent three weeks searching the country and Sabina, who's in L. A., could've known all along?" Jane felt forgotten slivers of heat slide along her skin and remembered Danalia's warning to be cautious of stress. She closed her eyes and took a couple of deep breaths to calm herself. "That's not important. Right now we should focus on the fact that we may have a new lead. Let me go in the house and find my phone. I'll ask her. You're too invested in this to remain rational enough to engage Sabina."

"Why aren't you invested in this as much as I am?"

Jane felt the anger bubble up inside of her. Despite her best efforts, she was having an increasingly more difficult time of controlling it and she felt powers start to leak out from behind the container that Danalia had placed them in. She looked over Tyler's head and saw Jared step out into the yard from the kitchen door and knew that her eyes blazed a bright blue-green. "Because I love her enough to let her go with the belief that she has a better life than this world can give her. There's nothing normal or stable about our lives. I can't feel bad that my sister has a chance at a life I can't give her. A better life. If she's a child there's even a chance that she'll never remember us or the pain that we caused her. That I caused her." Jane flicked a finger, exerting enough power that it shoved Tyler back into his chair. "You think that I don't want to find her, that I don't want my sister back? This kills me but I'm willing to live with that because I love her. You're not sure you love her. You're not sure where she is but you want to rip her away from wherever she is to find out. What if you're wrong, you don't love her and you ruin her life again?" Jane stepped in front of Tyler and ripped the sunglasses from his face so that she could stare directly into his eyes. "Before you do this you'd better make damn sure that you can protect her, that you can give her what Jared gives me. I will not lose my sister again because you're unsure." Jane stormed back into the house, past her husband who watched the scene unfold from a few feet away.

Tyler caught his brother watching him and shrugged helplessly, replacing his glasses on his face. "Not just a cuddly bunny is she?"

Jared laughed. "Did you really think she was?"

"I'm surprised that it is you who requested a meeting with me. I thought it would be Traegar." Sabina slid into the matte red vinyl booth seat across the table from Jane. She looked around the diner, noting with disdain the chrome and Formica interior. "You eat at the most...interesting places." Sabina wrinkled her nose and wiped at the table with her paper napkin.

Jane propped her elbows on the table and sipped her coffee while watching Sabina's dark countenance over the rim of her cup. "They have good coffee. Food's not bad either. This isn't a social call though."

"You want information from me, you might want to consider being more sociable." Sabina glared at her.

Jane met her stare but lowered her elbows. "What did you do to my sister?"

"Your sister's dead."

"I think we both know that's not entirely true. I'd like to know what happened the day Zane died."

Sabina shook her head negatively. "You're not asking the right question."

"What is the right question?"

"You'll have had a year next week to come up with it. I believe that you should tell me."

Jane closed her eyes and took a deep breath to calm herself. The last thing she needed was to release her power in front of Sabina and a restaurant full of unsuspecting humans enjoying their late morning breakfast. She forced her teeth to unclench as she opened her eyes, carefully regarding the succubus as she tried to view the situation from a different angle. "What did Karina want for her gift?"

"That's better." Sabina leaned back in her seat and smiled. "I offered Karina the same arrangement with Traegar that you have with Anyasis. Curiously, she refused even though it was her desire to accept. She knew that in Zane's death I would be losing the life I needed for survival. I was short on time, so I accepted her bargain. Her life for Zane's death and a chance for her to be reborn again."

"What was she reborn as?" Jane asked quietly, almost afraid of the answer.

Sabina laughed. "She's a human adult, of course. How else could she hope to pursue a relationship with Traegar again?"

Jane slumped back in her seat, not sure if she was disappointed or relieved. "That's what she asked for?"

"Technically, no, actually, yes. Karina did not want her life to end but she saw the good that her sacrifice would do, so she requested to be brought back immediately as an adult. Since she couldn't go into her old body and the time restriction made generating a new one out of the question we had to become a bit more creative. Given the special circumstances surrounding her and Zane's deaths her soul was given another chance for survival in a different body."

"Does she remember?"

Sabina smiled and shook her head negatively. "That was not a part of our deal. You know that these things should be made as specific as possible. Generalizations are always open to interpretation."

"What wasn't open to interpretation?"

Sabina smiled encouragingly. "Now we're getting somewhere. Karina was reincarnated as a female adult, approximately the same age as when she died. She is hidden so that none of you may find her using supernatural means but you can know that she is alive. She believed that if it was meant for you to find her that you would. Unlike when Anyasis brought your soul back, this is all of Karina simply in another body."

"So my sister is alive and basically an amnesia patient somewhere on the planet in another body?"

"In crude terms essentially, yes."

"So it is possible that she could remember?"

"It would not behoove you or her if she remembered any of this now. Your sister leads a very different and much simpler life now. There may be some things that you must accept on faith." Jane rose to go, pausing as she stood to stare curiously at Sabina who smiled a very strange, cheerful smile and turned to leave. "Good luck, Mrs. Stateton."

"I will find her," Jane told Sabina, snatching her coffee mug off the table.

"No, you won't. Call when you need my assistance with the other matter."

Jane gulped down the last of her coffee and slammed the cup back down on the table. "There is no other matter, not right now anyway. Thank you for meeting with me and for the information." She paused before leaving, staring out the scuffed windows at the passersby. When she turned back to the table Sabina stared up at her expectantly.

"Was there something else?" Sabina daintily sipped her tea.

"I meant what I said when I saw you and Zane in the sushi bar. If circumstances were different I really think we could have been friends."

"I don't have friends. And circumstances are never different, they just are. But if that time were to exist, I would have been honored."

"Did you ever love him?"

"Which one?"

"Zane. Did you ever love him?"

Sabina smiled brightly. "I love them all."

"Thank you."

"May I now ask you a question?"

"Of course." Jane took a single step back toward the table.

"Why do you still blame yourself for Zane's death? He was destined to die anyway. You did him a favor. At least in this way he was given judgment. If his soul had been recycled the judgment made during his life would be the determining factor and he would not have had a second chance. I am surprised that Anyasis did not tell you this. By Zane's soul being sacrificed to Alecto, you gave him freedom. His soul should be at peace."

A dark look crossed Jane's face and her eyes turned grey. "I was supposed to protect him. His soul was always supposed to be destined for greatness, for something more that I couldn't see. But I felt it; I knew it was there. But I failed. He's gone, I'm still here, and whatever greatness he should have accomplished died with him."

Sabina laughed. "Did you ever think that perhaps you were backwards? If his soul were destined for greatness he would have achieved it in the millennia he was here. Maybe a part of the reason he's gone is so that you can finally see who you were really meant to be."

"You think so?" Jane considered her words, letting them roll slowly through her mind.

"Short-sighted humans. You forget that I can see it. As I said, knowing you as my friend would have been an honor, Jane Stateton.

Trust me though when I say that the destiny to achieve is your own. You have not failed yet. You're only beginning."

Jane nodded, confused and feeling slightly overwhelmed by Sabina's strange revelation. She took two slow steps back then turned, shaking off the strange feeling as Sabina watched her leave the diner, the cryptic smile still on her face. Jane pushed the information to the back of her mind for the moment and pulled out her new smartphone, dialing her brother-in-law. "I know where to start."

"Are you sure about this?" Tyler eyed his sister-in-law curiously as she unfolded a map of North America next to her laptop on the wooden planks of the den floor. Jane glared at him and passed him Karina's brass-handled athame from her position on the floor.

"I'm sure. Well, relatively sure. She wants you, right?" Jane pushed on without waiting for a response. Her fingers flew so fast across the laptop's keyboard that Tyler could barely follow the flow of information across the screen. "So I need you for bait. She's drawn to you, Ty, so I need you to reverse it and tell me where to look."

"And how do I do that?" Tyler idly pressed the tip of the athame against his skin.

Jane took a deep breath and looked up at him hesitantly. "You're probably not going to like it. I don't think it will be particularly pleasant for you but you need to see if you can sense Karina's soul. If you can connect with her we might be able to figure out where and who she is."

"I think I would have noticed by now if I could sense Karina."

Jane smiled secretively. "I don't think so. You're not looking in the right place. For her to come back for a chance with you, to risk this life again, Karina's not something external to you anymore. At

94

least not if you really feel how you think you do. So," she smiled tightly up into his surprised face, "ready to have all your questions answered?"

"What do I have to do?"

"You have to bleed out."

"No the hell I don't!" Tyler eyed the small silver knife in his hands in disbelief. He wanted to find Karina but he didn't think it would do any good to find her if her location died with him in a puddle on the floor. Not to mention that the last emotion his brother would experience on his behalf would be anger. Jared would be really pissed if he ruined the reclaimed wood floors.

"Yes the hell you do. If you want to find her this is the best way I can think of. She's blocked from us so nothing that we do magically is going to find her. You're still our best shot and you've got to look deep inside yourself, deeper than your conscious mind will let you go, if you want to find her. The place inside of you that you need to go, most people only go there when faced with death. You've got to go there but we need to keep you alive while we do it." She clapped him on the shoulder effectively. "Ready to do this?"

Tyler swallowed nervously, suddenly unable to look at the face that usually reminded him so much of what he'd lost. What he thought he'd lost. Staring down the answers to the hardest questions in his existence he suddenly wasn't sure he was ready to know the answers. Tyler closed his eyes for the briefest of moments and saw a picture of Karina's smiling face in the sun, a snapshot taken from his memory, laughing at him. He saw her tortured expression as she faced her death, the wounds opening anew with the knowledge that her hesitation in facing death was for him rather than her. He owed her a simple, black and white life, not the shades of gray that they lived in. And yet he couldn't stop himself from wanting to find her, to once and for all know what was real and what his mind had turned into fiction without his consent. And Tyler had to admit he was a little afraid to look that deeply into himself. He pierced his skin with Karina's blade and watched his bright red blood trickle down the shining surface. Some things should stay buried. His potential girlfriend wasn't one of them. Finally meeting Jane's multi-colored gaze he nodded affirmatively. "What do you need me to do?"

Jane took the knife and sliced open Tyler's wrist, holding it over the map. "Cut your arm. I need you to die and tell me what you see. That's payback for the knife to the heart, by the way."

"I assumed." Tyler watched the blood slowly begin to drain from his body. "How much do I need to lose?"

Jane cradled her own wrist as she continued her database search. "Don't think about it. Think about the last thing you want to see before you die then find my sister. I'm going to check on Jared." With a final tap on the keyboard Jane stood, her hands slowly growing slick with her own blood. With a few whispered words the cut on her arm healed and Tyler felt his brother slip from his conscious mind, leaving him alone with his fears and the warm pain radiating from his wrist. The blood continued to flow steadily from his arm and Tyler closed his eyes tiredly, welcoming the pain and not for the first time wishing that a little suicidal cut was all it took to end his life.

"What now?" Jared heard the irritation in his voice as blood dripped from his hand and ruined the sheet music that he had been carefully crafting for the past six days. He rubbed his eyes, tired from having not slept well in several days, and balled up his ruined work, grabbing a fresh sheet of paper and starting over writing the arrangement. Jared looked up when his wife stepped through the doorway, a pristine white hand towel in one hand.

"Thought you might need this." She took his offered hand and wiped it clean, pressing a soft kiss to the unmarked inside of his wrist where a wound should have been.

"Would a little warning have killed you?" he grumbled, his eyes directing her to the pile of ruined paper that he had tossed to the far corner of the room. "What are the two of you doing anyway?" He pulled Jane down to sit on his lap.

"Nothing much, killing Tyler." She wrapped her arms around him and sighed into his neck, breathing in the spicy scent of his skin. "You won't miss him, will you?" Jane curled closer into his body and closed her eyes, completely relaxed as she allowed herself to become immersed in her husband and his cinnamon spice smell.

Jared smiled as he felt the tension seep from her body, his hands gliding slowly up and down her spine. "Will we get to stop bleeding every five minutes? I really liked that song."

"I already fixed that," Jane mumbled, content to stay exactly where she was.

"Can we have uninterrupted sex whenever we want?"

Jane's husky laugh vibrated through his chest. "We can try, but I think you'll still have to fire your overeager new assistant."

"She means well," Jared argued half-heartedly.

"She means to get into your pants. She gives me one more death glare and I'm going to turn her into a toad for looking at you."

Jared laughed at the mental image knowing that given half the chance his wife would have the college student sprouting warts and eating flies. "Leigh's a good worker. She may just have a--," he took a deep breath, his forehead pinched as he searched for the right word," she may have a slightly misguided notion about what will make her successful in this industry." He laughed. "She'll be really popular though and will probably be a good second or third wife for someone. Not me," he added quickly.

Jane bit her lip to keep from smiling as she dug her nails into the small of his back, causing him to arch into her ever so slightly. "Something you need to tell me?" she teased.

"What would you think about becoming polygamists?"

"I don't share you," Jane whispered, licking his earlobe. "But if you don't mind sharing me I know a couple of hot actors…" her voice trailed off when his teeth found the sensitive spot on her neck and bit down hard enough to leave marks. Her nails dug into his back in earnest and an involuntary gasp escaped from her throat.

"Do you really want anyone else to touch you?" Jared growled in her ear, his teeth scraping up her neck.

"No one else is getting a chance because I refuse to stop touching you." Jane bestowed soft little kisses across his face and curled back against Jared's chest with her face pressed into his neck.

"Can I ask you something and you answer me honestly?"

Jane raised her eyebrows, causing her husband to chuckle at the sensation. "Because I don't tell you the truth all the time anyway. Not that you can't pull it out of my head at any time." She snorted. "I think I may be insulted."

Jared kissed the top of her head. "Why do you love me? Things changed so quickly and I know that you're sure and things are just…this is amazing. I just want to know if you know what changed."

"When I fell in love with you?" Jane felt a knot form low in her stomach, her brain furiously filtering through all of the possible hidden meanings behind the statement. "I thought about it a lot in the beginning but the reasons didn't really matter to me, not once I knew you."

"You mean once we had sex?"

"No. Once I knew that you were probably the best part of me. That you'd been inside of me all along."

"That can't be right. You were destined for someone else. We weren't supposed to fall in love."

Jane sat up straight, adjusting her position to put more distance between them. "Says the man who literally moved heaven and earth to bring me back to life. Didn't you ever wonder what drew you to me, why you couldn't just move on?" Jane tried to ease the conflicting emotions running rampant across his face with the caress of her hands on his temples. "You've been inside of me, a part of me, for my whole existence. There's no way this could have happened if you weren't."

Jared wrapped his arms securely around her waist. "You really believe that, don't you?"

"You don't? I think that we were meant to be together all along, it just took us awhile to notice it." Jane looped her arms around her husband's neck and leaned into him casually. "Whoever is above your father apparently doesn't care that I'm a mortal. Was mortal." The idea was still so foreign that Jane couldn't really process it enough to allow the startled protest that echoed in her head. She leaned in close, her breath warm against her husband's cheek. "Why did you chase me for twenty years?"

Jared smiled as his heart rate sped up and he felt heat emanating from his body in every place that they touched. He pulled back far enough that he could see her bright aqua-violet eyes. "I chased you so that I can do this." Jane's eyes closed reflexively, her mouth waiting for his kiss. Jared grinned, his face close enough that she could feel it when he licked his lips. His fingertips slid down her sides until he found the most sensitive spot, and tickled it. Jane jumped, her jaw dropping and her eyes popping open in surprise. A giggle escaped her throat, encouraging her husband.

"All this so that you could tickle me?"

"Well I was a kid technically then." Jared grinned, holding her waist in a vise grip while she struggled to get away. "You may be turning into a goddess, but I'm still stronger than you."

Tyler stared at the blank white wall in front of him, fighting against his weakening body to take deep breaths to speed the process along. Despite the extraordinary amount of blood loss he still felt nothing, saw nothing. No light at the end of a tunnel, no life flashing before his eyes, nothing. Tyler just felt hollow. As his clouded vision began to clear, he turned his head ever so slightly to see that the wound on his arm was slowly healing. He sighed and through a supreme effort of will sliced his wrist back open. His head fell back against his sister-in-law's desk as he felt the first rush of blood slide over his arm and down his hand. As his blood washed out of his body Tyler felt himself relaxing and his mind starting to wander. No longer able to expend energy on focus, he allowed his conscious mind to bleed unchecked into his subconscious, visions sliding across the back of his eyelids like a film in fast-forward. Flashes of green interrupted the playback and Tyler patiently waited for the images to slow to see what was causing the interruption. He was annoyed until his inner vision came into focus and he realized that the green was shots of Karina's hazel eyes. The slide show slowed enough that Tyler could finally see the subject of his internal monologue. Karina.

She wasn't the Karina he remembered. She was taller, her skin tanned a few shades darker. Her chestnut hair was long, in loose curls. Though she was still beautiful, there was nothing remaining of the woman he had been seeking. Only the hazel green eyes that shone in his dreams remained. The woman whose image flashed before his eyes had a delicate oval face that bespoke of a French Creole heritage and long, thin fingers that desperately clutched at the kitchen sink in front of her as she fought some tremor in her body. She looked up and stared straight ahead. Tyler swore that she could see him as clearly as he could see her. Then she turned without a glimmer of recognition, responding to someone out of Tyler's limited range of sight. Tyler shook himself from his distraction, trying to note every detail in the room, anything that would help to bring her location into focus. Like watching a film, he couldn't see or smell anything. Tyler scrambled to hold on to the vision as she left the room. For the first time in his life his world was silent and he longed for sound. Her face was turned away from him, not giving him the option to read her lips as she re-entered the room. He willed her to sense his presence but received no response. Before he could find anything of further value, his tenuous grasp on the vision snapped, sending him reeling back into his own present and his aching body. When his eyes opened a familiar face filled his vision and he smiled for a moment before realization struck. "I saw her."

Jane sat back on her heels, releasing the arm she had just finished bandaging. "Welcome back. Tell me if you feel all right then you can tell me what you saw."

"Why in that order?" Tyler squinted up at her, still trying to remove the image of Karina's old face which seemed to have stamped itself all over her twin's familiar features.

"Need to know if you need a blood transfusion." Jane indicated the pile of bloody rags she'd used to clean the floor. "You've been out for a while. You stopped healing."

"Hence the bandages. I get it." He struggled into a straighter sitting position, falling heavily against the desk when his arms couldn't support the movement. "How close was it?"

"Close enough that Jared closed the cut on your wrist as much as he could and went in search of medical supplies so that we could give you blood from one of us because we weren't sure you'd make the trip to the hospital. Twice in as many days is enough close calls for the week. We can't do this again."

He saw the weariness in her eyes and realized how much it must have cost her to keep herself and his brother shielded. "You'd protect him if it killed you, wouldn't you?"

If she seemed surprised by his question, she didn't show it. "He wouldn't survive it, but to give him the chance I would, yes."

"We've come a long way in a year, haven't we?"

"Well it's better than despising each other for eternity," Jane remarked wryly, helping him to sit comfortably while he recovered. "So what did you see?"

"You don't look like each other anymore." Tyler continued to study her face for comparison. "She was handwashing dishes. She's still a she, by the way, though I might be the only one affected by that particular quirk. She looked so familiar, but not like you at all. I can't place where I recognize her from. I'll work on it." He struggled to stand, leaning on Jane heavily as his mind clouded over again. They carefully crossed the hall to the living room and the couch.

"Maybe she looks like someone you know," Jane offered, trying to be helpful as she carefully lowered him to sit on the couch. "Did you see anything that would give us a location?"

Tyler shook his head. "Nothing. She was in a kitchen washing dishes. It was day. That's all I got. I can't even tell you what time of day it was."

"Anything unusual about the room that she was in? Anything that would tell you what region or country she's in? You saw what you saw for a reason. Not we've just got to find out what that reason is." Jane held a glass of orange juice to his lips. "Drink this. The sugar will help to stabilize you until Jared gets back with the needles for a transfusion."

Tyler glared at her from cloudy eyes as he took the glass, carefully taking a swallow. "I can do it myself. I don't need a transfusion. I'm fine."

"You're not fine. I mopped up half of your blood from the floor and there's no telling how much seeped through the floorboards. I can't shield against you forever just because you're being stubborn."

"Jared's the healer; let him decide," Tyler grumbled, taking another, more confident sip of his drink.

"Fine. What did you see that could possibly be of help?"

"She's young, female, alive, dark hair, hazel eyes, tan skin, and seems to be some sort of housewife in a mid-century house that doesn't look like it's been updated since the 70's. She was talking to someone in another room so I don't know if she has a roommate, a boyfriend, or just had people over. Is any of that helpful?"

"Can you draw the room she was in? The architecture might help us narrow things down."

"I don't think so, Jane. I've seen dozens of houses like that all over the country. They all look exactly the same shade of hideous. And I couldn't hear anything so I wasn't able to get a read on an accent. I couldn't even see a clock to tell you what time zone she was in." Tyler closed his eyes, swallowing against the rising nausea in his stomach and feeling like a failure. "I found nothing that we didn't already know other than a face."

"So draw her face. Maybe we'll be able to find something that way." Jane paused, feeling Jared close by. "You didn't fail. I'm the one who failed her. She died cleaning up my mess." Her eyes turned from gray to black, then back to the blue-green that meant Jared was nearby. "What are you going to do if she's with someone?" she asked, watching her husband enter the room, anxiously carrying medical supplies.

103

Tyler followed her gaze then glanced back at her. "What would you do?"

Jane shook her head. "My answer won't help you. I couldn't let him walk away from me without fighting for him with everything I have. I want what's best for him, but I have no doubt that I'm a part of that. If I did, I would hope that I'd have the strength to let him go. But I can't answer and tell you with any certainty that I would. And I can't tell you what the best answer is for you." She smiled at her husband, easing his anxiety as he rushed over to her side.

"Will the patient live?" Jared tried to hide the fear in his voice.

Tyler winced as he tried to stand, his head swimming, his thoughts caught somewhere between his present and his fantasies of the past. "Alive. Give me a minute before I need to kick anything, all right?"

Jared used his body weight to lift his brother to his feet, nearly carrying him to his bedroom. "Was it worth it?"

Tyler grinned as he tumbled into bed. "Aren't they always?"

8

"What exactly is it that you want from me, Drew?" Anna dropped the hot casserole dish she had retrieved from the oven on the laminated kitchen tabletop in front of her husband. She groaned, her dark eyes closing briefly as she felt a tension headache building. "Please be as specific as you'd like so that I know what to expect." She sashayed back into the kitchen to search out her missing glass of iced tea.

"What do you want me to say? The economy sucks and no one who's hiring wants to talk to the guy married to the local spook. Why do you keep claiming to see things that aren't there?"

"Because I see them and I want it to stop! It's just bad dreams, Drew. I'm not telling people, I'm telling you. You're my husband. Why can't you keep your mouth shut?"

"What man is going to take that seriously? Woman, you come to me and tell me you're seeing shit that ain't there." Andrew laughed, helping himself to the rapidly cooling chicken casserole in front of him and enjoying the pain that he could see forming behind her eyes. "You should start writing that shit down. Bring in some money around here." He slanted his eyes upward to see what impact, if any, his words had on her.

"I had a job. You told me to quit because I wasn't spending enough time with you. The only reason we have any money at all is because you qualified for Unemployment. That's going to run out. You should think about that when you're sitting at the bar racking up more bills that we can't afford, regaling your friends with stories about your crazy wife." Anna sat down across the table from him, helping herself to the casserole. Her stomach groaned in protest. She spent the few minutes that they sat in silence pushing her food around on her plate. The more she cut it up in pieces, the more overwhelming the amount of food became. Much like her life, she wanted to toss the entire thing in the trash and start over. Not that it wasn't good, or at least serviceable, but it wasn't what she wanted. Anna had always pictured herself in a different life, a different place. She'd woken up about a year earlier wondering where all those dreams had gone, how this mediocre existence had become her life. It was all so stereotypical, so pedestrian, so not anything she'd ever wanted for herself. In a city rebuilding possibility from rubble, Anna had become nothing more than a housewife to a prom king with a tarnished resume. His cushy corporate "yes man" position had washed away with the broken levees. When the company had returned to the city, it was only to see what was salvageable in their building. Without inclination to move, Drew's job hadn't been one of the salvaged things. In a city nearly destroyed, they lived in one of the few neighborhoods that hadn't been completely torn apart by Hurricane Katrina. A sense of hometown pride had taken hold of many New Orleans residents in the wake of that disaster. Anna and Drew were two of those that had been born and raised in the outer parishes, moving to New Orleans together in the years before the hurricane to make a better life than the bayous provided. The city was steeped in superstition and a healthy respect for the supernatural. That was one of the things that hadn't changed at all in the days since the water had washed back out of the city. Some people took it very seriously. Others, like Drew, thought it was just a bunch of stories told to keep young people in line. Regardless, everyone approached it with some amount of caution. Anna hadn't thought much about it at all. Now she was beginning to believe the stories. She just didn't want to become one of them. And her husband using her "episodes" as a humorous story to tell friends at the bar wasn't helping matters. Looking at him now, overweight, lacking ambition, self-important, she wondered what it was that she saw in him, why she'd stayed married to him. There was something in there that was familiar to her. Watching Drew as he ate, Anna found herself entertaining the fantasy that Drew was just an opening, a gateway for her. That the only reason she was with him now was because he was supposed to lead her to something else, something different. Somewhere that she could be more than the crazy has-been waitress turned housewife that her life with Andrew had made her into. Anna loved the moments when she could escape into her fantasies. It started concerning her when the fantasies began to bleed over into her everyday life, taking over her mind and vision when she was occupied with other things, when the fantasies were the furthest thing from her mind. She didn't want it, didn't need it, and the graphic images of violence and death were nothing that she would have formed on her own at all. And yet it all seemed eerily familiar. She was sure that she had seen it all somewhere before. It played across her mind like scenes from a half-forgotten film. Except these were not spectacular enough to be captured on celluloid. They were just normal enough for Anna to believe that they were real. She just didn't know what they had to do with her.

I will find her. It's the mantra that echoed through Tyler's mind, the thought that filled his days, the obsession that woke him in the darkest hours of night. *I know it's weird. I know that I never loved her the way that my brother loves his wife. I may never look at her that way despite that it's what my new sister expects of me. I look for her the same way that I would any member of my family. I would tear the world apart for any of them. I would watch the world burn for them. Karina is one of the four members of my family. I should have made her like us when I had the chance. I wanted to be fair to her; I wanted selfishly to have my freedom. I wanted to squander my existence. When I woke up, when I realized, it was too late and she was gone. What I realized was that my sister-in-law was right: There are people that you protect, people that you'll kill for, people that you'll watch the world burn for. And then there are the rare few that you would personally set the world aflame for. I hadn't known that. I wish I'd known that. Now I know that no matter how many lifetimes I live after this I won't forget it. The casino chip that I carry with me like Catholics carry a crucifix or a rosary won't let me. It reminds me that stranger things have happened in my family than being raised from the dead. It reminds me of how strong she is, how determined. Of how much life she had left to live.*

I took it from her. I took everything from her. And I was the only one who could have saved her. Honestly I couldn't admit even to myself that she wanted me to save her until the end. And even then what I could do hadn't been enough to stop death's grasping hands or allow me to easily find her once she was gone from that body. The blood that she'd asked me for to save her sister, that she'd asked for again with the dying breath that no one else had heard hadn't done its job. At her death, Karina had been no more a goddess for taking my blood than she had been before. Admittedly it had been a desperate last act with no time for the vows or rites that bound Jared to Jane. In that moment though I knew we were both willing. She had taken my blood and she had still died in my arms. I should have had the courage to kill Zane myself. It's not like my people had never murdered anyone, I just hadn't wanted to be one of them. I've fought my heritage, fought for my humanity, for my morals, for my beliefs, for the sacredness of human life. It could have all been cancelled in that one act which I couldn't allow myself, even to save the sister I was growing to love and my brother's sanity. Despite my best efforts it had all been lost anyway. With one incidental wave of someone else's hand, it had all been lost.

Tyler's thoughts zigzagged through his mind as he contemplated the horizon. The sunset from the top of the mountains overlooking the San Fernando Valley was beautiful. He thought he should feel some of his Zen returning, some patience, some something that would begin to counteract the seemingly endless stream of negativity that had been flowing through him for the last several months. It had progressively gotten worse, as if a dam had broken in his brain when Karina died. Nothing he did calmed it and nothing he was doing had helped him to get any closer to bringing back what had been lost.

The pink and orange casting shadows over the blue valley made Tyler vainly wish for one of his cameras. That is until his view of it was interrupted by a bus load of tourists with a loud mouthed guide pulling in to the Universal City overlook, effectively destroying the solitude. As shutters clicked outside of his foliage-lined hiding place, the tour guide launched into a monologue describing the areas showcased below and recited a list of the area's known celebrity residents. *I did not know that an overly self-important, mediocre actor lived behind here in the overpriced house that doesn't have enough windows to fully appreciate the magnificent view, thank you, tour guide. I guess you learn something new every day*, he thought glumly. After the tour bus pulled away and the sun was hidden behind another mountain, Tyler rose, jumping over the barrier designed to keep tourists from tumbling down the side of the mountain as they overeagerly snapped pictures that they'd show to family and friends once before forgetting them in some dusty photo album. As he looked out over the Valley turning blue in the early twilight he vaguely remembered taking in this view a hundred years ago when there was nothing here but a few houses, trees, farms, and fledgling film studios. It had been beautiful then too. He'd never once thought that it would become this, that he would be sitting here staring at the same place through such different eyes. They were the same color, same shape, locked in the same face that he'd had in every life. Tyler briefly thought that maybe it wasn't his eyes that had changed, it was just him. He'd never before felt the pull of humanity as strongly as he did now. Now that he knew the sensation, he didn't much care for it. Tyler looked down at the people and cars traversing Ventura Boulevard looking like ants from his high vantage point and knew that he could throw himself down this mountain, step in front of a truck, and wouldn't die. The cheery thought didn't make him feel any less dead inside. He could be injured, he might come close to dying, like he did this afternoon, and to taking two other people he loved with him, but he wouldn't die, not really. It's slightly depressing to know that even that most basic of choices, to live or die, is denied. Rather than continue to contemplate useless thoughts comprised of fiction, Tyler concentrated on the images he'd seen of who Karina might now be as he drove, winding down the narrow mountain roads. He knew that he needed to get his mind back under control before either Jane or Jared took a trip to the dark side and saw what he was hiding in there. Tyler couldn't help but grouse to himself that what he thinking isn't always any of their concern. He knew they couldn't help it, the bleeding into each other's brains. Shit just happens. Since he don't want to see at a minimum half of what they are usually thinking about they've gotten better about shielding them from him and vice-versa unless they're in the same room. Though he appreciated the shields during the times when he wanted to be alone in his own head and their more intimate moments as a couple, it still irked him how Jane would just unilaterally decide who saw what and when. The last thing that Tyler needed was someone else telling him what he needed to do, how he should react and when. He knew that they worry that he felt shut off from the collective, like they're edging him out. Sometimes he does want to be shut off and that's a valid assumption. Sometimes it's nice to have some separation and others it would just be nice to not have what he was thinking and wanting assumed for him. They work together, they live together, they're in each other's thoughts. Overwhelming isn't the word for their rather unique set of circumstances. Certifiable might be more accurate. After all these years if his brother were really gone from his head Tyler thought he might truly go insane. The options aren't numerous for people like him. Looking down at the oceans of people going through the motions of their daily lives, Tyler couldn't help feeling that they were taking their lives for granted. As an immortal, at least a semi-immortal, he knew he has the luxury of taking his life for granted, knowing that in a predetermined number of years he'd have a total do-over. For the first few precocious years he won't even remember anything. Tyler would be no different from anyone else on the planet. Those years are his favorite. Well at least they are once he starts remembering. It doesn't take long for them to start to remember. At least that's one thing Jane won't have to get used to after this life; she remembers everything from birth.

Despite the horror that it sometimes caused him, Tyler did enjoy his humanity. There are some aspects of it that he loved, some that he would walk through fire naked to never have to experience them again. Tyler believed that this may be one of those things. He wasn't in love with Karina when she was Karina. He wasn't sure he was in love with her now. He never was, not really. He could have been. Well, Tyler thought he could have been. He did know that they didn't take the chance that they were given to find out. He could admit that he was interested. He still was. But Tyler also knew that she won't come back the same person that she left as. He just wanted to give back what he took from her. She's the closest he'd ever come to considering a companion rather than a mate. It all boils down to that in the end anyway. Tyler knew he would have saved her. He still will if he can. If she wants to be saved. Above all, he knew that no one else in their group would understand but he did. Tyler wanted to make sure that she was given a choice. She can choose whatever life she likes. And then he'd make damn sure that she got it. The person who sacrificed everything for everyone else gets a happy ending. Tyler didn't delude himself for a moment that he was anyone's saving grace or a knight in shining armor. She deserved better than this life can give her. Jane thinks that she's better off away from the collective. She wants to see her sister but she doesn't want to drag her back into this mess. Angels, demons, and demi-gods aren't exactly everyone's forte. Not that he was complaining. It has just become terribly important to Tyler that she has a choice. That being said, he was too chicken shit to find out what the other deal was that she made with Sabina before she died, the one that involved him. He thought that it might be that he's afraid of what that knowledge might do to him, what it may mean for both of our futures. He'd hoped Jane would come back with answers and all she'd gleaned from her meeting with Sabina was riddles. One thing he did know was that Jane won't let it go for long which means that he'd need to decide and he'd have to do it quickly. Sitting in his car, parked outside of the new-age bookstore where Sabina dains to work reading tarot cards for celebrities and tourists one would think that he'd already made his decision. Tyler knew that she already knows he's out here. He kept thinking that after the next deep breath he'd have enough resolve to get out of the car and walk through that door. Maybe it'll be after the next one...

"Jack Dawson. I have a six o'clock with Glenda." Tyler tried to keep the annoyance off of his face and out of his voice. He didn't want to raise any red flags for the cashier and he definitely didn't want to be recognized. Thankfully all psychic readings here are required to be paid in cash. If he's going to keep torturing himself he needed to know what he was doing it for. Jane's just let go of her sister. Tyler felt like he was already dragging her and his brother back into hell. Whatever Sabina has to tell him, he hoped that it clarifies the decisions that he was making.

While Tyler waited for Sabina to grant him the audience that he'd paid for, he idly perused the aisles of random items. Some of the things he recognized as being moderately useful, most were replicas or fakes. Tyler stopped in front of a display of shaped candles designed to bring the caster money, love, marriage, sex, the normal crap that people ask for when they need a wish granted. All the stuff that he'd thought of so long as mediocre or just plain. Things that his long life allowed him to take for granted. Tyler knew his hindsight was better than his foresight. One of the more detestable of his human qualities. He did wonder though, what wish a burning a penis shaped candle granted? As a man, the thought was just painful.

"Mr. Dawson. Did you not sink on James Cameron's version of the Titanic?" Sabina approached Tyler from behind. He felt her stare on his back before he turned and he didn't ask what she had been looking at. Tyler was pretty sure he already knew.

"Froze to death in the water, actually. Given the current state of my emotions I found it appropriate. Didn't Dorothy drop a house on you?"

"Wrong witch. I'm the one who made the twister that brought the house and Dorothy to Oz. Regardless your emotions are not frozen, they're active. It's an acquired taste. I do not care for it myself." Her nose wrinkled in a very human gesture, the expression alien on her face. Tyler kept waiting for one of her tattoos to escape from wherever inside of her she hid them while out in public. Whatever held them in place was old and powerful. Just like the woman standing before him, struggling to remain contained in the form of a being lesser than she. In all the years they'd known each other this was the first time he'd seen her struggle. There were stress lines around her eyes. They screamed with a quiet panic. For her to be weak enough for Tyler to see this much meant that something was very wrong. As she moved, he noticed that her skin slid across her bones like paper. Was Sabina aging? How had he not noticed this before?

"Everything has a season, Traegar, even me." She spoke softly as she led Tyler down a narrow hallway lined with velvet curtained cubes where other psychics were telling clients of future loves and fortunes. "There will come a day when even the son of Apollo will not come back to us as he is." She sat down across from him at a battered antique table and pulled out a deck of tarot cards. "So what is it that the prince wishes to know?"

113

"Put the cards away; you won't need them." Tyler took a deep breath and met her gaze directly. "There was a two part deal. You only told Jane half of it. What was the other part?"

"All right." Sabina nodded thoughtfully. "What else?"

"Why didn't it work?" He couldn't help leaning forward. Tyler had tortured himself with this question for a year. The only person he knew who'd done the ritual successfully had been his brother and he sure as hell couldn't tell him what he'd done or that it had failed. He'd never be able to keep it from Jane and she wouldn't understand. "I know that she was dying, that we didn't do the full ritual, but it should have at least helped heal her, brought us some time. What went wrong?"

Sabina laughed in his face. "You who senses magic asks me what went wrong. Your problem, prince, is that you assumed that your blood was the stronger of the two because of your brother's experience with Jane. In this you were mistaken. Karina had already been touched by magic far higher than yours. You were not of the same kind before, nor are you now. She also did not die a human, for to do so she would not have been reborn as quickly. Think about it, prince, and the answer will come to you. Remember how she died."

"She died in a car crash. I was there. I saw her last breath."

"What did you see in that breath?" Her eyes lit up as she prodded Tyler, pushing him toward the answer that his mind refused to accept.

"Fire. She wanted to live."

"No, she was being reborn."

"That's not possible. They're birds. They're extinct."

"They can take many forms. She chose to be human. And they are not extinct for one such as your sister, the creator."

114

"Danalia knew of this?"

"She'd wanted to try it for years. I just helped facilitate the opportunity."

"Where is she?" Tyler had suspected before but now he knew that his family had been involved in this catastrophe. Even better he now knew that they know where she is which increased the chances dramatically of getting a real location out of one of them.

Sabina shrugged. "I cannot help you there. You must find her on your own."

"Don't think that I won't tear the globe apart to search for her. A phoenix cannot be that difficult to find. She won't be able to be hidden forever." A thought occurred to him then and Tyler couldn't keep his next question from being blurted out. "Does she know?"

"She has no memory of these things yet she is wholly herself. Time for one more question."

"What was the other part of the deal?"

"She asked to be hidden from you but requested what she thought was a loophole. She asked that you be bound to your true soul-mate. Selflessly, she wished for you the happiness that she saw granted your brother. Karina assumed that if you were to find her that the two of you would be bound and therefore destined to see each other. If not, then she had no further purpose in your life."

"Did you do it?"

"I elected to give you the choice. If you want to be bound to your soul-mate, I will do it. However, I ask that you think on it, prince. To do this is an irrevocable thing. There are no guarantees that Karina will be the one that you get."

"I know the risks."

"Our time is passed, Traegar." She stood and passed a business card to him. "Think on it. If you wish it done, I shall do it. Know that once done, the magic cannot be undone, not by me and not by your phoenix. The consequences, whether they be good or bad, will be yours alone. And you won't get a preview. No one does, not really. Do not wait too long with your decision. These things have a timeline and your year's almost up."

"I have until Friday? That gives me just over a week."

"Think quickly. More quickly than your decision to ask the correct questions."

With that she was gone past the curtain to greet another client. Tyler left her portion of her fee on the table and left out the back door, not wishing to see anyone else on his way out. His confusion stayed with him as far as the threshold. Tyler turned and caught the door just before it closed in his face. Not surprisingly, Sabina was standing there waiting for him expectantly. "Do it."

She smiled. "As you will it, so may it be, prince."

"What did you do?" Jane's angry words rushed at Tyler as soon he entered the house. "I felt something change. What did you do to us?" She shoved him, causing her brother-in-law to stumble back into the wall.

"I went to see Sabina today. Is that all right with you or should I have gotten a permission slip from you and Jared?" He shoved her back, just enough that she allowed him to pass.

"Honestly, you haven't been thinking that clearly recently and you still haven't answered my question."

"Stop fucking yelling at me and I'll tell you!" he roared.

"Children! What the hell are you doing?" Jared stomped into the room dramatically, laughing at the two of them. "Do I need to send you both to time-out?"

Tyler noticed that Jane backed off immediately when Jared entered the room. The sudden uncharacteristic reaction made him wonder how much of their relationship she willingly showed his brother. And how much of their new-found friendship was faked for Jared's benefit. When she turned back to Tyler there were still flames behind the loving sea green of her eyes and something that he hadn't seen in a long time: Panic. Clearly whatever Sabina had done to him, his brother's wife had felt it deeply, more deeply than Tyler himself had. All he'd felt was a little mental tug and a sense of awareness that hadn't been there before. A quick scan of Jared's brain brought up nothing out of the ordinary. Whatever it was, Jared hadn't felt it which meant that Jane was once again playing shield between the two of them. Tyler knew that it was in her to protect those she loves, particularly Jared. But he felt that they seriously needed to have a talk about her stepping between the two of them like this all the time. Tyler didn't want their rampant thoughts of sex. It's none of his business and all of the ways that he could see his brother, the fetishes that the two of them have with each other pushes even Tyler way beyond his limits. There are some images that an eternity won't erode from his brain. Then Tyler appreciated the constant shielding. However for his brother to not know that anything was different about him meant that Jane was taking this to a whole new level that Tyler wasn't entirely sure that he was comfortable with.

"So who's gonna tell me what's going on or is Jane going to drop her shields enough for me to find out on my own?" Jane's eyes turned a stormy gray for an instant before they resumed their usual color. Jared stumbled back a step, his mind reeling as he took in all of the information that he'd missed while their collective mindset had been temporarily disabled. "So, who's the lucky girl?" His voice was a little breathless as the color began to gradually return to his face.

"I have no idea. That wasn't one of my options. It was kind of an either or situation. If it gave us a shot, I thought it was worth the risk. Apparently Karina was okay with it, this being her initial idea and all." Tyler shrugged, his eyes downcast as he reached up to rub the back of his neck.

"Don't do it!" Jared warned, his words stopping Tyler in mid-movement. "That means you're worried about something. You can't reassure me that this was the right decision if you're worried about it."

"You have no right to lecture me in this area." Tyler pointed an accusing finger at Jane who continued to remain silent. "Exhibit A to your insane madness."

"In case you've forgotten, this time it's not about me."

"Nice to have the tables turned, isn't it?" Tyler sneered. "Don't look down at me from your lofty, privileged perch for making a decision concerning me and my soul-mate without consulting the two of you first. From my perspective that particular decision has absolutely nothing to do with the two of you."

"It concerns me when it concerns my sister who you seem determined to prevent from living in peace!" Jane stepped up to him, her face so close to his that they were almost touching. "You weren't this interested in her when she was alive, Tyler. Why the sudden fascination now? What happens when you find her happily living another life? What if just seeing us brings back a whole host of memories that she'd rather not have? We could destroy her, Tyler. Do you really want that?"

He took another step closer to her, a snarl marring his normally handsome features. "And what the fuck makes you think that of all people you would know what she'd want or what's best for her? If memory serves me, she died cleaning up your mess." Jane's fist swung, catching him square in the jaw. Tyler smiled, pushing it back into place with a sickening pop. "That's what I thought. Guess the barrier's gone without Danalia's help." His gaze rose to meet his brother's and he felt the confusion mingling with Jared's overwhelming need to protect Jane that he saw there. "Maybe you should keep your cat on her leash more often. She so enjoys being tied up." Tyler dodged the fireball that Jane lobbed at his head, scooping up his keys on his way out the door.

Jared started out the door after his brother, holding Jane back with a look. "What the hell was that?"

"Sometimes your wife needs to be put in her place. I was just reminding her of that." Tyler stopped suddenly, turning to face his brother. "Do you even comprehend how far between us she's gotten? You felt nothing when Sabina worked that spell on me today, did you? I know every nuance of every second of your binding to Jane and believe me, there is a lot of it that I did not want to know. But I couldn't stop it, even with shielding and massive amounts of alcohol. You felt nothing. Nothing, Jared. She registered enough of it that she attacked me the second I crossed the threshold into the house. Our house, if you remember. What about that is right? Do you remember the last time that you got a clear, uninterrupted thought from me that was more than passing commentary on some inconsequential thing?" He paused, waiting for the response that never came. "Yeah, I don't either. If I had died today, would you have noticed before the police showed up with my body? I don't want to know about your sex life, not that I can't hear it, but I don't want to be shut out of your life either."

"She doesn't do it to shut you out. She was trying to do what you asked and give you a little silence, protect you and me from the powers building inside of her. Trust me, we don't care if the whole world knows that we enjoy each other. Hell, we'd probably fuck in the streets if we wouldn't get arrested. You wanted privacy, to be shut off. If that's not what you want I'll tell her to toss the shields. We'll go back to the way it was, no problem."

Tyler groaned. "How can you not see that something is horribly wrong? It shouldn't come to this! We shouldn't be standing in our driveway screaming at each other after our third was throwing punches and fire! We've spent a year burying our heads in the sand, pretending everything was all Brady Bunch great when it wasn't. All this shit started the day Karina died. We've nearly lost our opportunity to fix this. I'm making this right, Jared, even if you won't." Tyler turned and stomped across the driveway to his car. He was cranking the engine when the passenger door opened and his brother got in.

"All right. Where are we going?"

Tyler let out the breath he'd been holding in a quiet *whoosh*, more relieved than he wanted to admit. "To hunt a phoenix."

9

"When I very dramatically left my very angry wife to jump into the car with you I had no idea that this was where we were going." Jared sighed deeply, glancing up at his brother to see his reaction.

Tyler didn't look up from the library book resting on his lap. "Not my fault that you didn't ask before we got in the car. You really just didn't want to have to deal with Jane's little pyrotechnic fire display after I left, did you?"

"You shouldn't have made her so mad that she pushed past the barrier Danalia erected."

"I don't think she got past all of it. Looked to me like she was slowly leaking which is probably better than just removing it or breaking the whole thing down at once. If she'd been at full strength she would've done a lot more than dislocated my jaw." Tyler continued to flip through the reference book he was holding, ignoring the synapses in his brain that he could feel sparking and melding with someone else's. He just hoped that when it was all over the person he was linked to would be Karina. Otherwise he was stuck with someone he didn't know rambling around in his brain forever. "I don't know how to find a phoenix, do you?" Tyler abruptly changed the subject.

Jared took the redirection of conversation in stride, assuming that if Tyler was okay with what just happened with Jane, he shouldn't push him any further right now. Besides, he really wanted to know what a phoenix had to do with anything. To answer his brother's question, Jared shook his head negatively, snapping closed the book he was holding and adding it to the discard pile beside his chair in the atrium of the downtown Los Angeles Library. "No. Why do you need a phoenix? Will it lead you to Karina?"

"It is Karina." Tyler didn't even look up from the passage he was reading to see his brother's reaction.

"Excuse me? I know I didn't hear that correctly."

"Karina is a phoenix. It's how she was reborn so quickly. Danalia made her a science experiment and turned her into a phoenix."
"They don't exist. They haven't in more than a millennia. And now I really have no idea why we're in the library. You won't find her here, in a book. If Danalia created her, she must know where Karina is. Why wouldn't she just tell you rather than sending us on some impossible quest?" Jared slumped further down into his chair, rubbing his temples to keep from yelling.

"Danalia won't tell us. You know she won't. She has little sense of urgency and to her, this is just a game. I'm going through mythology books to find something that could possibly be of use," Tyler replied calmly.

"Those are nothing but children's bedtime stories, you know that."

"I think we're both proof that they're not all just stories carved out of someone's imagination." Tyler passed his open book to his brother, indicating a passage with his index finger. "Only one phoenix can be created at a time. The last one disappeared from record over two thousand years ago. Apparently they loved our father."

Jared read. "He's drawn to their song. We're his blood so we would be too. All you've got to do is get her to sing. Start hanging around karaoke bars." Jared dropped the book back down on the wooden table where it landed with a thud that echoed in the quiet space.

"I have to be able to hear it. And I don't think that singing is going to work unless she's become a musician in the last year."

"Do you think that her new incarnation took her ashes to the old country?"

"No. I'd be willing to bet that she's got an urge to go though and she doesn't know why." An idea suddenly occurred to him. "We have her ashes. She'll come for them."

"We buried her ashes and she may come for them eventually. It's been a year and they're still safely buried in the graveyard. Keep in mind that she's a woman with probably limited understanding of what she is and little to no inclination to ruin a manicure by digging up a grave. My guess would be that just the idea would freak her out enough to keep her from exhibiting that particular quirk."

"Are you sure about that?" Tyler met his brother's eyes. They both dropped their books and nearly ran for the doors.

Jared shoveled more dirt out from around Karina's grave marker, squinting to see inside the hole with the help of only moonlight. "I don't think that anyone's disturbed this other than us."

"Have you gotten to it yet?" Tyler leaned over the small hole to check his brother's progress.

Jared glared back up at him. "Does it look like I've gotten to it yet? Am I digging this hole for fun?" He tossed another shovel full of dirt out from under his feet then paused to glance up again. "Why am I the one digging up your girlfriend's grave anyway?"

Tyler yanked the shovel from his brother's grasp as they traded places. "She is not my girlfriend. She never was."

"Then why are you here?"

"Because I owe it to her. How many times do I have to explain myself to you?" Tyler channeled his frustration into the shovel, flinging dirt at his brother's feet. After a few moments the shovel hit something hard. Jared jumped in to help Tyler clear the remaining soil by hand.

"Well I guess she's still here." Jared leaned back against the dirt wall. "What are we going to do now?"

Tyler pulled the sealed box of ashes from the crumbling earth and climbed out of the grave, dragging his shovel with him. "We're taking these with us. One the off chance that she'll come back for them they might as well be somewhere that we can have visual surveillance. I don't want to lose any chance that we're given, however slim." Tyler didn't meet Jared's eyes as he covered the box and gently set it safely aside. "Help me cover this?" He used the shovel to scoop up some of the loose dirt they had displaced, refilling the now empty grave.

"What's Plan B?" Jared picked up another shovel, hesitantly helping his brother to speed things along. He thanked God that the graveyard was on their property. Otherwise he would be worried about discovery by the police. Or the press. Jared briefly wondered what reputation grave robbing would earn him. Especially since it was the grave of someone he knew.

Tyler patted the earth into place and replaced the patch of grass he'd carefully removed before they started digging. When he was done he glanced up at his brother. "This is Plan B. Plan C is to figure out why that vision of Karina, the new Karina, that I had earlier is giving me déjà vu. There's something really familiar about her, not about her surroundings. Or maybe I'm just projecting and wish there was something about her that could lead me closer." Tyler rubbed the back of his neck with one hand, closing his eyes tiredly.

"We have to try everything." Jared patted his brother on the shoulder to try and encourage him to keep going.

Tyler looked up at him through eyes bleary with exhaustion. "We've got less than a week left."

10

Andrew awoke in the middle of the night to his wife's screams. He reluctantly rolled off of the couch where he'd fallen asleep watching some easily forgettable sitcom and walked to the bedroom. Anna was lying in bed, twisted in the covers, her mouth open in a scream. Drew sat down next to her, roughly shaking her into wakefulness. "You're dreaming again." He knew that the words were tired, impatient, but he didn't care. These dreams had been going on for months now, had removed him from his place in the bed, and he was sick of it. He wanted her to suffer for what she'd done to him but the screaming was just too much. Anna was the one who was supposed to be tortured, not him. Right now he just wanted her to shut up and be normal for a minute so that he could get some sleep. The more she kept this kind of crap up, the more he wanted to be away from the house and her which put a serious kink in his plans. It was also possible that she was starting to remember things that he wasn't quite ready for her to remember yet. Drew had a plan and he didn't want his "wife" to derail it. Just thinking the word "wife" almost made him giddy with glee.

It was starting to be a serious problem that the woman never seemed to do anything anymore that wasn't wrought with drama. He almost longed for the memory of simple life that they'd shared where she did all of the housework, he went to work, and they ate silently in front of the television together at night. Nothing had been wrong with that life. Anna's growing independence was starting to grate on his nerves though. Rather than staying home and doing just as he told her she was going out for these runs every day. Last week she had taken the car without asking and disappeared for an entire day. He knew that he would have to come up with a way to keep her from the idea that she could venture off on her own. He'd already fixed it so that his ball and chain was the town kook, a joke. No one in town or the nearby areas would take her seriously as anything else. His once trophy wife had become the thing that all the other townspeople whispered about when they thought she couldn't hear. He knew what they said about her, what they said about him, and he fed the stories every chance he got. He did appreciate that rather than acting normal and trying to dispel the rumors, Anna was feeding right into them. As she continued to moan in pain in her sleep, Drew briefly wondered how hard he was going to have to work to totally break her spirit. He shook her suddenly still body again, refusing to leave until she looked him in the eye and he knew she had regained her senses so that he could finally get back to sleep.

Anna awoke, curling into herself, her eyes blinking slowly open. In her mind she saw herself reaching out, trying to help someone whose face she couldn't clearly see. Then there was a loud crash of glass around her and an indescribably blinding pain that radiated throughout her entire being. Anna still felt the shadow of the sensation of having her life ripped out of her. Looking at Drew who watched her with a resigned tiredness, Anna saw the face of a man that she shouldn't have known, but that she clearly recognized. Something deep inside her psyche was trying to tell her something. She knew it as well as she breathed. She just didn't know why remembering the things that had happened to someone else was so important. If these were memories, and that was the only logical conclusion that she could come to, that they belonged to someone else. What could it possibly have to do with her? This woman had obviously died. What help was there for her now? Anna started when she realized that she was assuming they had happened to someone else. Having never suffered a head trauma she knew that these memories weren't, shouldn't be hers. And yet here she was screaming for her life in the middle of the night in her own bed. Seeing that she was finally awake, Drew padded silently out of the room, returning to the couch where he spent most nights since her dreams had started. Anna felt bad that her constant tossing and turning kept him awake but her need for answers was more pressing that her need to protect her husband's sleep patterns. As dreams began to pull her back into a dark oblivion she released herself, welcoming the visions of herself in another life. This time she dreamed of green on the backs of her eyelids.

"Ow!" Jared rubbed his shin, glancing up from the book he was reading in their sitting area. "What the hell?" He observed his wife's angry demeanor and clamped his mouth shut. "All right, I guess I deserved that."

Jane crossed her arms over her chest, standing in front of him and refusing to budge. "What happened? Something happened today with that spell and then the two of you just disappeared. Now I can delve into your brain, possibly causing you some pain, and pull it out but that's not really fun for either of us so why don't you save me the trouble and start talking."

Jared sighed, placing his head in his hands. "Sabina told Tyler that Danalia turned Karina into a phoenix. She's shielded from us so

129

that's why the spell didn't work. I had already assumed that much. As a precaution, we dug up her ashes in case she comes looking for them. Tyler has them. Right now that's all I know."

"That's it? That's all you've been hiding from me? Seriously, Jared?" Jane felt some of her elemental powers slip past the barricade in her mind, causing phantom flames to light along her exposed skin.

"Tyler has to handle some things his way. You have to let him."

"When he does something that affects all of us, you can't tell me that I can't step in, that I don't have a vote. This is my life too, the life that you brought me in to, asked me to be a part of. I have just as much of a vote as you and Tyler."

"Not in Tyler's life, you don't. He isn't Zane; he's not going to kill you, me, or anyone else. Just trust that we're making the best decision for everyone. You don't have to be in control of everything."

Jane took a step back from her husband. "Wow. I cannot believe that you of all people just said that to me. Is that what you've been waiting on, for me to snap one day and start treating you like an incompetent moron? If that's the goal then you've got a few more steps before I can become the psycho wife. Go fuck your assistant, a handful of fangirls, and then we can talk, Jared."

"That is not what I said!" Jared raked his hands through his hair in frustration. "Do not blow this out of proportion!"

"Do not treat me like a 1950's housewife! I am not your property. I have a voice, I have an opinion about what happens to my life. You advocated for me to have that. Being my husband does not give you the right to take that away from me."

"You don't have the right to take that away from Tyler either," Jared pointed out quietly. "He didn't particularly like it when we got married, when I unilaterally made the decision to bind myself, and him by extension, to you. But he trusted me enough that he stepped aside and allowed me to do it because that was what was best for me. All we're asking is that you extend him the same courtesy. I know it's scary, but even if you don't trust him, trust me," he pleaded with her. "I won't let anything happen to you."

Jane sighed deeply and closed her eyes. "I know that. I just don't want the two of you making decisions for me all the time. I need a family, not caretakers. I'm not a child." When she opened her eyes the color was slowly changing from dark gray to blue. "I'm sorry for snapping at you. This thing is coming back slowly and it's making me crankier than usual."

Jared smiled, pulling her into his arms. "We just had our first fight."

"Nope. First fight was in Vegas. You are not a good drunk, if I remember correctly. You bumped your head here," she kissed him gently on the nose, "here," her mouth moved to his forehead, "and here I just enjoy kissing." Jane turned his head to the side and kissed the sensitive spot behind his ear. A small noise escaped his throat, causing his wife to smile against his neck. "I love that noise."

"You know, I didn't do that before I met you."

"Good."

Tyler lay down on his unmade bed, his mind desperately trying to spindle together some sort of plan of attack that made sense. How do you hunt a phoenix that doesn't know she's a phoenix? Would her powers remain dormant because of her ignorance of their existence or would they flare to life without warning? Would she panic and cause a scene that would be reported in the local media? If it was, would he know where to find record of it?

131

For the first time in longer than he cared to remember, Tyler closed his eyes and prayed to the Christian God for a way to find Karina without hurting her or causing her distress. The knowledge that she was now more of an immortal than he was only intensified his longing to find her. She was the only one of her kind. There was no one else to help her with that transition, no one who could be trusted with that information. Existence as a truly unique being had the definite drawback of being completely priceless and your life being envied. Karina in pieces would already be a huge commodity. That she wasn't aware of it made her easy prey. Should she ever fully recover her memory, Tyler vowed to remind her that any future deals with Sabina needed to be stated in terms that were as specific as possible to avoid loopholes like the one she was unwittingly experiencing now.

His mind moving in increasingly illogical circles, Tyler closed his eyes with a groan. Several deep breaths later found him sliding into the arms of sleep. His mind's eye flared to life, drawing him into a dream. In this dream he was wholly himself, sitting on a bus bench, staring at a crossroads alone. The road, the background, even the bench he was sitting on was all white. Out of all of that stark, bright white came Karina, moving slowly but purposefully toward him and it made his heart ache a little just to look at her.

"What are you doing?" She stood in front of him, a smile playing across just the edges of her lips like she was enjoying some great secret joke.

"I'm waiting for direction," Tyler answered honestly, not rising from his seat.

Karina took the seat next to him on the bench. "I'll wait with you." She slid her arm through his and rested her head on his shoulder, staring straight ahead as they waited together for the bus that wasn't coming. When he looked down Tyler caught a glimpse of the gold tattoo on her hand and realized with some sadness that Karina was truly gone and that it was Jane holding his hand.

Tyler woke up in the middle of the night drenched in a cold sweat and dreaming of his sister-in-law. *Yeah, that's normal.* He remembered the crossroads as having four directions, one that he had come from and three to choose from. The way he saw it, while everyone always thinks that revisiting the past is an option, in reality there's really no going back, only moving forward and standing still even as the world moves and changes. He didn't really recommend that one. Tyler knew that even if he decided to do nothing right now, not go forward with the search for Karina that terrified him even more with the newly imposed timeline, inevitably he would end up moving in one direction or another whether he wanted to or not. When he woke up at 4 a.m. after approximately ninety minutes of sleep with thoughts of Jane burning holes inside his skull Tyler decided to pick a direction himself. Screw waiting on fate or destiny. For whatever reason it seemed to behoove him to act quickly. A time clock that he hadn't previously been aware of seemed to have suddenly started ticking at a rapid pace and Tyler didn't want to waste any more of its precious seconds. Tyler got up, took a shower, and packed a bag. The one thing he knew for damn sure is that Karina wasn't sitting in front of him here in Los Angeles. Unlike his brother's fantastic success story, Tyler didn't think it likely that he'd happen across Karina coincidentally in a sushi bar. If he was going to find her then he needed to actively start pursuing her without help from his friends or family. To do that Tyler needed to get out of Los Angeles and find a good starting point. He'd finally recognized something from his vision of her: water marks on the walls, which suggested somewhere in the south that had been flooded so it would have to be a low-lying area. That combined with her looks, uncannily similar to the woman he had met in the bookstore, suggested New Orleans and its outlying areas. It was still a needle in a haystack search but one that he felt he had at least a prayer of succeeding at. *What if she was that woman at the bookstore?* Tyler shook the thought out of his head. He really didn't think that he could stand it if what he had been searching for all this time had been standing right in front of him, had touched him and he hadn't realized it until it was too late. He couldn't even remember her name. He did remember the thin gold band on her hand and wondered if it was just a trinket or if it really did mean that she was married. Tyler shoved the thought away for later contemplation. The chances that Karina had been standing in front of him and that neither of them had realized it were extremely slim. It was far more likely that she was related to the woman he had met which would account for the close resemblance. As he slipped quietly through the house, Tyler only felt slightly guilty for not waking his brother as he ran out the door rushing to the airport but not enough to leave a note. Jared would already find him sooner rather than later.

Jared awoke a few hours later with a start, a sudden feeling of momentary weightlessness overtaking him as he lay in his wife's arms. His gasp woke Jane who had been having restless dreams of her own. "Tyler's gone."

Jane gently pulled him back down into her arms, laying her head against his chest so that she could hear his heart beat. "Aren't you the one who told me earlier that he needs the freedom to follow his own leads? Let him go. We know where to find him."

11

Two hours. Two hours since Tyler had been on the ground in New Orleans. Two hours since he'd left his safe tourist hotel near Bourbon Street and gone off in search of answers. Two hours of blessed silence. The last thing his brother had said to Tyler was that he loved him. He knew it but he didn't think they'd verbalized the sentiment in years. It showed Tyler just how much it was killing Jared to leave him alone. If anything it was Tyler's trust in Jane to let him pursue Karina on his own that let him do this without guilt or thought about how it was affecting other people. Tyler trusted her to keep his brother safe but to keep him home. Their relationship was not the best. It had obviously started disintegrating over the last few months but he knew that if he couldn't rely on anything else, he could rely on

Jane to protect Jared, even at her own expense. If anyone else was to ever understand how important this was to Tyler, he knew it was Jane. She had just as much at stake in this as he did, but she knew she couldn't do it. Not the right pieces in her head, she said. Tyler knew that for her to trust him to find her sister was a big deal. The way he saw it was he trusted her with his brother, her with her sister's well-being. Guess it really is a two-way street after all. There was never any question in Tyler's mind that Jane's loyalty lies with Jared. That's what it should be and she won't be able to keep him distracted in Los Angeles indefinitely. Tyler just wished he could feel Karina's spirit as well as he could hear the internal clock ticking in his head. The damn thing might be imaginary but the time that it was keeping is very real.

Tyler left the tourist trap of the Quarter for the other wards. Foremost in his mind was that he needed to do his homework. Karina's home was still standing after all of the storms and the water hadn't risen more than four feet on the inside. There had to be a way to narrow down the area of town by the damage sustained and how close the bookstore was to where she lived. If she knew about the book signing then she had to have shopped there before making her a local. As far as the water marks and architectural details he'd seen in the house, historical markers wouldn't cut it and there were at least a dozen parishes outside of Orleans that had sustained significant storm damage over the last several years. Tyler needed to narrow his search area down further, to see what his mind had been attempting to tell him through visions more clearly. Since his extended family had fixed it so that Karina maintained her element of anonymity where he was concerned, Tyler needed to seek out someone with powers comparable to his but in a different line of magic. Luckily, Cajun country was chock full of conjure men and women. You just have to know where to look for one.

Terrebonne parish is one of the largest parishes in Louisiana. Anna knew this because she'd studied it. She also knew that it's one of the least densely populated areas of the state despite its rather close proximity to New Orleans. After Katrina, Gustav, and every other storm that's tried to wash away Anna's home there were still half of the previous residents remaining who had been here before. About three-quarters of them were born and raised here or somewhere nearby. *So why is it that Drew and I are the only ones who really remember how long they'd lived there?*

Anna was actually enjoying a day out. Drew had let her take him to a job interview so she had spent the late morning running errands unattended. It didn't sound like much, but to someone like Anna, who was constantly under her husband's thumb, it could mean everything in her day just to see the sun shine up close and personal rather than through the glass of a window or the barrier of a screen. She went to the grocery store, nothing out of the ordinary, nothing the least bit unusual. She really just wanted Mexican rice for supper. Encountering Rebecca Stewart made her forget all of that.

Rebecca had been Anna's best friend in school. The two women had gotten married the same year. Rebecca had even been one of Anna's bridesmaids. That's part of the reason that Anna really didn't understand why Rebecca had reacted the way she'd done that day. Maybe that's not true. Maybe she was just too afraid to believe.

"Rebecca! You forgot your keys!" Anna chased after her long blonde hair, the yellow all she could see between cars in the crowded parking lot. Rebecca's hunter green SUV was parked near Anna's late-model beat-up sedan. A testament to the vast differences that had taken place in their lives over the last ten years. Rebecca's keys were housed on an expensive Coach keychain. Anna's were on the mood ring that she had found in one of Andrew's jacket pockets a year ago, a forgotten trinket from some county fair or another that she and Drew had attended in better days. When she finally turned around, Rebecca's face was a perfect blank of smiling happiness.

"Thank you." She took the keys from Anna's outstretched hand and used them to open the back of her SUV. "Was there something else, Anna?"

"No, I just was thinking that we haven't spent much time together in the last few years. Maybe ya'll would like to come over for dinner one day next week? Catch up on things?"

"I'm sorry, I don't mean to be rude, but why would we do that? We barely know each other beyond polite conversation and comments at community gatherings. Of course we haven't gotten together recently. We've only known you and Andrew for a year and you keep to yourselves so much."

"What are you talking about? Drew and I have known you for years. We went to school together." Anna wasn't pretending to be confused, she *was* confused. If the woman wanted to pretend like she didn't know her, at least she should have the courtesy to not do it to Anna's face without even the smallest audience to witness her humiliation. She and Rebecca were from the exact same neighborhood, exact same upbringing. That she moved out of the bayou and into town didn't make her any better than those who had chosen to return. Except maybe in her own mind, that is. She seemed to be having no problem flashing her shiny designer rings in Anna's face while she put her in her place. Here she was, trying to be nice, and Rebecca was treating her like garbage. It made Anna so mad that she could've spit nails.

Rebecca loaded the last of her bags into the back of the SUV and closed the door with a sigh. "I knew an Anna Bryant in high school but you aren't her. I don't know how they do things where you're from, but here in Louisiana this isn't how you try to make friends." She tried to push her empty shopping cart past the other woman. Anna blocked her exit and recovered the use of her voice.

"Where do you think that I'm from?"

"What are you on, Anna? You're from Los Angeles. At least that's what Andrew told my sister, Emily, when she sold him your house. And drop the make-believe Southern accent. You sound ridiculous."

"We bought that house nearly ten years ago. Why are you saying these things?" Anna felt knots forming in her throat and stomach. It was all of a sudden too hot and she couldn't breathe well. This was way beyond any measure of a cruel joke that she could imagine.

"Check the mortgage paperwork. You bought that house nearly one year ago. I remember because it was my son Tommy's birthday and Emily had to leave early because you and Andrew demanded to sign the paperwork immediately and you wouldn't wait til Monday like decent people." She glanced down at Anna's hands still on the shopping cart then back up to her dazed face pointedly. "Do you mind? I still have a birthday party to prepare for."

"When is Tommy's birthday?" The words were almost an incoherent mumble to Anna's ears. She wasn't quite sure how Rebecca understood them.

"Friday." Rebecca left Anna standing there alone in the parking lot next to the dirt-covered sedan that she wasn't entirely sure belonged to her anymore. She looked down at her hands as she fumbled for the car keys, feeling like she was seeing their tanned skin and long, thin fingers for the first time. As Anna climbed into the driver's seat she glanced across the street into the window of what everyone knew was a hoodoo shop and she could almost swear that a man with green eyes was staring at her. He looked a lot like the man that she had met at the book signing and it freaked her out and thrilled her a little bit that he might be watching her. Anna drove out of the parking lot, glancing back into the shop window as she passed. The only thing looking back at her was a large red and gold bird in a gilded cage. She felt that it looked at her and recognized something that it saw in itself. Anna wasn't entirely sure it was wrong. More and more she felt that she was beginning to resemble that bird in its cage.

"Why hasn't he contacted us?" Jared paced the small space beside Jane's desk.

She groaned her frustration, staring through splayed fingers at the mess of papers littering the desktop. Jane covered her eyes, wished the mess away, then carefully peeked through her fingers. The papers were still there, her husband was still mumbling incoherently as he paced, and now she was slightly disgruntled that nothing had changed. "Stop it, Jared."

"Stop what?"

"Stop mumbling, stop worrying, and stop freaking pacing. You're making me crazy." Jane half-heartedly lobbed one of her reference books at his knees.

Jared side-stepped the book, staring blankly at her. "What the hell is wrong with you?"

"You stopped pacing." Jane smiled smugly, returning to her laptop screen. She mentally cheered herself on for the win. "I have to work. You have to stop worrying about things that you have no control over. Tyler will not combust because he is out of your range of sight. He's a big boy. Let him do what he needs to do. Be supportive. Weren't you the one giving me this lecture two days ago?"

"What if something happens? What if he needs me and I can't get to him in time?"

"What if you're freaking out because you love your brother and you can't fix this for him?" Jane gave up on the pile of papers and went to her husband, hugging him tightly. "I know it's an impossible thing for me to ask, for you to try and separate yourself from him, even for a moment. But we can't interfere. She's my sister and I can't step in to the middle of this anymore than you can. You know it and I know it. I want to know that Karina's all right and living a happy life, but I owe it to Tyler to let him go and see whatever it is that he needs to see without him feeling like I'm breathing down his neck. He can't look at this situation, at her, with any measure of objectivity while you and I are around him. When he needs help you'll know it. Hell at the rate it's been going lately we'll probably both know simultaneously." She released him and walked the three steps to the couch, sitting down tiredly.

"How bad has it been for you?" A terrible thought occurred to Jared then, one that stilled both his feet and the breath in his chest.

"Not that bad." Jane shrugged noncommittally, her eyes returning to the work on her desk rather than to her husband's face.

Jared stepped in front of her and sat down on her desk, blocking access to her paperwork. "You're a really bad liar."

"You can read my thoughts. I think that would be considered cheating." She tried to push him and her thoughts aside.

"You've been blocking me and I've been trying to give you your space because I feel that you should be allowed some measure of privacy in your own mind. So would you care to tell me what's really going on?" He reached for the hands that were vainly attempting to remove the notebook directly under his ass. "Don't get frustrated, you'll just burn the only existing pages of your book."

Jane gave up and sat back down in the desk chair. For the first time Jared noticed the deep purple shadows under her eyes. "I'm just tired. A little confused, extremely frustrated, and very tired. It's difficult for me sometimes to carry both of you inside my head is all. When you're both extremely emotional it just becomes that much more difficult. Some days it's hard enough to be me without having to distinguish between my thoughts and yours and Tyler's. It makes me feel a bit like I'm losing myself."

"Why didn't you tell me?"

"What are you going to do about it? Worry? Wear a hole in the floorboards pacing? I didn't want you to be concerned over nothing."

"For one I'd tell you to quit trying to shield between us all of the time."

"If I don't do it, who will, Jared?"

"Who says it has to be done? Yeah, there's a lot of information that would normally not be shared, but so what? We'll deal with it. I know that you're afraid that there's some residual powers that will adversely affect us, but I promise we'll be fine. Tyler and I have been fine for a few thousand years without your shields. You can't add that much craziness." He paused. "I worry that it's tying you too strongly to Tyler."

Jane's head jerked up to meet his gaze. "Is that what's caused it?"

"What are you experiencing exactly?" Jared reached out for her, trying to pull the words that she refused to speak from her mind. What he saw before she shut him out was worse than anything he had imagined. Jane wasn't just getting random thoughts or images from Tyler's mind, she had a direct link to everything he was consciously or unconsciously experiencing. The most direct route that his wife had to his own thoughts was routed through his brother and it was still nothing compared to the all-access pass she had to Tyler. Everything he'd ever done, every place he'd ever been, memories, thoughts, feelings, it was all laid bare in Jane's mind with no filter to protect her from the onslaught of information. A far cry from the link her mind shared with Jared's. This made their shared telepathy look like a cheap parlor trick. "How long?" His voice sounded weak to his own ears but he didn't have the mental fortitude to try and hide it from her. For the first time in his life, Jared was legitimately afraid of his brother.

Jane watched him and chose her words carefully, speaking quietly so as to not alarm him further even though she knew the gravity of what she spoke. "This is why I was so upset the other day, when he came back from seeing Sabina. Not because he made a decision for himself but because this is what it did to me. I've been trying to stop it. You've no idea how hard it's been to keep this from you."

Jared's hands dropped down to his lap and he noticed for the first time that the notebook he was sitting on contained spells and incantations rather than the fictional dialogue he had been expecting. "Have you been helping him?"

Jane nodded, reaching again for the notebook that he released without comment. "Hoodoo. He thinks she's somewhere in Louisiana, somewhere recently affected by hurricanes. In the vision he had she was in a kitchen that had high watermarks on the wall. There was brick dust just inside the doorway and window. If she believes then it might help him find her."

"He knows about this?" Jared chose to ignore the angry note that entered his voice.

"We were just about to get into it when you came in the other day. We haven't discussed it since but yeah, he knows. There's no way for him to not know. He trusted me to do what I can but also to keep you safe and as far away from this as possible. There's nothing you can do to help him that you haven't already done and he can't take the risks he needs to take without knowing that you're safe."

"What risks?"

"Have you ever used hoodoo?" She handed him the notebook. "It's not religion, it's not pure ability, it's straight magic and it can go really well or really bad with very little in between. Despite having been born on the bayou this time your little Greek god asses know nothing about this kind of earth magic. And I would prefer it if no one works roots on my family for being stupid."

"What do you know about it?"

"I know that it's not something to play with. No god, living, dead, or otherwise has much to do with it and that your intent is a lot stronger than any feeble attempt at free will. I've seen people do some fucked up shit to each other and using this stuff scares the hell out of me. But so far no New Orleans conjure man or woman has been willing to help Tyler with it so I will. My life as James was not my first trip into the bayou, nor do I expect it to be my last. Speak nothing aloud that you see in my notes right now, don't even read it with intent. I'm not sure how much of what I've found works and what doesn't but until I do know, none of us touches it."

Jared nodded blankly. "How will you know?"

"As James I had a teacher in one of the smaller parishes outside of New Orleans. I'm trying to find a way to contact her now. If Tyler just showed up at her place without an introduction he'd likely not escape with him memories intact and while there's a lot about my past that I'd like to forget, I don't really want to lose it that way. There are some things that even being a goddess can't fix."

Jared gave voice to the thing he feared most. "You're Tyler's soul-mate, aren't you? Not Karina, or whoever she is now, but you."

Jane nodded slowly. "Sabina did say that he might not like what he got out of the deal. We all wanted to stay together after this life. Now we're a regular Jerry Springer episode."

"What are you going to do?"

Jane shrugged. "I'm open to ideas, if you've got any. Right now, I don't know."

Jared's face took on a pale, sickly hue. "It can't be undone."

His wife met his eyes directly for the first time in the conversation, their hazel green color matching his brother's exactly. "Would you really undo it if you could?"

12

"Soul-mates come in all forms, Jared." Tyler inwardly groaned at the conversation he'd known was coming for a week. After the third day of insistent screaming messages, both mentally and literally via voicemail, he'd finally decided to take one of his brother's many phone calls. He knew through Jane how her initial conversation with Jared on the subject had gone. Tyler was personally trying to avoid as much confrontation on the subject as possible. "No, I do not want your wife! What god-forsaken fucking crazy pills are you on?" He paused for a moment, listening to his brother's angry ranting. "Well, I kind of can't help that Jane is listening in on this conversation and neither can she. Everyone in a three state radius and probably Japan can hear you screaming…Trust me, we weren't each other's first choice for this either." Tyler rolled his eyes and fell back across one of the two pristinely made beds in his hotel room. He'd been in New Orleans for nearly a week and was no closer to finding Karina than he had been in Los Angeles. He could almost feel her. Every time he turned a corner he expected to find her there, waiting for him… Waiting for him to what? To ride in like a fairytale knight and sweep her off her feet? To save her from whatever her reality was and take her away with him? Take her back to what? To Los Angeles, to a sister that she doesn't remember, to a life that no longer exists, to looking over her shoulder and knowing that all of the monsters are real? Unless Karina was lying in a coma with the brain function of a zucchini, Tyler was failing miserably at seeing how anything that he had to offer her was better than whatever she was living with now. His brother's worried barrage of questions wasn't helping at this point either. This conversation was beginning to feel like the Spanish Inquisition all over again. And that hadn't ended well for him either.

Through the cell phone that he held up to his ear, Tyler continued to be berated by Jared's one-sided discussion on the gravity of his actions. Like he needed the reminder. Funny how Jared wasn't too overly concerned until it intimately involved his wife. Tyler wondered briefly if the new closeness he was experiencing with Jane was what was at the root of Jared's worry more than his general concern for their collective well-being.

"Do you know what you've done? You officially know more about my wife than I do. And instead of trying to find a way to fix it, to shut yourself off from her, you're asking her to use that link more, to help you and to keep me out of it. The concern is flattering but it's completely misplaced. I can handle myself. I cannot handle my wife going insane and wearing herself down to nothing to try and help you, to keep something from me that there's no possible way you could have hidden. Why did neither one of you tell me?"

Tyler took a deep breath, silently counting to ten before answering. "Obviously we did hide it from you, however briefly, therefore it is possible. Also you must have been told by one of us because we sure as hell haven't been sharing this with everyone we come across. Otherwise we wouldn't be having this conversation…Do *not* interrupt me, I'm not finished yet. The reason that you were not included is that we knew you would react in exactly this way. You would wig out and try to take charge and you cannot take point on this one. I wouldn't involve Jane but I have no choice. I will not involve you. I cannot afford the distraction." Tyler sighed and closed his eyes tiredly, groping blindly for the dark sunglasses he had dropped beside him on the bed. "Yes, now I'm finished. Please, feel free to continue." He found the sunglasses and slid them on, dropping the phone to lay speaker side up beside his ear. Maybe enough layers across his eyes would shut out the cacophony going on behind them, he thought. Maybe.

I wear my sunglasses at night so I can…

So I can try to distract myself from my life, he thought glumly. *So I can hide that for the first time in my existence my eyes are blue instead of green.*

Jared's voice on the other end of the phone faded in his mind until it was background noise. Really what was the point in having the argument? It didn't solve or change anything. It did succeed splendidly in making Tyler frustrated with his brother, another time-consuming human response for him to obsess over. As if having himself and his new soul-mate relying solely on him to locate Karina's soul wasn't enough to deal with. And it wasn't like he asked for Jane. He sure as hell didn't want her and yet there she was, blaring like a homing beacon inside his mind, all shiny and full of red warning lights. Tyler had always assumed that Jared was his soul-mate. They'd always been tied together. His brother's wife who he could barely stand up until recently hadn't even entered into the equation as a contender. Sure, there'd been a tiny, faint hope that Sabina's spell would bring him closer to Karina or allow him the peace to let her go. He'd instead landed in a self-made hell where he had fewer answers than he'd begun with, more complications than he cared to acknowledge, a useless soul-mate and one very pissed off brother. As a bonus Tyler did know for certain that Jared had exactly as long as the end of eternity to continue to be pissed off and berate him for undoable things that were out of his control. And for some reason everyone was yelling at him. Jane yelled, Jared yelled. Tyler was willing to bet that if he shut the phone in the closet under three pillows and stuck his head out of the window he could hear his brother without benefit of the tiny electronic device. It nearly made him scream, or resort to calm logic, neither of which his brother was willing to entertain at the moment. Just what he needed: eternity with not one but two people who treated him like an intruder in their lives. Like he had a choice in the matter. Like they'd really let him have it if he'd been gifted with choice. Ah, the illusion of free-will and how quickly it fails you. His brother's tirade continued, echoing twice inside of his head. For once, he just wanted Jared to shut up and let him think for himself. After five thousand years that really wasn't too much to ask, was it? To be simply left alone in his own mind with his own thoughts. Just for a moment. What difference, in the larger scheme of things, would his telepathic absence from his brother and Jane make, really? Sighing, Tyler knew that it could be a larger turning point in his existence than he dared to comprehend. It could mean the difference between life and death. That's really what all of this boiled down to: his life with his brother or the death of that long-held connection. They'd fought, struggled to find a way to stay together after this life for nearly two years, ever since Jared had married Jane. They'd had no idea that her soul was still unbound, that this could ever happen. And no one knew that a butterfly flapping its wings in Cape Town could cause a tsunami in Japan. Now that the virtual tsunami had crashed on his head, Tyler could see with amazing clarity how perfect this solution truly was. Its elegant simplicity stunned him. Jared was fulfilling a decades-old obligation to their father and both of them potentially got to stay together in the lifetimes after this. Jane was bound to Jared, soul-mated to Tyler, and Tyler wasn't left in a position where he'd be alone for the next millennia, vainly searching the globe for his other half. It really was perfect if you looked at it from the outside. It was exactly what Jared had been wishing, searching for. If you could overlook the tiny caveat of Tyler now being linked more closely to his brother's wife than to Jared. Gods didn't tend to deal in little minute details like that. All they were concerned with was that the job got done, forget how it was done. The joys of dealing with middle management. And the higher-ups on the deity food-chain wouldn't even glance at a problem so vainly trivial. Seraphim didn't much care for demi-gods nor their affairs unless politics were involved. Those closest to the true God, Alpha, and his Goddess had bigger concerns to suck up their unlimited contractually obligated terms of servitude. Like the continually impending apocalypse. While the development of humanity had greatly shortened the life-expectancy of the ball of astral matter they called Earth the Big Show was still a good ways off in the distance. From his calculations, Tyler figured that they were only a couple of million years off with their 2012 assumptions. Just because the Mayans hadn't had enough foresight or will to plan another of their cycles further into the future didn't mean the damn planet was going to implode. It did mean that they needed to find someone else to make a calendar. Tyler glanced at the screen of his iPhone and wondered briefly if there was an app for that. Probably.

Tuning back into the tirade continuing to bubble out of the phone's small speakers, Tyler did notice that his brother's one-sided conversation had changed topics. Apparently either Jared had used his somewhat keen mental powers to figure out that Tyler wasn't paying attention or he'd gotten out everything he needed to say at this moment on the subject and was just assuming that Tyler agreed with his assessment. Sadly Tyler assumed it was the latter rather than the former and reluctantly tuned his hearing back in to the words rushing out of his brother's mouth.

Oh, now that was interesting…

Jane stared silently at the name and address in front of her, clutching her cell phone in one hand and re-reading the phone number for what she assumed should have been about the millionth time.

Hi, this is James. I know I'm supposed to be dead, well I guess James is technically, but I was wondering if you could help me and my family with something?

How do you reintroduce yourself to someone who knows you to be dead without getting hexed? Jane looked down at the scraps of paper in front of her with her hastily scribbled handwriting and concluded that she had approximately three options: phone, email, or snail mail. It was almost laughable that a hoodoo priestess would have email. Even the bayous had to modernize sometime, she mused. Jane's eyes scanned the information again, summoning all of her powers to try and glance into the future to see which option was least likely to get her killed. What good was foresight if it only worked in hindsight anyway? Frustrated, she left the phone on her desk and went in search of her husband. She knew already what way she needed to approach Cecile. And she knew that her husband was not going to like it. She found him slumping tiredly over sheet music in his office. "I'm going to New Orleans."

Jared didn't even glance up from the work in front of him. "I was wondering how long that would take." He lifted his head, swiveling around in his desk chair to face her. "Why do you want to go now? I thought this was Tyler's fight?"

"He can't see Cecile without me and the only way she'll believe I am who I say I am is if I'm there physically."

"And if she still doesn't believe you?" Jared raised a questioning eyebrow in his wife's direction.

"Then I either convince her or hope she doesn't hex me." Jane crossed the room to wrap her arms around her husband's waist. "Would you miss me if she killed me or turned me into a toad?" Jane pouted, batting her eyelashes at him.

Jared stood, his hands sliding across her skin possessively. "What if I told you there was another way?"

Jane pushed back a bit to look more closely at his face. "I'd wonder why you didn't say anything sooner."

"I just figured it out, impatient." He reached behind him, sliding over a book that had been resting beside his sheet music so that she could see it.

"What language is that in?"

Jared laughed. "Farsi. Persian," he amended seeing her confusion. "Tyler and I have lived a lot of places. Anyway, whoever created the phoenix can activate it, call it into its power, make it essentially embrace the phoenix side of its nature."

"So we get your creator half-sister who pretty much hates your guts to do us a favor and call her amnesiac phoenix into power?" Jane paused for a moment. "You're either truly brilliant or completely insane."

"Yeah, I'm not sure if it would blow up in our faces or not but right now it might be the best shot we've got."

"What happens when her powers are active? Will she survive?"

"She'll survive. I'm just not sure what else will happen. For all I know she could turn into a giant red and gold bird that spits fire."

"And this sounds better to you than visiting a two-headed doctor to see if the magical veil imposed by your father can be lifted?"

"Honestly either way is a shot in the dark." Jared pulled her back into his arms.

"You don't want me to go."

"Of course not. I'm selfish."

"You're worried."

"I'm not worried." He plastered a smile on his face, dipping his head to kiss her.

Jane ducked to the side, placing her hand over his lips. "You're jealous then. One of the two."

Jared licked her hand, hoping to either encourage her to move it away from his mouth or drop the current topic of conversation. Her intent green stare made him groan knowing that she wouldn't back down. He wondered how often his wife's eyes would resemble his brother's now that they were bound to each other. "I don't like it; that's not a secret. I would also prefer to have my wife here, safe, with me rather than in danger chasing ghosts with my brother and hoodoo practitioners. I can't keep you safe if you're not here, Jane. And if something happened to you or to Tyler I can't get there fast enough to save you."

"And you can't go with me," she finished for him. "I promised Tyler I'd keep you as far from this as I could."

"Thank you for promising to protect the protector," he remarked drily.

"I'm the protector. Remember Zane, the me getting killed repeatedly over the last thousand or so years because I was programmed by the gods or whoever to spend my life trying to save him from himself?"

"Yes, but Zane's dead and you're slowly turning into a goddess. You're not a protector anymore. Our family already has one of those."

"What am I then? Don't say the destroyer because that's really not sexy."

"You're my wife. Other than that I'm not sure which is another reason I'd prefer to keep you close by and out of Louisiana and whatever rain of shit that's about to come down there. Unless Tyler can find whatever body Karina's spirit has taken up residence in and bring her back here quietly with her powers still dormant, he's looking for a bomb with an unknown timer. We don't even know that she's still dormant, we're just assuming. She could theoretically level half the state in fiery rubble if she wanted to and she might just do it accidentally because she got mad. I don't want you in the line of fire, Jane. It's already bad enough that I can't sleep at night because Tyler's thrown himself in it."

"You can't hide me from the world, Jared," Jane remarked softly. "I know you're worried but we're all adults here. You may just have to trust that we're all doing the best we can given the situation. No one wants to be injured, no one wants to die. And thanks to you and your gifted healing powers, both Tyler and I are a lot harder to kill than the average person. And this thing between Tyler and me, it's just going to take some adjusting on all of our parts. We'll be fine." She hugged him tightly, burying her nose in his neck and inhaling the scent of the man she loved. "You will not lose me." Jane caught sight of her gold tattooed wedding band, a gift from Jared's true mother, and silently prayed to whatever deity was listening that she hadn't just lied to her husband.

"Anna, what the fuck!" Drew ran past her, spraying the fire extinguisher before he was even in the kitchen. This was the second time this week Anna had unintentionally set something on fire. She'd been on edge ever since she'd found out that no one else retained the same memories she had. When Anna had come home after the confrontation with Rebecca she had point-blank asked Drew what he remembered. He had laughed and told her she must've been crazy. The thing is Anna felt like she was going crazy. She know that Rebecca believed what she'd said. And Anna knew that Drew was lying to her. It sounds too unbelievable to contemplate in her own mind but she wasn't sure that her thoughts really belong to her anymore. When Anna thought about it, when she got distracted by it for an instant, that's when the fires happen. She didn't do it on purpose, it's like whenever she came near something while upset the fire just jumped out of her. It's like a stress reliever. Well, at least it made Anna feel better. She glanced into the broiling oven with a sad sigh, observing the blackened meat and the random flames that burst into life every so often. The hens that she was cooking for dinner had probably seen better days. Anna could still hear Drew muttering over it, cursing as he continues to douse the smoldering remains with white foam.

He lied to me. Out of everything that was going through Anna's head right now that would be the part she couldn't wrap her head around. It should be nothing, it's not like this is the first time that Drew's ever told her something that wasn't partially or all the way untrue. Anna thought it might hurt more to know that he's intentionally hiding something like this, what their past really was versus the plethora of memories that she had that no one else shared. Her more rational side couldn't help the nagging thought that maybe she was the only one who was confused, that it was just her, that she was paranoid for some reason that she couldn't identify. *What if the problem isn't everyone else? What if it's just me?*

Anna caught her reflection in the small hallway mirror and cringed. Dark curly hair, darkly tan skin, dark hazel eyes. *How drab and depressing am I? I'm even wearing brown. I'm monochromatic. No wonder I'm losing my mind. There's no originality inside of me anymore. I'm not sure what's inside of me anymore. I'm too thin, there are dark smudges under my eyes, I don't remember the last time I saw the sun for longer than it took to walk to or from the car or go for a run. Maybe there is something wrong with me.*

Drew finally emerged from the kitchen covered in foam and coughing from smoke. "Would you like to tell me what the fuck is going on? You've never been the best cook but this is damn near ridiculous." He dropped the empty fire extinguisher and the burned platter of blackened Cornish hens on the kitchen table.

"I…I don't know." Anna's voice was softer than she had intended it to be, partly from fear of what would come out and partly because she feared what Drew would do. The last time he had been violent with her was nearly a year ago. Anna had awoken from her first dream about the car crash to find Andrew standing over her, staring. God, he was so angry. Anna immediately apologized. She didn't know what for, she just wanted to make that expression go away. But it hadn't. When Anna spoke it got worse. She remembered him dragging her out of the bed by the throat, throwing her against the wall. There were bruises on her neck for a week afterwards. He spit on her, called her "Jane". When she managed enough breath to say her name, Anna, it looked like he had been struck. He stepped back and let her go. Anna thought it was over. Then that mean gleam entered his eyes again and he punched her so hard that she felt her teeth rattle in her head as she went down. Anna remembered her head colliding with the dresser. She woke up hours later sweetly tucked in her own bed. Drew moved out of the bedroom to the couch that night. Always said it was the nightmares that had run him off. Looking at him now he has that same look in his eyes, the one that he had when he called her by another woman's name and had gotten so angry. Anna was afraid of what he might do if he got that angry again.

"You don't know or you don't want to tell me?" Andrew's voice brought her back to the present with a vengeance. That's exactly what it looks like, that evil gleam in his eyes: vengeance. And Anna didn't know what she'd done to deserve it, but it frightened her, a lot. So much so that she felt herself backing away from him as he advanced on her, even though she didn't mean to.

"I really don't know, Drew. I was just putting the hens on to cook. That's all." Anna wanted to raise her hands in front of her body but she knew that if she did he would see it as a sign of weakness.

Instead Anna forced her gaze up to meet his and kept her hands fisted at her sides.

To her surprise, Drew reached out and grasped her shoulders gently. Anna couldn't help the involuntary flinch. At just under six feet with a slight build and the beginnings of a beer gut, Drew was not an imposing man. When he got angry his shoulders seemed to grow wide enough to leave God in shadows. "Anna, you need to talk to someone. This can't keep happening. You're endangering yourself. I'm going to make an appointment for you with someone in town." He hugged her and she felt her eyes well up with tears borne from confusion that wouldn't be shed.

"Why doesn't anyone remember me?" Anna's voice was small and fragile even to her own ears.

"Sweetheart, everyone does remember you. It just might not be in the way you think. You're just a little mixed up. We'll work through it." Drew released his wife's overly tense body and stepped past her toward the kitchen and the telephone.

Anna turned toward his retreating back. She knew that it probably wouldn't help her already precarious position but she had to know. Anna needed to know if the things she was seeing in her head were real or not. "Did anything happen to me a year ago?"

He stopped and faced her. Only for a moment, a split second, Anna saw the hesitation in his step, in his face. "Anything such as..." he let the question hang in the suddenly thick air between them.

"An accident, a traumatic event, a move, anything. Something that changed suddenly about me." Anna threw up her hands in an act of frustration that was unlike her. It felt good, just acting to act. The righteous anger that filled her at the idea that she shouldn't show a reaction startled her. "Why do I feel like everyone is keeping something from me?"

"Anna, no one is lying to you and nothing is being kept from you. Nothing bad or traumatic or anything else of note happened to you a year ago or any time before that. We're just like we've always been, living in the house we've always lived in, stuck together until the earth ends. Nothing ever really changes, does it, Jane?" Drew turned and walked into the kitchen.

Suddenly cold, Anna wrapped her arms around herself. It felt like she was holding herself together, refusing to break. It took everything in her to resist the urge to slump to the floor and collapse into a puddle of defeat. "My name is Anna." Still numb, Anna heard him pick up the phone and dial. She heard his voice as he explained to whoever was on the other end of the line that she was having some sort of breakdown, that his wife was losing her mind. The more he spoke in that calm, placating voice, the more it infuriated her. She wasn't crazy. Some of what was in her head had to be true. Anna was not sure if it was the idea that she had at some point had a life outside of this hell-hole or that a life, any life, might exist for her outside of all the things she hates, all the pieces of what she'd settled for that caused such self-loathing.

The stronger these thoughts grew in her head, the more her conviction grew until she could see it as a physical thing in her mind. The heat grew inside of her but this time Anna caught it before it burst forth from her body, channeling it into that thing in her mind, superheating it until the physical properties of her will were malleable and she could mold it to what she wanted, something that a long-dormant part of her recognized. Taking a deep breath Anna drew strength from this new thing inside of her and marched into the kitchen.

"My name is Anna."

Drew turned away from the telephone that he was holding, an evil smile lifting the corners of his mouth ever so slightly, twisting his face into something cruel. "I know your name. It's you that seems to be forgetting."

"You will not convince me that I'm crazy. I am not confused. You are trying to trick me."

"Why would I try to trick you, Anna? You're speaking nonsense." Drew's voice was annoyed and slightly amused as he turned back to the phone. "Did you hear that, Doctor? Yes, that was my wife, Anna. She's having these delusions—"

"You *will* hear me, Andrew!" Anna had never heard her voice come out that loudly. Or known what it looked like to stand that close to a fire. One minute Andrew was standing in front of her. The next, he was covered in flames. Horrified, Anna watched as he screamed, dropped the melting phone to the floor, and ran to the sink, dousing the flames on his arms in dirty dish water. She did slump to the floor then. She had no inclination to save him. Anna listened to the doctor's worried voice, sounding tinny and small as it came through what was left of the plastic receiver. She heard Andrew's pained shrieks as the heat slowly died away from his burned flesh. Anna sat on the floor with her head against the wall, staring at the blister mark that the phone had made on the cheap linoleum tile beneath her. All she could think as she continued to cough up smoke was that she should have cleaned the floor better. Anna was still sitting there, staring at the dirty floor and long-dead receiver when they came for her.

13

"Sit still and keep your eyes closed."

Jane impatiently followed her husband's directions. She still didn't understand how sitting in the middle of the floor in the lotus position was going to help her talk to Danalia.

"Take deep breaths, clear your mind."

Jane's eyes popped open to see Jared sitting calmly across from her, watching her impatience. "I *am* taking deep breaths. This is not what you and Tyler do before you *poof* out of existence and pop on an alternate plane full of gods and goddesses."

"I'm not teaching you how to travel between planes, I'm teaching you how to meditate and clear your mind. Moving between planes takes a lot of energy and concentration that you don't have yet. I'm not even sure that you're enough of a goddess to do it yet."

"I am enough of a freaking goddess to do this," Jane ground out through clenched teeth.

"Patience is a virtue."

"How long have we been married?" She glared at him.

"Two blissful years." Jared ginned at her irritated expression, causing her heart to flutter with an extra beat and her face to relax in a smile. She enjoyed that his gift particular to her was that he had an uncanny ability to always make her smile, melting away any bad mood that had momentarily claimed her. She secretly suspected that was the reason for the extremely low occurrences of angry words between them.

"Then you should know that patience may be a virtue but it is not one of mine." Jane laughed, falling forward, twisting so that her head landed comfortably on his legs. She reached over her head, her fingers slipping beneath the hem of his shirt to gently caress his back. She always felt better just touching him. "How do you do it?"

"It's the magic in our blood. It calls us home. For us, it's simply a matter of giving in to that feeling, of accepting for the moment that Olympus is our home that transports us there. That's what I'm trying to get you to find within yourself, that urge to go somewhere that more fully accepts your true self than this plane does. Unfortunately it's either not there yet or it's lost in a combination of other things. I can't feel it though and neither can you or you would've teleported by now."

"Why doesn't it work on this plane?" Jane spoke softly, turning her face in toward the pale hand that had been stroking her long dark hair.

"Because it's not keyed to this plane of existence. That is how we get around on Olympus though. Here we generally have to resort to everyday mundane human means of transportation." Jared leaned forward and kissed her on the forehead. "It'll take some time but I'm sure you'll be able to get used to travelling by car, airplane, on foot." He shrugged noncommittally, trying not to laugh.

Jane grinned, poking him playfully in the side. "I think I'll manage." She laced her fingers in his, pulling their intertwined hands down to rest on her stomach. "I'm sorry that I've been so hormonal lately. I don't know what's wrong with me."

"You're changing," Jared answered simply. "You've been under a lot of stress, on top of which you've been changing, physically. It's gotta be taking an emotional toll on you. That's why I haven't said anything. I don't want to add to your burden."

"I won't stay like this, will I?"

He laughed. "I hope not."

Jane mock glared at him. When she spoke though the concern in her voice was real. "Not exactly the reassuring answer that I was looking for."

"I wasn't trying for reassuring platitudes, no matter how well-meaning they might be. I'm trying to be honest with you and tell you what little I know. I don't know everything about what's happening to you. I never went through this. No one I know's been through it. There are stories but none that I know of that have really ended well for the human. Trust the advice that Danalia gave you. She knows what you're dealing with, though not from first-hand experience."

"What does that mean precisely?" Jane slowly sat up, her dark eyebrows knitting together in concern. "What happened to the other humans?"

"Their new-found powers caused them to lose their minds and gods had to…relieve them of their burden." Jared winced at her startled expression. "It won't happen to you, Jane. It can't. You're not like they were. You weren't human to begin with and you're so strong. So much stronger than any other goddess I've ever known. I promised you that I'd never let anything hurt you."

"Even when the thing hurting me is your blood? Don't you think that this might be something that you should've mentioned? Possibly before our first date? Something along the lines of "hey, I'm a Greek god. Sleeping with me could lead to insanity, mood swings, and death" would have sufficed." Jane tried to take a deep breath, focusing on their intertwined hands. All she could see was the gold tattoo band around her pale, finger, the Latin reading "to know light in darkness", a gift from her mother-in-law and a stark reminder of how closely she was bound to the man beside her. "Jared, if something went wrong, if I lost my mind, you and Tyler…"

"Will not let that happen," he replied firmly, redirecting her dazed eyes to his face. "I was never sure of what would happen to whoever I chose as my mate. But I am sure of you. You will not break. Compared to the hell you lived through with Zane killing you every twenty years this will be a walk in the park. You've already been through most of the change without even noticing it. The only thing you're missing is the last little bit. Hopefully," he amended hesitantly. "As soon as I find out what that is, we will deal with it and you'll go back to your normal, charming self." Jared cradled her face between his hands forcing her to stare into his eyes. "I will not lose you to anything. Not even my family, not even to my blood. My father swore to protect whoever I chose. He will uphold his end of the bargain."

"Because you mean that much to him?"

"Because he wants the god child and you're his only shot at getting it. He knows that if you die he gets nothing from me. He holds Tyler to no such bargain."

"I'm a mini-god incubator. How exciting." Jane rolled her eyes. "Oddly that does make me feel a bit better. Guess once I've given birth I'll have to start worrying about what ghoulies and beasties will come out of the woodwork to try and kill me again." She laughed, dropping back to rest against her husband's chest.

"What is with you?" Jared ginned, pulling her closer. "When are you going to accept that your life is not all blood, death, and the four horsemen of the apocalypse anymore?"

"Sorry, it's taking some getting used to. I don't know how to not operate on high alert."

"Relax!" He massaged her shoulders. "I promised you that I'll take care of everything and I will." He kissed her cheek, causing her to smile and her eyes to lighten to the bright blue-green that they turned when she looked at him.

"That's an awful burden to place on you, everyone's happiness and well-being. I don't need you to take care of me." Jane twisted around to look at her husband's face.

"After a thousand years of indentured servitude as Zane's protector it's about time that someone took care of you for a change. It's much easier if you let me." Jared held her just a little tighter, trying to chase away the demons of what could have been that were playing havoc in his mind. It didn't matter anymore; he had won her, Jane was safe, and Zane was dead. That Zane's demise was the debt that Jane's twin sister had paid for with her life placed a chill up Jared's spine that he hadn't seemed to have gotten rid of since Karina's car accident. Some days he felt that they would never be free of Zane's memory, of Jane's past. Tyler's obsession with Karina's resurrection made Jared selfishly worry for his future with Jane. He knew that the past was dead. It just never seemed to be truly gone. The past being a part of who you are is one thing; the past constantly resurfacing to slap you in the face was something entirely different. Aside from Karina's death and Tyler's subsequent melancholy their lives had been good for the last year. Jane was happy, productive, slowly assimilating to her new life and new abilities. She'd written two books in the past year that were doing very well and the first feature film based off of her series of fantasy novels was in post-production. Jared knew he was happy. His father, Apollo, had finally backed off, stopped pushing the terms of their deal in Jared's face. Jared had the woman he'd wanted, the career as a musician that he'd worked for, and despite the rather interesting complication, he now knew for certain that he most likely wouldn't lose his brother after this life. This life which was steadily proving itself to be so uncertain but so happy after many millennia of monotonous certainty. At least he knew no matter what happened next he'd never again be bored. However his greatest fear, that Jane would one day be gone from his life, was an ever-present voice in his ear, a dark angel on his should. And Jared knew that he could never mention his fear to his wife, never let it fester in the parts of his brain that their shared telekinesis gave her access to. If Jane knew what he feared she would begin to doubt him, to doubt herself. And that he couldn't bear to see in her multi-colored eyes again.

"You don't admit defeat well."

"That's because I don't fail. Failure is not acceptable in my world. In my experience when you begin to fail is when you begin to die. I'm not nearly ready for that." Jane pressed her lips together tightly, determination forming little creases across her forehead.

"You've got a long, happy life still ahead of you this time."

"Well as we both know I don't know how to deal with that either." Jane pushed to her feet and faced him, silently praying that her face reflected more bravery than she felt.

"It doesn't," Jared replied to the unasked question, hearing the thought as it floated across her mind. "Even if I didn't know you, your eyes would give you away," he explained, indicating the changing colors of her mood ring eyes with his forefinger. "Tyler gave me one of these," Jared extracted a small slip of paper from his wallet, passing it to her. "Oddly he was right. The color change in your eyes does correspond to the mood ring jewelry color code." He laughed, returning the tiny color chart to his wallet for safe keeping.

"You know that body temperature is what changes the colors in mood rings, not emotions." Jane grinned, pulling him to his feet.

"Don't knock it; it's surprisingly accurate. So why are you afraid?"

"Because you once told me that this trip to the other side might kill me. Because I don't know what to expect but I know I need to go and that I have to do it now. What if they don't like me?" the question exploded out of her, making Jane fervently wish that she could shove the words back in.

"Faced with a world full of gods and goddesses your two biggest concerns are that either they'll kill you or not like you? Only one of those is irrational."

"How would you feel if every figure you thought to be a myth turned out to be your very real in-laws? It's a little strange and a lot to deal with, especially when I'm turning in to one of them and I'm not even wholly sure what "them" is." Jane took his hands in hers, pulling him closer, willing him to feel her earnestness past the fear that she knew was coming off of her in waves. Being married to an empath had definite drawbacks. "I never believed in these things before I met you. I had one God and one Goddess in my heavens and that was it. I know it's real because you're standing here right in front of me, irrefutable proof that the stories are at least somewhat real. But I've been catching up on my mythology and it's frightening that I'm becoming an unknown version of these things I've read about."

"I am one of those things. So is my brother. My family may be dysfunctional but they're the one I've got. They're not "things"."

"They're not human either."

"Neither are you. It hasn't stopped you from being a person. Just because we live on this plane doesn't make any of us human but you've never held it against me or Tyler. Give my family the same courtesy. Please. In her own way Danalia is trying to help us. As much as I hate to admit that Tyler was right, Tyler was right. We need help."

Jane sighed. "I didn't mean it in a racist way, Jer, I just don't know what to call them. I'm scared. I don't know what's happening to me, I don't know what I'll become as a result of it, and my body's changing internally in ways that I don't fully understand." She threw up her hands in frustration. "It's like I'm a teenager going through puberty all over again! It's slightly annoying," she amended, lowering her voice an octave. "I don't like not being in control. I don't like not being able to formulate a plan because we don't know what we're dealing with. Sitting back and riding things out isn't really my forte."

"I know that you like to have a plan, a plan to back up the plan, and a contingency for that plan too but unfortunately that's not how this works. In all aspects you're going to have to learn to adapt to the change. Ignoring the fact that your body and your abilities are changing is just going to backfire and end badly for some poor, flammable, hopefully inanimate object." Jared clasped her hands in between his, staring at them intently. "If nothing else, do not forget that you're an elemental and the only one that we know of. You wield and control fire. You have the potential to level an entire city block in a hailstorm of fire and ash if you can't control yourself and your emotions. Bottling things up, trying to spare my feelings by hiding things from me, these are luxuries that you can no longer afford. You've had nearly two years to adjust to life unbound from Zane's non-magical idiocy which is also enough time to come to terms with what Tyler and I, and now by extension you, are. We're all gods from the Greek pantheon. Our children will probably blessed from birth with powers that neither you nor I can imagine. And yes, I know that it's a lot to take in, but this isn't exactly new information. When you think about it, is it really so different from a witch who remembers one hundred or so past lives and shoots fire out of her fingertips?" Jared looked up from those fingertips, warm in his hands, to search her face for answers and found none that he was looking for.

"My issues, the things that I'm dealing with now, have nothing to do with Zane." Jane pulled away from him, silently counting to ten in her head before continuing. There was no point in trying to have this discussion with him now. They were both stubborn and neither would budge from their stance, on opposing sides of the same issue. At least Jane felt like they were on opposing sides. Regardless she was very quickly growing tired of the arguments with the same consistent topic: her lack of wanting to take her place in Olympus, the alternate plane where her husband's family resided. The ritualistic bloodletting that had married them had also transferred Jared's Olympian blood to her, causing her blood to change, morphing her slowly but surely into a goddess. A destroyer goddess. The entire transformation would take another few years to complete as her body finished building new cells to replace all of the old ones but she could already feel the differences. By the time it was over with it would take a lot more than the knife Tyler had shoved into her heart to kill her. Jane wondered too how much giving birth to the little gods and goddesses that she knew her husband wanted would accelerate the process. Giving up who she'd been for the last millennia had sounded like a brilliant plan when she'd still been tied to Zane and his stupid talent for getting them killed at a young age. Now that they were unbound and his soul had been claimed for eternity by Alecto, one of the Furies and Jared's cousin, the reality of the change was weighing heavily on her. It didn't help that when she had asked the goddess to bind her to her true soul-mate two years ago she had opened herself up to being bound eternally to Tyler rather than Jared. Whoever said Fate didn't have a sense of humor had obviously never encountered the being. When she'd met Jared one of the first things that had drawn her to him was how comfortable he was with who he was, how confident he was in his abilities, in his place in the world. Now that seemed to be the very thing that was beginning to drive a wedge between them. He had been confident and she had been resigned to a loveless, monotonous destiny of death, protecting the man who at one time would have been a prophet. Now that the consistency of Zane was gone and Jane's life was well past its normal expiration date, she felt at loose ends, wholly uncertain about what fate had in store for her and wondering if she had enough inner strength left to forge her own destiny. In the past these were the things that she would have discussed with her twin sister. Karina would have listened patiently and then laughed. She would've told Jane how ridiculous she was being, how lucky she was that Zane had had an affair with Sabina, a black witch and succubus who had been able to undo the ties that had linked Jane's life to Zane's. Karina had always been the voice of reason inside the whirling vortex of Jane's inner turmoil. Now that Karina was gone, Jane mostly kept these thoughts locked inside of her, questions without answers, hidden away where even Jared couldn't find them. Despite knowing that Karina's soul walked the earth, Jane didn't share Tyler's opinion that they could get back the Karina that they had lost a year ago. Jane knew in her heart that her sister, the only ally that she'd had in a millennia of existence, was well and truly gone.

"If you take me to Danalia, am I goddess enough to survive wherever she is?"

Jared nodded solemnly in response.

"Will you take me there?"

14

"It's all right, honey. You're in the psychiatric ward at Bedford Clinic."

The sweet motherly voice pulled Anna away from foggy dreams of car crashes, witches, and men with green eyes. "Thank you." Anna blinked, readjusting her vision to the bright sunlight streaming in through the thing curtains. "How did I get here?"

"That I can't answer for you, child. The orderlies brought you in here about five o'clock last night. It's Sunday, just after noon, in case you were wondering," the woman added helpfully. Anna looked around her now, noting the drab gray walls, the two twin beds, one of which she was in, and the woman, apparently in her mid-to-late forties, who was smiling sweetly at her in scrubs and a bathrobe.

"Are you a nurse?"

"No, I'm your roommate, Iris. I made the mistake of telling the wrong someone that my son was a god. I've been here ever since." She shrugged, still smiling.

"My name is Anna."

"Oh, I know. Heard tell that you tried to kill your husband."

"I wasn't trying to kill him; it was an accident," Anna whispered fearfully, hugging herself tightly.

"What did you do?"

"I lit him on fire."

"Is he a bastard?"

"I'd say that he didn't used to be but I honestly don't remember. That's been bothering me, all the things I thought I knew but that I don't remember." Anna shook her head to rid herself of the thoughts and the faraway look that she knew was in her eyes. "I'm sorry. You probably didn't want to know my life story."

"Oh we'll know a lot more than that about each other before either one of us gets out of here. It's good that your husband's a bastard. Means that he got what was coming to him for putting you in this place." Iris lowered her eyes before Anna could be frightened by the ghosts that resided there.

"How long have you been here?"

"Two years. Involuntarily, if you wondered. I take it you're involuntary too." It was more of a statement than a real question. For the first time since waking, Anna was very much aware of how precarious her situation really was.

"I didn't volunteer, if that's what you're asking." Anna clapped both hands over her mouth, shocked at her uncharacteristically sharp, sarcastic tone. "I'm so sorry. I don't usually talk like that."

"Not to worry, dear." Iris rose, walking the few short steps to Anna and patting her knee comfortingly, the thin hand that she extended looking too strong, young, for the way that the woman spoke. Anna looked up, taking in the tiny woman's strong features and athletic, graceful frame. Her black hair didn't show evidence of one gray hair. Her bright green eyes were surrounded by smooth skin. Anna began to reassess her judgment of the other woman's age.

"How old are you?"

"A lady never reveals her true age, darlin'." Iris laughed and it sounded like silver bells chiming in a light breeze. Were the setting different Anna would've thought she was holding court in a garden over iced tea and mint juleps.

"I'm sorry; I shouldn't have asked," Anna murmured, forcing herself to glance away.

"Stop apologizing, child!" Iris admonished. "We'll work on that. I'm sixty-nine years young, to answer your question." She stood up straight and spun in a circle. "Not bad, right? The doctors around here think I'm all kinds of anomaly."

Anna couldn't help but laugh. "I guess I'm an anomaly too. Well, more specifically Anna Molly, but I seem to accidentally cause fires a lot lately."

"Arson?"

"Firestarter. Though I'm pretty certain that won't be my official diagnosis."

Iris studied her new roommate carefully. "You've no idea what you are, do you, Anna Molly?" Anna blushed and shook her head, smiling in spite of herself.

"Fuck the doctors. Not to worry, dear. We'll figure it out. Might as well use the time constructively."

"What brings Anyasis's little goddess prematurely into my presence on this plane? You're either advancing far past your scheduled capabilities or my brother has assisted you for some reason." Danalia glared at Jared from where she rested in a bed of peonies in the middle of a field of clover. The place was beautiful but as it had no discernible end or beginning. Jane assumed it was a place of Danalia's imagination, where she could create without the hindrance of human interference. "You do not need my help to remove your powers from the container I created. I see that they're already leaking out, as I told you they would."

"I didn't forget what you told me about not using them, I just got a bit angry. Jar-Anyasis," Jane corrected herself, the name feeling foreign on her tongue, "brought me here. I need to talk to you about your phoenix."

A quick smile flashed across Danalia's aesthetically beautiful face before she bowed her head, shaking it sadly. "My greatest triumph and my greatest tragedy. I fear she has failed me and will be lost to the abyss."

Jane looked to Jared for a translation. He shrugged helplessly, negatively shaking his head. His wife turned back to Danalia. "What specifically does that mean?" Jane had learned very quickly that when dealing with her in-laws it was best to deal in specifics. They might not outright lie to her but they would dance around a straight forward answer all day unless otherwise prompted.

"She had but seven days to come into her powers. Otherwise she is lost and my creation has failed." Danalia gaped at the other woman like she had brain damage, as if the answer should be obvious.

Jane took a deep breath to fight her losing battle with her patience. "That's why I'm here. I need you to call her, to bring her into her powers."

"Why would I do that? If she cannot earn them herself then she does not deserve the power I have gifted her with."

"You've also gifted her with amnesia. She doesn't know she's a phoenix. How can she search for something inside of herself that she doesn't know exists?"

"I did not give her amnesia. As it was not my doing I do not believe I am obligated to give allowances for it. The contract stands. She has seven days remaining."

"What happens at the end of seven days if she doesn't realize what she is?" Jared placed a hand on Jane's arm to caution her against the edge in her voice.

"She will turn to ash and another phoenix will take her place."

"She'll be reborn again?"

"No, you silly girl. Do you not listen? Anna will be incinerated, destroyed, and another who is more worthy will take her place." Danalia turned away indifferently, her attention returning to her flowers.

"Anna?" Jane prompted, trying to keep the note of excitement out of her voice.

Danalia laughed, the sound of tiny bells ringing. "Yes, of course. Who did you think we were discussing? My little Anomaly. I thought of everyone you would appreciate the joke, little Destroyer."

"I didn't realize that was public knowledge yet," Jane muttered, her voice hollow.

"If even Anayasis can tell then it will be obvious to anyone of magical power who sees you. With your temperament it should come as no surprise that Zeus chose you to carry the destroyer power. Besides, the last one was such fun."

"What happened to the last one?" Jane peered at Danalia curiously, though the other woman refused to answer. Jared placed a hand on her arm to caution her against asking any more questions.

"Danalia, I know that what my wife asks is not something you would normally do, but if you will not call the phoenix into power, will you tell us where to find her? We'd like to at least be able to say our goodbyes if we cannot save her."

"If she cannot save herself there will be no point in finding her. She will have no memory of you without her powers." Danalia waved them away as she created a small, beautiful pond and several large trees to grow on its banks.

"Why can't we be given the opportunity to help her save herself?" Jane knew that her voice was angry but she didn't care. She was beyond trying to reason with this woman, who despite having helped Jane, was unwilling to help her sister, the phoenix that she herself had created. Jane wanted to set the whole field of plants on fire just to see if Danalia cared as little for her plants as she did for the human life she was risking.

"Anyasis, why does she ask questions I have already answered?" Danalia's voice was indifferent as she ignored Jane's question.

"She repeats because she does not accept the answer," Jared answered, his voice hoarse with worry. "Is there a way to find her before the phoenix consumes her?"

176

Danalia laughed. "They've both already encountered her. If my phoenix is found, it must be done without the use of your god-like powers. That was at Karina's request and not something that I or Sabina imposed upon her soul. As it was a part of her deal, I cannot change it no matter how much I would like to." She sighed heavily, regarding Jane and Jared sadly. "Believe me, I want you to find her. But I cannot give you the answers that you seek. However, should you encounter a full blooded human who can find an alternate way of locating her without using a locator spell, I would dare say that you might have a fighting chance." She rose gracefully to her bare feet and strode across the field, the plants parting to form a path before her. Danalia reached out, clasping both of Jane's hands in her own. "Please know that I am on your side in this. I cannot cross the barriers set before me and I can do nothing to anger our family. The less they know of you until you reach your full powers, the better. It is common to have to fight to secure your place in our world and you are not yet prepared. I will do all that I can to help you prepare and when you are ready, return to this plane and this one only. I will know when you appear here and will come as quickly as I can. Anything you say or do here will be safe. I understand that for your own sanity you must complete this quest. I just caution you to do it quickly. Our time is almost certainly limited. I feel your powers expanding rapidly. You are advancing quickly and it will not be much longer before word spreads that you are coming into your powers. When that does happen, you will be expected to return to Olympus." Her large green eyes pleaded with her brother. "You have to keep her from exhibiting any large displays of power. Help her get through this, keep her safe. You know the consequences if she cannot be controlled."

Jared nodded to Danalia, put a hand on Jane's shoulder and pulled her back with him into the dim light that appeared at his back. Jane felt her stomach drop and was momentarily blinded as they were hurled back to the living room of their Los Angeles home.

"When are you going to tell me what that was about?" Jane blinked to readjust her vision as she stumbled back into the room.

"Everyone of our heritage has an assigned job, powers that they inherit to do that job with. You are the destroyer. It is a very powerful position and one that must be treated carefully and with respect."

"We already knew that but we've not really discussed it. I guess we have to now." Jane started pacing the length of the room, dragging her fingers through her long hair. "Please tell me that's not one of those self-explanatory titles and that in your family a destroyer cuddles kittens or something."

Jared grimaced, bowing his head and shoving his hands into his jeans pockets as he suddenly became keenly interested in his neon blue sneakers. "It's probably a little worse than what you're thinking. The last destroyer my kind saw was a destroyer of worlds. Atlantis, Babylon, our own planet. If the legends are to be believed he went on a rampage before he was stopped, wiping entire races off the planet. I never encountered him but Tyler did once and came home with his tail between his legs. The destroyer is one scary motherfucker. I can see why they would choose you for this. You're strong enough to not break under the weight of the position, the power, and you're controlled so tightly that it won't control you."

"Somehow I don't think that was a compliment." Jane pushed past him and entered the kitchen, returning with a shot glass and a bottle of Patron Silver. She sat down on the couch, took a shot straight from the bottle, and poured another one. "It's really just a bad joke if you're an alien." Her eyes rose to meet his as she drank her poured shot. "Are you an alien? Really?"

Jared sat beside her, taking the bottle from her grasp. "No, we are not aliens. Our world used to be a lot bigger than just one area with a mountain that's not even that impressive. Our world covered the expanse of Earth, co-existing with this world on another plane. These were not the only two planes though now this is the only one that is still known to exist in its entirety. They've been broken apart, destroyed by war, famine, anger, time, love."

"How does love destroy an entire world?" Jane interrupted.

"What would you do to save me? For example. In the most extreme of circumstances, what would you do?"

"In the most extreme of circumstances I would watch the world burn for you." She through about it for a moment. "No, I take it back. I wouldn't watch the world burn; I'd set it on fire myself."

"That's my point. That is precisely my point. And that's also why you're the destroyer."

"What if I don't want to be the destroyer? Do I even get a choice?" She correctly took Jared's silence as her answer. "What happened to the last destroyer? What are the consequences that Danalia was talking about?"

Jared shook his head. "Later. You should call Tyler. Tell him that we have a name."

"We have part of a name. It's also a song title. It doesn't give us much."

"It does if we hack into the DMV."

"Only if she used her middle name when she applied for her identification."

"Why wouldn't she? My middle name's on my driver's license."

"Mine's not. My maiden name is listed as my middle name."

"Do you think she's married?"

179

"Do you think she thought ahead enough to specify that she wouldn't be? It's worth a shot to check every possibility, just in case. Do I want to know what your plan is for checking all of these not-so-public records?"

"Tyler can be…very persuasive when the situation calls for it."

"You're going to ask him to manipulate a clerk's emotions to get the records?"

"Probably several clerks and a few bystanders. Are you appalled?"

"No, I'm impressed." Jane reached a hand out, stopping Jared as he attempted to stand. "Wait. You have to tell me. What happens if the destroyer inside of me goes horribly wrong?"

"It will fall to me to bring you under control. When called you will operate much like a soldier. You will do the bidding of those higher than yourself, like the rest of us."

"What will I destroy?"

"Anything you're called to destroy."

"Even you?"

"Anything."

"Can we stop it?"

"No."

15

"There's a name?" Tyler couldn't help the wash of relief that went over him. He'd been searching for days, visited every magic-related person in five parishes who would see him and had come up empty-handed. It was discouraging, depressing, and as Tyler was quickly running out of time it really made him start to doubt his own abilities. This life was turning out to be chock full of new experiences. At this moment he was not terribly certain that he was overly enjoying any of them. Tyler guessed this was what happened when everyday people experience a life-altering event. One significant thing happens and suddenly nothing is ever the same again. He didn't want to be resentful; it's not who he is. It was just the idea that everything that's altered his existence so completely happened without his knowledge, consent, or even input made his teeth clench and his neck twitch on a regular basis. It's not that Tyler begrudged his brother his happiness; he didn't. He just often found himself annoyed that he seemed to be the outsider stuck in the middle of it forever. Part of Tyler wished that Jared had just let him go. That Tyler could have accepted. This, this was hell.

"You've got to be kidding me. That's not a name, it's an alt-rock love song."

"I'm aware of that and trust me, I had the same reaction, but right now it's all we've got to go on." Jane's voice sounded small and tinny through the cellphone. Or maybe it was just the constant pounding in his head. The woman's thoughts never stopped. Tyler didn't know where she found time to talk or to breathe.

"Danalia confirmed it? That's really her name?"

"Danalia thought it was funny," Jane explained. "It's a first name and a middle name. It doesn't help us with a last name and it may not help much at all if she's married." Jane went silent, waiting for his response.

"Why would she be married? She's only been gone for a year."

"Without her memories. I married your brother after a few days."

"I'd like to think that you're more the exception than the rule." Tyler couldn't help the sarcasm that entered his voice. Bad week didn't even begin to describe it. He just hoped Jane wasn't lurking somewhere in his thoughts. The last thing he needed right now was his brother on his ass for being a bastard in his own head. It does truly suck to not even have privacy in your own thoughts, even worse to constantly be made aware of it.

"Danalia did say that we've both encountered her and didn't know it."

"Oh shit." Tyler's free hand gripped the back of his neck almost painfully. "That's why I came to New Orleans. I met a woman who looked a lot like the vision I had of Karina. Her name was Anna. She wanted you to sign a book for her." An unbelievable tiredness crept over his entire body. "I came here to look for her because I thought they might be related. I didn't really think it was her. Why didn't I know it? Why didn't you know it?"

"Damnit!" To say that Jane sounded pissed would be an understatement of epic proportions.

Tyler heard his brother cursing through the phone just before it cut out. He tried calling back a few times then finally gave up, closing his eyes and shoving aside the psychic barriers that blocked him from Jared and Jane's heads. He felt his sister-in-law's anger and his brother's frustration as if they were physical entities radiating through his hotel room. Once he received acknowledgement from Jared he backed off, his presence receding just enough that he could eavesdrop without them fully realizing that he was still lurking in their minds. Tyler's attention was drawn from the conversation taking place in Los Angeles when his phone rang. He saw his brother's name on the screen and had to fight the urge to laugh. "So Jane melted another phone?"

"I don't know how to keep explaining this to the cell phone company," Jared sighed. "Can you check with the DMV, see if you can find a match to the description or name?"

"I've already been trying to find her. What do you think I've been doing down here?"

"Twiddling your thumbs and praying for a miracle that you just happen across the same woman twice?" Jared suggested helpfully.

"Fuck you," Tyler snarled half-heartedly. "I'll see what I can do. When is Jane getting here?"

"Tonight. We're leaving for LAX soon." Tyler couldn't hear it but he knew Jared was watching her while she was packing. Even trying to block it he was keenly aware of what she was putting in her suitcase. Tyler mentally sent her a note to pack pajamas that weren't composed entirely of scraps of silk and lace. They'd already long passed the barrier of too much information but that might cause him to gouge his own eyes out. He mentally felt body her stop, change direction and as she reached for a tank top and sweatpants he sighed in relief.

"I have a rental car. What time should I pick her up?"

Rather than continue to relay messages, Jared passed the phone to Jane who eagerly snatched it from his hand. "Seven-thirty, Delta flight 0726. I already spoke with Cecile's grand-daughter. We have an audience at eleven so that gives us enough time to exchange notes and make it out to the swamps of Terrebonne parish."

"Terrebonne?" Tyler started at the name. You want me to go out there at night? Are you crazy? People die and disappear out there."

"Yeah, they do." Jane's voice was impatient and distant. "People die everywhere, Tyler, and we die harder than most. Don't worry, I'll protect you," she teased. "Besides," her voice turned serious, "Cecile won't come out to the city to meet with us. We have to go on her turf, on her terms and we're running out of time. If you've got any other brilliant suggestions of someone who can locate another person without using a locator spell when all normal human methods of searching have failed, please let me know and save me the plane trip. This would be so much faster if we could just flit around this planet or plane or whatever the same way that we can just vaporize on to other planes."

"You can't vaporize onto other planes without help yet anyway," Jared gently reminded her. "You're the one who didn't have the patience for a lesson today." Tyler fought the urge to snicker, smothering the slight choking noise he was making behind his hand before it could be heard through the phone.

"Shut up," Jane commented affectionately and Tyler heard the zipper on her suitcase slip into place. "We're getting in the car now, Tyler."

"Can I ask how you got mixed up with a hoodoo practitioner in Louisiana when you lived in Biloxi?"

"Like usual, as James, I left home as soon as I could to search out Zane's soul. "I travelled some. I had to go around a lot to look for my charge's dumb traitorous ass. While I was travelling around Louisiana I ran into Cecile. She accepted me as her student and I stayed with her off and on for a week or so every once in a while to learn. If you really need the whole story we can talk about it when I get there. Trust me, it's not a big deal. What's more important is that she can cast any spell you sit in front of her and she might actually be willing to help us."

"I'm not arguing against your choice of magical practitioners. If you say she can do it, I trust you." Tyler closed his eyes, briefly wondering if he had time for a nap before he had to leave for the airport and even if he did, what the possibility of him actually getting some sleep was. The shadows around his eyes were starting to make him wish he could wear tinted lenses all the time. They were making him feel old. Jane was silent for so long that Tyler started to wonder if she'd hung up while he'd been distracted thinking about his sleep patterns. "Jane? Still hanging in there with me?"

"Yeah. You've just never…" she let her voice trail off. "Forget it. I'll take care of things here and see you soon."

"No, I'll take care of things here, you're getting your ass on an airplane." Tyler heard the thump of a car door and assumed that Jared had forced Jane into the car.

"If we have a minute we should go visit mom." It occurred to Tyler then that he hadn't seen his mortal mother from this life in a while. Not that he really felt any particular attachment, he and Jared had a lot of mothers, but Tyler did care for her and he knew she understood her role in their lives but that she still thought of them as hers even though they really weren't.

"She's still alive?"

"Yeah. I talk to her every couple of months, or I did before all of the insanity took over our lives. I quit visiting because it started freaking people around her out when we stopped aging at twenty-five."

"And moved to L. A. where no one would notice." Jane laughed. "If slow aging scared her, I'm gonna freak her the fuck out."

"Nah, you won't scare her. Do bring the colored contacts though. Just in case."

"Do you think it will be that noticeable?" her voice was uncharacteristically quiet.

"I'm honestly not sure." Tyler sighed, feeling her fear and frustration, catching himself just before rubbing the twitch out of his neck. "You'd have to ask Jared. I wasn't alive at the time and his memories of James are so clouded and locked up for me to push it with him would be like opening Pandora's box. And honestly, you're a celebrity of sorts so you can expect that if she recognizes you as anything it will be that, not the reincarnated version of the person who used to babysit her kid. The contacts are more to keep you comfortable and less about what anyone else would think."

Tyler felt her relief before he heard it in her voice. "Good. Contacts are in the bag and we're on our way to the airport. Won't it be kind of awkward for you to introduce me to your mother?"

"She's not my mother." Jared's mumbled words sounded almost garbled through the phone.

"She gave birth to you, took care of you and was always very nice to me. Shut it." He felt Jane smack his brother on the back of the head while he drove and Tyler couldn't help but smile. Things like this reminded him of why he knew his brother needed Jane in his life. Tyler just wasn't sure he wanted her as imbedded in his as she seemed to have become. And now he had to even watch his thoughts about it because as his soul-mate Jane had unprecedented access to everything he felt and thought. *How much more complicated can my life possibly get?* Tyler immediately cursed himself for the wayward thought. Things could almost always get worse. He didn't need to be encouraging the Fates to prove it to him.

"Text me, message me, alert me, whatever when you take off so I know the plane's on time. What can I do in the interim?"

"Look for people with fire problems?"

"You think I haven't already done that?"

"What about miraculous accidents? People who shouldn't have survived but did?"

"Nothing. At least nothing that was reported. You know how it is down here though. People protect their own. It could've happened and no one said anything." Tyler sighed as he fought the crowds on Bourbon Street to get back to his hotel. He had spent the day searching for anything that could possibly point him in the direction of Karina or the woman that he had met who looked like her. It might have speeded things up if he had known he was looking for one person instead of two. Tyler had searched records for twelve hours and found nothing. Found less than nothing. The ticking clock in his head was growing louder every second and those seconds were becoming precious few. Karina's seconds were running out very quickly. Tyler knew he would live. If they didn't find her in the next 26 hours she wouldn't. She'd probably spontaneously combust into flames and there would be nothing Tyler or anyone else could do to save her, even if he was standing there looking at her. It wasn't looking good. *If were a casino, I wouldn't bet on me,* he thought glumly. And the worst part is that she has no idea.

"We'll save her. She can't hide from us both, Tyler, no matter what shell Danalia put her in."

"Stop reading my thoughts."

"I can't. They're just…there."

"We need to figure out how to establish boundaries. I can't take this for the next millennia."

"I didn't ask for you either," Jane shot back irritably.

"I didn't mean it. We'll talk about it when you get here," Tyler amended, closing his eyes and silently counting to ten. "Just add it to the damn list of things to talk about. I don't think I've ever been forced to have this many serious conversations with a woman in my entire existence combined, especially one that I wasn't sleeping with. Jared's getting all of the benefits while I have to provide emotional support."

Jane laughed out loud and felt some of the tension slide out of her body. "Do you really want that particular benefit? Besides, I get plenty of emotional support from Jared. Being in a relationship with you both is kind of exhausting," she teased. Jane ended the call and leaned back into the leather seats of her husband's SUV.

"What are you repeating in your head? I can hear it but just barely." Jared smiled at her as he wove through the early afternoon traffic on the 405 interstate.

Jane cracked one eye open in his direction and smiled at him. "I'm repeating to myself over and over again that I won't strangle Tyler when my plane lands in Louisiana. He talked to her and didn't even realize it. We could be done with it, you and I could be home having sex and Tyler and Karina could be doing whatever it is that they're going to end up doing. I think that's really why we're now joined at the hip; so I won't get pissed off and kill him."

Jared laughed. "I'm not concerned."

"I'm poised to become the destroyer now, so who knows? If it did come down to a death match, who would you bet on?" Jane teased.

"Neither."

"Why not?" she laughed. "Don't want the kids to know who the favorite is?"

"No, it won't come to it because neither of you would survive. And even if both of you for some reason were suicidal, I'm not and neither of you would kill me. So it seems that we're all just stuck together. I probably don't like this as much as you don't but we're all going to have to find a way to live with it. My brother having an all-access pass to my wife's head isn't my idea of a good time either." Jared's hands tightened reflexively on the steering wheel as he maneuvered the vehicle to the exit ramp. "You don't have to do this."

"Yes, I do. She's my sister. She already sacrificed everything once for us. Karina, Anna, whoever she is now, I can't let her die a second time because of an open loophole in a deal that she's not even aware of making. We have to try." Jane touched his shoulder gently. "We're coming back, all of us."

"I can't lose you to that fucking bayou again."

"You won't. I'm a goddess, thanks to you. I'm harder to kill and I'll embrace whatever powers I have to make sure that Tyler and I come out alive. But we have to try."

"And I have to stay here," he finished for her.

"Yes, you do. Someone has to keep an eye on Sabina. And other than searching, this is not a dangerous mission. You have absolutely nothing to worry about."

"Nothing to worry about?" Jared glanced over at her as he drove through the airport checkpoint. "In less than a week you've been bound to my brother instead of me and launched a hoodoo scavenger hunt to find and save a phoenix who doesn't know she's a phoenix and might burst into flame leveling half of Louisiana if you don't find her and convince her that she's a phoenix and you're not crazy, in under a day. Having you and Tyler in the blast zone, no, that's not dangerous at all. I have no idea why I'd be worried."

"I will call you and update you and you can read both my and Tyler's thoughts and emotions. I'll keep the shields down unless it starts to hurt you or Tyler and if it does you have to tell me. You will know everything as it happens in real-time. You have nothing to worry about. So don't. I don't want to come back to a husband with wrinkles and frown lines." She reached over and smoothed the creases out of his forehead when the car stopped at the curb in front of the airport terminal. "That's better." Jane kissed him sweetly on the cheek and opened the car door. "Thank you for the ride."

"What the hell was that? That was not a kiss." Jared reached across the gearshift and yanked her back, pulling her almost into his lap. His mouth found hers and he crushed her to him, wanting to remember nothing but the feel of her in his arms, against his skin, when she was gone. When he finally broke the kiss Jane was staring at him with wide aqua eyes, gasping for breath. He pulled her back to him, burying his face in her neck. "This is the first time that I won't fall asleep with you in my arms since we met."

"I'm having separation anxiety too. If you can't sleep, call me. We'll sit on the phone all night, even if all we do is listen to each other breathing. It'll be just like I'm there."

"Except I can't touch you." He grumbled as she pulled back, reluctant to let her go.

"Sure you can." She pulled back enough to see his eyes and smiled. "Just close your eyes."

16

"How was your therapy session, dear?" Iris was sitting at a round table in the common room playing cards with a woman who looked like she'd never seen a deck of cards in her life. In fact, the more Anna watched the woman the more it looked like she'd never seen anything outside of her own head. Her dishwater blonde hair was stringy and stuck out all over her head. She stared at the cards on the table in front of her with glazed over unseeing eyes. Iris for her part simply ignored her lack of response and took turns playing her hand and peering at the other woman's cards to respond properly. Anna briefly wondered if Iris would let the other woman win.

"I spent an excruciating ninety minutes attempting to explain how I managed to set my husband on fire without use of an accelerant." Anna sighed, sinking into a battered old easy chair behind

Iris. She had a momentary feeling of kinship with the chair, feeling that they had both once upon a time seen better days.

"What did you tell them?"

"That I had the gas turned up too high on the stove and the pilot must have ignited it. It was an accident. If I'd been aiming I would've lit his crotch on fire." Anna clapped a hand over her mouth, as surprised at her own words the second time as she was the first when she said the same to the therapist.

Iris just laughed. "Oh you've nothing to be ashamed of. Stop trying to stuff those words back in, it'll do you no good. Your husband sounds like something of a bastard. You've had to live with him. You have a right to feel however you feel. No one else knows what's gone on behind closed doors." Iris reached back, patting Anna reassuringly on the shoulder.

"How terrible is it that I'm in a mental institution, under guard, and this is the most relaxed I've been in years. The only thing about my life that I miss here is that I can't get a little yard time to go out and jog. That's the only way that I ever got out of the house without Andrew insisting I stay and do something for him or make up some excuse that makes me feel guilty for wanting something for myself. As long as I can remember it's felt like Drew was punishing me for something," Anna said, staring absently out of the barred window in front of her. How had it ever gotten this bad, that Drew had finally resorted to putting her behind any form of bars that he could muster up in order to get rid of her? How did any relationship ever get that bad? Last Anna had checked divorce was still legal in Louisiana. It took a while, at least twelve months, but it had to be more humane than this. This was just cruel. Anna knew that she was being mentally and emotionally tortured by doctors who called it "therapy". She was pumped full of drugs at every opportunity. As if everything else she was going through wasn't bad enough, Anna just felt weary, emotionally spent. Maybe she was having a breakdown. Maybe Iris wasn't a God-given guardian angel or a devil in the guise of a kindly older woman, encouraging the fantastic notions running rampant through Anna's swirling mind. Anna had never felt so helpless in all her life and crazy or not, she clung to Iris like a life-line. She stared longingly out the window and wished for her running shoes.

"And how far back is that, dear?" Iris continued playing the card game by herself, oblivious to the listless actions of the woman seated across the table from her.

"Pardon?" Anna shook her head sharply to clear it of her melancholy thoughts.

"How far back do you remember? Really remember?"

Anna frowned thoughtfully. "I don't know," she finally admitted. "Everything prior to the last year is kind of fuzzy. It all changes and disappears a bit every time I poke at it."

"What's the first thing that you remember?" Iris put her cards down, turning to look at Anna eagerly.

"I remember waking up next to Drew in our bedroom at our house in Terrebonne and thinking that I felt different than the day before. That's the first, concrete thing that I remember. It never changes, nothing about it."

"And when was that?"

"Almost a year ago to the day. It will be a year on Friday, actually. That I remember clear as a bell. Everything else before just kind of feels wrong."

"Everything else before that? There's nothing that sticks out clearly?"

"No, nothing."

"And you're sure you've never had a brain injury? Never been hit real hard on the head?"

Anna laughed callously. "I've been hit plenty of times. Just not hard enough to do any lasting damage. Drew never wanted a reason to have to call a doctor."

"He's abusive." The thought was a statement rather than a question, as if Iris had already surmised as much.

"Yeah. Back to the "punishing me for sins I didn't commit" obsession. I wish I could remember why I married him." Anna shook her head in disgust.

"Are you sure that you did?"

"Of course! He's my husband. If we weren't married I would've left a long time ago, trust me."

"You should've left him anyway," Iris commented tartly. Observing Anna's shocked expression she shrugged unapologetically. "Sorry, dear, but it's true. There's no good reason for a woman to ever stay with a man that hits her. You'll never hear anything from me that's not the truth unless it's directed at the staff. With them I'm not quite so forthcoming. That's what ended me up here in the first place, being too honest with folks. Are you sure you're married or do you just think you're married? Do you remember it?"

Anna thought for a moment. "Vaguely."

"What did your dress look like?"

"White. Long." The delicate skin across Anna's forehead creased as she tried to concentrate on the recollection of her memory. "I ran into one of the women who had been a bridesmaid at my wedding the other day at the market. She said she did not know me, that Drew and I had only just moved to Louisiana a year ago. But I have an accent. I remember growing up here."

"Do you really? Where does your mother live?"

"New Orleans."

"When was the last time you saw her?"

"I don't know."

"When did you meet Andrew?"

"When we were children."

"When specifically? How old were you?"

"I don't know."

"When is your anniversary?"

"June."

"June what? What year?"

"I don't know. At least ten years."

"If you don't know the year why are you so certain about the timeframe?"

"I just am! Why does it matter? Maybe our relationship just went so far wrong that keeping up with the year and day that my life essentially ended didn't seem so vastly important anymore."

"That the relationship went sour is more of a reason to remember the date than romance, don't you think? I would torture myself with that date all the time like making marks to gauge the passing of time on a prison cell wall."

"Maybe I'm just not like you."

"Oh I highly suspect that you're not," Iris laughed. "I'm just your everyday garden variety human. You, my dear, most definitely are not."

"What do you think I am then?"

"Well you smell like a bird but that can't possibly be right." Iris took a sniff of the inside of Anna's arm then leaned back in her chair a bit and sighed. "If my son was here he could tell you for sure. That boy could take one look at you and tell you what you are like that!" The older woman snapped her fingers in illustration.

"Any chance you could get ahold of this son of yours before they give me a lobotomy?"

Iris suddenly looked sad. "I don't know. Haven't heard from him since I was put in this place and I doubt they placed a friendly call and let him know I was here."

"I'm so sorry." Anna stood and placed her arms around the other woman's shoulders. "They haven't given you phone privileges to call him?"

Iris shook her head sadly. "Court ordered. No contact outside of my ward and the doctors. That's the way it is here."

"It doesn't have to be. Surely they have to at least give you a phone call. Inmates in prison get a phone call. Hell, even when you're arrested you're allowed one three minute phone call."

"Look at your chart, dear. I'll be that you don't have phone privileges either."

"Who said I was asking anyone's permission? Legally, they can't keep me from making a phone call."

"That's a dangerous thing that you propose, Anna. You don't yet understand what they'll do to you if you're caught."

"What, give me more therapy?" Anna lowered her voice to a whisper. "They won't catch me. Could your son get you out of here?"

"I don't know."

"If he could solve my mystery and get you out of here then maybe it's worth the risk."

"Anna, I can't guarantee that he'll be able to answer all of your questions."

"Right now I'm willing to settle with the idea that he might be able to answer one of them. Nothing that I know is real. And I keep having dreams about this car crash…"

"But it wasn't you in the crash?"

"It feels like it was me that was hit but I know that it couldn't be. No one could've survived that kind of accident."

"Maybe you didn't survive."

"And what, I'm a ghost, you're a medium and this hospital is hell? Come on! I might be crazy but I'm not that gullible." Anna laughed. She noticed people watching her and quickly clapped a hand over her mouth to muffle the giggles that slipped past her lips. For some reason the situation she proposed to Iris was absurdly funny.

"That's not what I meant." Iris waved the other woman's laughter off impatiently. "Have you ever heard of past lives?"

"Of course, but I'm not sure that I believe in them. Why?" Anna forced her face into a more sober expression. There's no way that her dreams were memories from a past life. Anna could buy a lot of things but the idea that what she was being tortured with was something that had happened long ago and couldn't possibly do her any good now was just more depressing than she was willing to deal with. Even if the alternative was that she was remembering a life that she'd already lived and that there was another life hanging around out there somewhere just waiting for her to remember who she was and fall into it. Anna wasn't sure which option sounded more improbable. If this was the way she was thinking maybe she did deserve to be in a mental ward.

"Perhaps that is what you're remembering. Yours just might not have been that long ago," Iris offered helpfully. "I'm sure that it's probably not as insane as it sounds, dear. Try not to worry. You'll give yourself frown lines. These things tend to work themselves out in time."

"I don't think that what's wrong with me is that fantastic or strange. I just want to know what it is so that I know for certain who I am."

"I don't think you're asking the right question, dear. You know who you are. I think the question that you need answered is what you are."

"I know what I am! I'm a person!" Anna screamed in frustration. Iris's forgotten cards burst into flames.

Iris reached out and calmly tipped over her plastic cup of water, dousing the flames quickly before anyone else noticed. "You're the only one I've ever met who can do that."

"You did that on purpose."

"Your hair's turning red," Iris commented calmly, ignoring the question. "You look like a firebird."

Anna pulled a lock of hair over her shoulder to examine the deep red and gold mass curiously. At this point she wasn't even mildly surprised that her hair had spontaneously changed colors from a deep bronzed brunette to an intense garnet red with hints of burnished gold and bronze overnight, she just wondered who other than Iris had noticed. "You don't think I'm human, you think I'm a mythical bird? If I'm a bird why can't I just sprout wings and feathers and fly out of here?" She shook her head, throwing the loose curls back over her shoulder. "You might be crazier than I am."

"Not crazier, more accepting maybe, but not crazy," Iris countered good-naturedly. "It's natural to be frightened of the things that we don't fully understand. It's self-preservation; keeps your curiosity down and your body alive. But sometimes we have to throw caution to the wind. It's the only way we find out who we really are, Anna."

"What if I don't want to know?"

"The truth is always better than ignorance, child. It might be astonishing at first but, once you figure out how to wrap your head around it, you'll find it easier to live with than not knowing why things are affecting you the way they are. Could you live with yourself if you made a conscious decision to ignore the truth when it was right in front of you? Besides, it was you that wanted to know who you are. I'm just offering a suggestion."

Anna didn't look up from her examination of her hands and arms to see if there was any discernible difference from a moment ago. "I'm not sure that I have a choice in the matter." She returned her hands demurely to her lap, shaking off the thoughts plaguing her mind, preferring ignorance for the moment and the temporary peace that it granted her. "Tell me about your son."

Iris's face lit up. "You wouldn't believe that my youngest is in his mid-thirties looking at me, would you?"

Anna laughed as Iris struck a pose. "You probably look more like his sister than his mother. How many children do you have?"

"Two boys. Would you like to see a picture?" Iris stood and motioned for Anna to follow her down the hall to their room. Anna stood, swiping the charred playing cards from the table, stuffing them in her pocket where no one else could see what she had done. When she reached their shared bedroom, Iris was already seated on her bed with a small photo album. "Close the door, dear. They don't know that I have this and I prefer to keep it that way." Anna did as she was told and crossed the room to take the offered seat next to Iris on the worn coverlet. "These are my boys, Tyler and Jared. Jared's the oldest," she indicated the tall dark haired boy in the picture. "He was sixteen here. That's him with his first love. Oh, he loved that car. Still has it, I think. I don't know. He moved out as soon as he could and I don't really speak to him much. Haven't seen him in several years."

Anna studied the smiling teenager and the silver sports car he was standing beside curiously. She couldn't quite put her finger on it but something about it looked so familiar. "Is that a Corvette?"

"A Stingray. Used to belong to our neighbors."

"It's a lovely car. I can't believe they sold it to a teenager."

"Oh, they didn't. They died when he was just a boy. Always surprised me a bit that he remembered them at all, though given the circumstances I guess nothing about him should have surprised me. Always such a quiet child." Iris shook her head sadly. "Not at all like my Tyler. Always happy and ready with a joke. Anything to make you smile. Jared grew up and left. Didn't have much use for an old lady I guess. He never was one to form a lot of emotional attachments. Except to his brother. He adored Tyler from the moment he knew I was pregnant. I've never seen anything like it. Five years old and nagging me worse than the doctor to make sure that I ate right and got enough sleep." Iris chuckled to herself, flipping the page. "This is Tyler from the last time he visited me. Tyler stayed with me until his brother called him out to live with him as soon as he was old enough." Anna fixated on the picture of a smiling man with dark blonde hair and green eyes posed with a tanned arm around his mother.

"I know him!" The words fell out of Anna's mouth without her consent. "I-I think I know him. He looks so familiar."

"Oh, I don't doubt that, hon," Iris dismissed the comment with a wave of her hand. "Both of my boys are famous musicians. They're in a band called Metamorphosis. They won a Grammy," she announced proudly.

"That's amazing! Do they still live in the area?" Anna continued to wrack her brain to try and remember where she had seen Tyler before.

"No, they never did once they got old enough to go out on their own. I raised them up in Biloxi and then after that horrible accident we moved out here. I just don't think that Jared ever recovered after James died."

"You had three boys?"

"Oh, no! Just the two. James was a girl, our neighbor when we lived here. She was Jared's babysitter. She and her boyfriend died in an accident in that car." Iris flipped back to the picture of her eldest son and the Corvette. "Such a shame. They were so young. Jared took it so hard, swore they were murdered. Never could convince him otherwise. I kept the car, had it restored for him so that he had something to remember her by. Never did see him take to anyone else like he did to her."

"Where do they live now?"

"Los Angeles. They have their big lives, big careers. Not a lot of time to come out to the swamps anymore."

"May I see the picture of Tyler again? Please?"

"Of course." Iris turned to the correct page and placed the book in Anna's lap.

"What is it about your sons that landed you in this place?" Anna idly traced the handsome face smiling up at her from the picture with her finger.

"Well I feel like they're mine because I gave birth to them but they're not my blood."

"You were a surrogate?"

"No, their parents are gods. Just needed a human incubator for them to be reborn."

That caught Anna's attention. "Excuse me?" her head jerked up to meet Iris's level gaze. "Immaculate conception? Like Jesus?"

"Oh no, nothing like that. Something more akin to partially informed consent to a less invasive kind of in vitro fertilization than most people are used to."

"Are you sure?"

"Meet my boys. You'll see there's no mistaking it." Iris looked confident; Anna tried to not look worried.

"Who are the parents?"

"Oh, I'm not sure. Some god and goddess or another. Really they're all pretty much the same. Except for my sons. At their creation they chose to be humans so they aren't immortal. They're born every couple hundred years to a different mortal woman. As restitution for carrying them and caring for them as children the woman gets to live as long as they do and doesn't age like normal. I've also got a nice pot of gold buried in my adoptive mother's backyard."

"That's literal, isn't it?"

"Well technically it's not a pot, more like a large lockbox, but it does the trick just the same."

"They make banks for a reason."

"The banks work for the government. I don't trust them."

"So you were committed for believing that your sons are gods?"

"No, I was committed for being too good at my job as a psychic. Scared the hell out of the wrong people. Then they started noticing other oddities about me. So here I am, locked up to stop me from being a public nuisance."

"Can't you just convince them that you're not crazy so they'll let you go?"

"Child, that only works in the pictures! Out here in the real world they lock up the things they don't understand and throw away the key. A beautiful world being run and ruined by the small-minded. It's a damn shame. And now they've thrown you in here too. So young with your whole life ahead of you." Iris sniffed, straightened her shoulders and pulled herself out of her melancholy. "Don't worry about me, dear. I've already lived my life and I've got a lot more to go. Let's worry about getting you out of here."

"So what is it that this hoodoo priestess friend of yours is going to do to help us?" Tyler drove his rented Prius through the interstate traffic back to the French Quarter from the airport.

"I don't know exactly. Honestly I'm just hoping that she can and will help us. No one else seems to want to." Jane leaned back in the passenger seat, closing her eyes tiredly.

"That's a lot of "maybe" for this being our last shot at helping Karina."

"Has anything you've done worked so far?" Jane fought the electricity crawling under her skin, responding to her irritation. "Right now Cecile is our best shot. If this fails we're out of options, ideas and time." She took a deep breath and blew it out slowly. "I'm sorry. What's happened isn't your fault, it's mine. You're just trying to clean up my mess."

"It's not your mess, it's Zane's. I've thought a lot about this in the last few days so hear me out. If it hadn't been for him fucking around with that succubus four decades ago, none of this would've ever happened. James would still be alive, Jared would have maintained his sanity, Karina would've been born not knowing any of this and you and I wouldn't be bound to each other for eternity."

"How do you know this isn't exactly what was supposed to happen? Do you see nothing but the negative? If none of that had happened Jared and I wouldn't be together because I would be thirteen years older than him, probably with kids or dead from something else by the time he hit his twenties. I wouldn't have a sister. Karina wouldn't have you. Where do you think you would've ended up in all of this? Working in some backwoods bar in the bayou? We are who we are and somehow we would all have still had this life, even if we had to wait a few years to begin another lifetime to work toward it. I know this isn't easy, this has been horrible for you and I didn't even need to read your thoughts to know that you don't particularly care for being in the same room with me. Trust me, I didn't plan on being tied metaphysically to you forever either. But when I made the decision to be with Jared I knew that I was signing up for you and I to be tied together forever in some way. This is just a little more intimate than I bargained for but it's nothing that we can't handle. I believe that you're a good guy, a great brother and not a bad person to be stuck with if I have to be tethered to someone other than my husband forever. Is being bound to me really so bad that you would give up everything that Zane's one act of stupidity has gained us?" Jane opened her eyes and turned sideways in her seat to look at him. "For once I thought Zane's stupidity had a somewhat positive result, other than his soul being banished to purgatory forever. You would really give up your career, Karina, my and Jared's happiness, our family, everything that the four of us have fought for these past two years?" She continued, cutting off his reply. "Even if that hadn't happened, if we went with your idea of bliss and I had lived as James, if Jared had maintained his lack of emotional trauma, do you really think that this would have turned out any other way? You were born in the house next door to where I lived. I already knew your brother. Do you honestly think that you would be totally rid of me?"

"No, I just thought after this life that you would be rid of me," he muttered under his breath, aware that even if he had chosen not to speak at all that she would have still heard him clear as a bell.

"Why on earth would I want that?" Jane asked softly, placing a hand on his arm.

"Because you and Jared are happy!" he spat out scornfully, swerving through traffic. "Why would you want me around? Shouldn't I be allowed to go out and find what makes me happy? Jared has you, he doesn't need me anymore, not after this life. No one ever bothered to ask if I wanted to be stuck like this forever, it was just decided for me. All of it was decided for me as if I don't have a voice, vote or opinion. I don't want you in my head for the rest of my life. I don't want to be the third wheel in your and Jared's relationship watching your happiness from the outside. I didn't choose this and I sure as hell didn't want it! I'd ask who I killed in a previous life to deserve it but I already know the answer. Nobody! I remember all of my previous lives." Tyler slapped the steering wheel in frustration. "Why couldn't he just let me go?"

"Because it never occurred to either of us that you wanted to be let go," Jane whispered as she recovered use of her voice. "All that time we spent searching for a way for all three of us to be together after this life and we never knew that it wasn't something you wanted. Why didn't you ever say anything?"

"I didn't think I'd have to. No one gets two soul-mates and we all thought you were Jared's. If I didn't say anything then we wouldn't know until it was too late and then you wouldn't be able to find me because we'd be separated. It never occurred to any of us that the two of you could be soul-bound in another way. I never thought we'd find an answer so I never thought I'd have to say anything. I just thought that would be that. I'd get to watch you guys have kids, grow old with you both once and then we'd all move on. That some sick bastard of fate would soul-mate the two of us together never once entered my conscious thought processes and if it entered my unconscious thoughts I never knew about it." He stopped the car at the curb in front of the hotel, allowing the valet to open the door for him. Tyler gave the young man a tip and walked around the car to meet Jane on the sidewalk. "The lady's luggage is in the trunk. Please bring it to room 407." The young man nodded at the instruction, clutching his tip. Tyler turned, putting a hand at the small of Jane's back to guide her into the hotel.

"I can carry my own bag," Jane protested under her breath.

"While you are here you will do as I say. We are not partners, I am in charge of you. Nothing happens to you, you make no unilateral decisions. I may not be in charge in Los Angeles but I am here and you will not throw yourself under a bus to save your sister, killing me and probably my brother in the process and at the very least ruining Jared's perfect happiness and the remainder of my existence. Do you understand?" he finished as the elevator doors snapped closed in their faces and they were whisked up to the fourth floor.

"No. I understand where the words came from and while I appreciate your need for dominance the answer is no. I am an adult and I will do what I damn well please without your permission as long as it doesn't get me seriously maimed or killed. I am the destroyer and

I will happily start the new job that I didn't ask for with you." Jane marched through the elevator doors as soon as they were open, heading for their hotel room.

"You don't have the key!" Tyler called after her in a sing-song voice. He stepped up beside her, nudging her aside to unlock the door. "So you're embracing your new powers, huh? He held the door open, allowing her to enter the room first. "Kind of makes sense that you were picked to be the destroyer if you think about it." The door clicked shut behind them.

17

"We're going to figure out a way to call your son tonight," Anna whispered conspiratorially across the dinner table to Iris. Iris raised an eyebrow but said nothing as she continued to sedately eat her mashed potatoes. "Well?"

"Well what? You get caught and you'll spend your life in here like me." Iris emphasized her point by jabbing her fork in Anna's direction. "I don't want you to get caught and punished on my account. I've been taking care of myself in here for a good bit now. You've either got to learn your place around here or they'll teach you real quick and they're not nice about it. Solitary confinement is a real thing and it's not a joke."

"If I don't get caught we might both get out of here and whatever punishment they can come up with won't matter." Anna leaned across the table. "We can do this. We can both get out of this hell."

"We can both get out or we could both get scheduled for lobotomies."

"Oh come on. You're not scared, not really. And I can breathe fire. We'll make it, Iris." Anna touched the other woman's hand briefly before returning to her dinner, not wanting the guards posing as orderlies to take note of their conversation.

How do you plan on doing this? Iris mouthed silently.

Phone number? Anna replied silently. Iris gave a nearly imperceptible nod. *Tonight.*

Tyler groaned as he followed Jane's directions, driving so far off the beaten path into the swamps that he knew not only could they be killed out here and no one would know, but there was a high chance that their bodies would be barbequed, fed to the gators and they would never be found. "Are you sure this is the right way?" Tyler knew that he sounded like a broken record but damnit, he did not want to drive down yet another partially flooded dirt road leading further away from civilization and working cell phone towers. He may have been born here this time but he didn't grow up like this. Tyler didn't consider himself a city guy or a snob. He just really liked modern conveniences. This is like the place that time forgot sometime around the year 1900. Every road the car turned down, the sound of insects grew louder and the ramshackle shotgun houses grew fewer. Tyler wasn't sure if that made him feel better or worse. Honestly, he felt bad about the entire situation. Anything that dragged them out here in the middle of the night couldn't end well. They may not be able to outright kill them in the swamps because of their heritage but they'd sure as hell know that Tyler and Jane were not part of their society. And as Tyler was quickly relearning, there are a lot of things worse than death.

"Yes, I'm sure. Turn right there." Jane pointed to a barely visible dirt path off to the right.

Tyler rolled his eyes and turned the Prius down the unmarked road. At least the rental car was low-jacked. The police would find that if nothing else.

"You know it's been awhile since you've been out here. Maybe we should call for directions. Or a guide."

"Google Maps doesn't exactly work out here. Knowing where to go is part of the test. If you're not worthy then you don't deserve to find the place."

"We've only got twenty minutes left before we're late and I swear that we've passed that log a dozen times already."

Jane consulted her cell phone. "Your clock's wrong. We have seventeen minutes and not surprisingly there's no cell service out here so you're just going to have to trust me."

"It's not that I don't trust you, Jane, I just don't want to get hexed for being late."

"It's called "crossed" in hoodoo, not "hexed" and if you don't believe in it, it can't hurt you."

Tyler nearly stopped the car in the middle of the muddy road with only the fear of it getting stuck keeping him from slamming on the brakes. "Do you seriously believe that after all the shit I've seen that I don't believe in magic?" Wisely Jane remained silent and Tyler kept driving. A few minutes later music began streaming through the open car windows, seeming to float out of nowhere through the humid night. He looked to Jane for an explanation. She said nothing, mentally or otherwise as she stared out into the blackness surrounding them. It was the first time that her mind had been totally silent in the days since they'd been linked. Rather than being a comfort it made Tyler more concerned about the clandestine meeting they were about to attend.

"How close are we?"

"Close."

"We can hear them. I assume that music is where we're headed?" When Jane said nothing, Tyler opted for a different question. "Can they hear us?"

"No," she answered finally, turning to face him. He felt her mental probe as she curiously tried to follow his line of reasoning.

"Is there anything I need to know about anything at all, before we go in there tonight?"

"Like what, Tyler?" Jane snapped back. He didn't take it personally because he knew why she was scared. Tyler looked out the windows and saw the general darkness of the night. Jane saw ghosts that counted her among their numbers. Before he took the opportunity to reply, Jane corrected herself, a horrible, haunted look crossing her face and causing her eyes to pale out to an almost white-gray with sadness. "You may learn some things about me that you'd wish you didn't know. If that happens, promise me that you'll let me be the one to tell Jared. I know that you probably couldn't care any less for me than you already do, but as you know with our kind there's always something more behind the surface than meets the eye. I've done awful things, Tyler, some that Jared knows about, some that he doesn't. Cecile knows everything. She was trying to help me find a way out when I died as James."

Tyler did stop the car then, slowing it gently to avoid making any gouges in the soft mud. "Jane, it doesn't matter who you were or what you've done. We're not lily-white on the mortal sin scale wither. What does matter is that you're my sister now. For better or for worse now my life is joined to yours."

"Isn't that why we're here though? Because who you were, the things you've done, they do matter. Look at us, at this mess. That should be more proof than you'd ever need that your past doesn't always let you go."

This time Tyler kept silent and his eyes on the road ahead as he continued to drive.

"Give me your son's phone number," Anna whispered to Iris, watching the night guard patrol the hallways through the open crack of their bedroom door.

"You can't risk this. I've done it. I got caught. They threw me in solitary ward for a week." Iris sat on her bed, her arms stubbornly crossed over her chest. "You don't get much food or water and all you've got is a six by five cement block cell that you can barely lay down in. The lights stay on all the time and all you can hear is water dripping and other women screaming from the madness. I'm not risking it. If it's meant for me to get out of here, I will. You're new. There's a chance a court could let you out. You shouldn't risk it either. Definitely don't do it for me. Please, Anna."

Anna gently closed the door with a barely audible click and sighed, crossing the room to stand in front of Iris. "This was your idea. These are your sons. They need to know where their mother is and that she needs their help. The people in this city, their fear, it cannot win. If they want to live in ignorance, fine, but we don't have to make their choices. We have to fight, Iris. They can't keep us locked up here forever unless we allow it. I know you don't want to be here. So what are you so afraid of out there?"

"What if they don't come for me?" Iris asked fearfully. "Right now they don't know where I am, what's happened to me, so there's that. If they don't know and don't come then it's because they didn't know. But if they don't come and they know I'm here? I couldn't bear it." Iris shook her head, ducking her face toward the wall to hide her tears from Anna. "I don't want them to see me reduced to this."

"Iris, they're your sons, no matter where they came from. They won't want you living like this. When it's my life you are afraid of nothing. Why are you afraid of this for your own life?" Anna didn't know where the sudden rush of frustrated confidence in her voice came from but she relished the feeling. For the first time in her life she felt powerful. As soon as the thought crossed her mind Anna knew instinctively that it was wrong, she had felt this way before. Better, actually because it was recognized by another. A quick flash, like a memory from a forgotten time slipped across her vision and disappeared just as quickly. It was of two people, a man and a woman. They appeared to be dancing but the image was distorted, haloed in gold, like a reflection in an old gilded mirror. The image filled her with a stronger desire than she had ever felt for her husband and that desire made her feel alive, confident that she could have whatever it was in the world that she wanted. Anna didn't know how much time had passed but when she blinked slowly to clear her vision she knew by Iris's expression that her face had revealed too much.

"What did you see?"

Anna shook her head slowly, still not trusting her voice to not betray the strong emotions still vibrating through her being. "Nothing," she croaked out finally.

"Don't try to pull the wool over my eyes, girl. I know that faraway look to you. I've seen it on my boys when they're hearin' or seein' something that's not there. Now what did you see? It might matter more than you know, Anna," the other woman finished quietly, her eyes downcast.

"I saw a man and a woman, a couple, dancing in an elevator."

"Who were you?"

"I don't know." Anna thought about it for a moment then corrected herself. "I think I was the woman. Do you think it's a memory?"

"I think it's a clue to who you really are."

"Do you think that someone wiped my memories?" Anna laughed. "Even with my limited knowledge I still think that's ridiculous."

"No." Iris examined her face curiously, paying particular attention to Anna's eyes. "I don't think this is your life. It never was. What you see in your head, that's what's real, that's who you really are."

"Then why hasn't anyone come for me? In all of those memories there were other people. Wouldn't there be friend, family, someone to miss me?" A note of sadness slipped into her voice. The sentiment for a life that existed in her dreams filled Anna with an unreasonable anger.

Iris reached for Anna, cautiously touching her heated skin. "Don't set me on fire, but I don't think this was your body. I'd be willing to bet that they don't know you're alive or where to look for you. Don't be angry with them; unless they put a bullet in your brain this not their fault. They just may not know any better."

"You think the people in my head are really out there?" There was so much hope in Anna's voice that it made her feel physically ill. Nothing should reduce her to fantasizing about a life with complete strangers who would probably freak out if she suddenly showed up on their doorstep claiming to be their dead loved one whose name she couldn't remember.

"Yes, I believe that they're very real and out there somewhere. At least they were when those memories were made. If you've got no way of dating them then there's no way to tell how old they are. I can't see what you see, not really anyway, but if push comes to shove you can always make a guess based on things like wardrobe or hairstyles." Iris shrugged her shoulders. "You need to be prepared though; if the memories are old there might not be anything left to find. There's no telling how long you've been like this or how much time transpired in the in-between times."

"I don't think that it was that much time at all. What I see looks very much like now but definitely not Louisiana. If I could find them, the people that knew me before, do you think they'd know what's wrong with me?"

"There's nothing wrong with you, child," Iris admonished. "A little different's done this world more good than harm. You shooting fire, or whatever it is you do, doesn't cause anything to break that's not already broken."

"Yeah, but if something like that was happening to you wouldn't you want to know why? Wouldn't you want to know what you are?"

"Will it help you sleep better at night, the knowing?"

"It might help bring some peace, to help me understand and cope with what's going on inside my body. If I have to keep living like this, Iris, without any answers then maybe I'm better off locked away in here where they can limit the amount of people I can hurt. I don't know what this is and I can't control it."

"You can't control it that well," Iris corrected sternly. "I've seen you control it, concentrate it. It can be done. You didn't have anyone tell you you're human did you?" Anna shook her head "no" and Iris forged ahead. "So you don't have anyone to tell you what you are this time either. Doesn't mean that you can't figure it out on your own. You don't need someone else's permission to be who and what you are. All you need is your own acceptance and the rest will fall into place. One thing I've learned from my two boys is that no one decides your fate but you. So don't let someone else take that away from you."

"Nice speech from the woman who's too afraid to let me call her own son." Anna raised an eyebrow in challenge and held out her hand. "Are you going to decide your fate or let these doctors do it for you? Your choice. There's no one out there to get me out. Even if there was, they don't know me. You're different. You have your kids and they deserve to know what's happened to their mother, no matter the relationship." Anna paused for a moment. "I know that this is none of my business but I'll ask any way. You seem to have a good relationship with your sons, at least with one of them. How did they let this happen to you? Why are you so frightened for them to know that you are locked in here?"

"My sons are…different. They're mine, I birthed them, I raised them, but in every other way they're not mine and they know it." Iris shook her head sadly. "If I tried to explain the rest you'd think me just as crazy as the people who put me here."

Anna laughed. "If I'm going to be accepting of my life, I'm a mythological firebird that literally just rose from the ashes without a memory. How much weirder can you be?"

Iris pushed her shoulders back, visibly fortifying herself. "All right. I'm the current mother of two demi-gods who remember time before Christ."

"I admit, that's weird," Anna acknowledged. "But in the larger scheme of weirdness in my life lately, that sounds downright normal. Though almost every mother believes her child to be something special and out of the ordinary. If I hadn't had my recent experience with the strange and otherworldly, I might not believe you. But right now I shoot fire out of my body, my hair changes colors, my husband's locked me away in the psych ward and you're the only person who believes that I'm innocent of trying to kill him. If I'm some sort of firestarter then it's no less illogical for your sons to be demi-gods." Both women laughed as the tension eased out of the room.

"You don't think I'm crazy?"

"If you are then so am I. I do think you need to give me at least one son's phone number before the guards change shifts again so that we can both get out of here." Anna held out her hand expectantly.

219

"What is that?" Tyler nervously eyed the orangey-red dust laid in a thick line across the doorway of the small, weathered house.

Jane didn't even glance down to see what he was looking at. "Brick dust." She stepped across the line and into the small foyer cramped with well-worn furniture and dust covered knick-knacks. "Don't disturb it. It just keeps the bad things out." When Tyler hesitated to follow her, she turned and glared at him impatiently. "It won't hurt you. Laying a line of brick dust across openings keeps people who would do you harm from entering. If you break the line the magic won't work so step over it."

"We should've made you bathe in this when you met Jared. Would've saved us all a lot of trouble," Tyler grumbled, stepping gingerly over the line and entering the house.

Jane glanced back at him. "Don't look so nervous. If she was going to kill you she wouldn't have let you through the door. If you were going to kill her then the dust wouldn't have let you enter."

As they stepped further into the house Tyler took in their dim surroundings in the ramshackle house carefully. He couldn't help but notice that Jane stepped forward confidently, completely unafraid of what could be lurking in the shadows. "You've been here before."

"Many times," Jane smiled at the memories.

"Great. Then maybe you can tell me what this is."

The strain in his voice caused Jane to turn around. Tyler was standing very still with the sharp white blade of a knife held tight at his throat. A small, wizened old woman with wiry gray hair and skin the color of coffee stood at his back, holding the blade and using his body as a shield. "The thing at your neck is a bone knife that's probably almost as old as you are. Who's holding it is Mama Cecile." A wide smile broke across Jane's face as she addressed the old woman. "How have you been? Do you know who I am?" She stepped into the light so that the old woman might see her better.

Mama Cecile pushed Tyler aside hard enough that the man stumbled, catching his balance against the wall. She lowered the knife as she approached Jane, her eyes never leaving the other woman's face. She grabbed Jane by the chin, pulling her face down several inches so that they could meet eye-to eye. "Change for me," Cecile commanded.

Jane thought about her sadness at her sister's death, her anger at herself for how it happened and her deep love for her husband, almost physically feeling the color changes in her eyes as she experienced each emotion. After a few moments Cecile made a satisfied sound and released Jane. "If I hadn't known you was ma' girl, I wouldna have recognized you 'cept by them eyes. Ain't nobody else ever had them eyes."

"It's good to see you too." Jane grabbed Tyler by his shirtsleeve and dragged him behind her as she followed Cecile through the house crowded with dust and old relics.

"I didna say it was good to see you. I prayed that after the last time you had finally found some peace. I see now that was not meant to be." Cecile eyed Tyler darkly. "What has this one done to you that's brought you back to darken my door after all these years?"

"Tyler's done nothing untoward to me. He's trying to help me."

"You've lost one of your numbers. I know that. What I don't know is what you're doing with this one." The wizened old woman never took her eyes off Tyler. "He's not the same one as before but you don't love him neither. So why do I see those tiresome silver strands hanging between you?" The little old woman sank gratefully onto a faded floral couch, gesturing for Jane and Tyler to sit. Jane took a padded, weather-beaten wicker chair near Cecile while Tyler chose the remaining chair, a decrepit wooden and basket-woven affair stationed across the coffee table from Cecile and her perch on the couch near the door. Tyler knew to not underestimate anyone that had already gotten the drop on him once, not even a wrinkled old lady half his size. That and the only other seats were the cramped, dust covered floor and beside Cecile on the couch. Tyler opted for the uncomfortable straight-backed chair and just hoped it didn't break under his weight.

"He's one of our four," Jane answered Cecile. "I married his brother. The other one is dead."

Mama Cecile shook her head negatively. "That cowl around your neck may have been removed but he's not gone from this world. Some spirit of him lingers and it's angry with you. The malevolence I feel is somethin' awful." Cecile shivered. "Enough about the past. I want to know what he is." She pointed to Tyler who remained uncharacteristically mute. "I canna get a read on him and I don't trust it."

"He's a demi-god. Greek," Jane answered, cutting off Tyler before he could voice the protest she heard screaming in his mind. If they were going to ask for help they needed to be completely honest with Cecile. "So is his brother."

"Trust my girl to fall in love with the stuff of myths and legends and find a way out of her purgatory." Cecile squinted at Jane and Tyler knew she was seeing something that the rest of them could not. "You're one of them. Were you reborn this way or made?"

"Made. Almost two years ago," Jane admitted.

"The power in you is enormous. It's something to be feared, but also embraced and understood. You'll master it; don't fear the responsibilities and burdens that your body now holds. It will not destroy you but it will require a firm hand to control it."

"Mama Cecile, we need to find our fourth, my sister." Jane tried to move the conversation away from the uncomfortable topic of her newfound destroyer heritage. "She died but was reborn in another body. We have only a few hours left to find her, to help her, before she is lost to us forever."

Cecile didn't object to the turn in topic. "Who was she before she left you?"

"She was my twin. The more grounded, confident, logical of us two. We shared some of my powers for a time."

"Which abilities did she have?"

"She could see the light. Her casting abilities were very good. We shared mental telepathy."

"Kari could read people. She didn't have many active powers but she was very good at knowing things about you that you didn't want known," Tyler interjected, his green eyes glaring from across the room. "Anything else that you want to know? About me? About her?" he jerked his thumb to indicate Jane.

"What does Kari mean to you?" Cecile watched Tyler's jaw tighten and his eyes lower. "That's your motivation. It's not for the woman, this is about you, what you want. For the very first time you don't know what you want and it scares the bejeezus outta you, boy. This canna be about you; your power for this, it comes from a selfish place. What we do to find her, you can't be involved. With your influence, everything would just circle back around. It's probably why everything you've tried has failed and led you to darken my door."

"What can we do, Mama Cecile? Karina's running out of time and so are we. Once the clock stops ticking we've no idea what will happen to her. I don't think it will be good."

"What has she become that has you so worried, child?"

"She's a fucking phoenix," Tyler growled. He extended a finger, freezing the surprised look on Cecile's face. "And we do not have time for this." He turned to Jane. "I get that you're enjoying the traipse down memory lane that the old woman provides but we are down to hours. Hours, Jane! Hours before Karina spontaneously combusts from powers that she does not understand and cannot possibly control without our help. We need to get her back to Olympus, get her help before something worse happens that she can't control."

"You think I've forgotten that? Cecile cannot help us if she doesn't fully understand the mess that she's stepping into," Jane argued. "If you're worried about time, you're wasting it now. Unfreeze her." She sat back in her seat, crossing her arms and looking at Tyler expectantly.

"Your sister is a ticking nuclear bomb. We don't know where she is or how far away that might be. It's in our best interests and hers to move this along quickly." Tyler pushed himself to his feet and walked toward the door.

"Where do you think you're going? You're as much a part of this as I am."

"Your friend can't work with me here. I'm too selfish to be of help in locating Karina so I'll wait in the car. You finish this and do it fast." Tyler walked out, slamming the front door behind him.

Cecile unfroze almost as soon as Jane heard the car door open. "Your friend isn't lacking in practical magic."

Jane rolled her eyes. "He's fairly unaccustomed to not getting what he wants. As a warning he can also hear anything within a one mile radius and has a direct link to my brain so don't think that he's really gone just because he left the room." She ran her hand through her hair nervously. "Mama, we're running out of time. What do you suggest we do? We have to find her."

"What do you know?" Cecile placed a comforting hand on Jane's arm.

"She's a human adult, a woman. When Tyler saw her in a vision she had dark hair and eyes, Creole skin. Her kitchen had flood water lines in it. He didn't see much else. We know from the…thing that made her deal, brought her back that she's a phoenix. We don't know what powers she's already developed, if any. I'd assume that she has because we were told that if we don't find her, help her realize what she is and how to control it her creator will allow her to be destroyed or worse, to self-destruct."

"Isn't that a tiny bit cruel on behalf of a maker?"

"Greek gods aren't a particularly benevolent lot."

"You fear becoming like them."

"I do. I fear my sister exploding like a nuclear bomb and taking out half of the state more. What do we need to do?" Jane repeated firmly.

Cecile patted Jane's arm again then stood slowly, motioning for the other woman to follow her into the kitchen. "It's real simple, honey. We're just gonna ask her. It could be a mite bit uncomfortable for you though."

Jane sighed. "Of course it will be. How much blood do you need and how much time do I have once it's done to figure this out?"

Cecile pulled a glass bowl down from a shelf and placed it on the large round table in the center of the room. She put on an apron and reached out for Jane's hand, the bone knife clutched in her fingers. "Only need a drop, dear. As for time, we can't keep you swapped for too long. You might get stuck then we'd be in a real mess. Don't need you swapping bodies again."

"Don't tell me; I don't want to know what you're thinking of doing. Just do it." Jane obediently held her arm over the bowl.

"Jared, I don't know what they're doing. I was exiled to the car." Tyler paced in the soft gravel beside the rental car.

"I trusted you to take care of her!" Jared's distorted voice buzzed through the bad cell phone connection. "How hard is it to keep an eye on her and for the two of you to not do anything stupid?"

"Have you met your wife?" Tyler shot back irritably. "You try to convince her to not take any stupid risks and let me know how that works out for you. You don't even know what's going on in there. They've just been talking for over an hour."

"Why aren't you listening in on them?"

"I'm trying but it's kind of hard with someone screaming at me over a bad cell phone connection! If we live through this the two of you need to get the fuck out of my head. I can't keep going like this. You're driving me crazy."

Jared took a deep breath and Tyler could feel him rubbing his forehead. "Try to understand this. You're in this, whether you want to be or not. Hell, you started this search for Karina so it's not like you can claim ignorance and ask for a pass now. The four of us, we're a family and we're pretty much all we've got so you have to learn to deal with that."

"I never asked for this, Jared. I love you, but I didn't want this. This is your life now. Not mine, not ours, yours. And there's no spot in it for me. I just wanted to repay the debt I have to Karina and get the hell out of this mess."

"Can we not do this now? What's going on in there? I can't get a read on Jane."

"Shut up for two seconds and I'll try." Tyler released the mental block that he'd constructed to hold off most of Jane's thoughts from wreaking havoc in his head when they were together. The five thousand or so thoughts that crossed her mind at once slammed into his consciousness, causing him to stumble from the metaphysical impact. "She's still there," Tyler replied weakly, pushing the mental blocks back into place and shoving Jane's thoughts from his mind. As her thoughts began to recede, the jumble coalesced into complete sentences that his mind automatically filtered through for information. One sentence caught his attention, causing him to drop the phone amidst his brother's protests and run back into the house. As soon as the thought reached Jared's mind he grabbed his keys and drove toward the airport.

"Jane!" Tyler burst back into the house, stumbling through the dark, cramped hallway until he found the kitchen at the back of the house.

"Calm down, boy." Mama Cecile stepped in between him and where Jane knelt with her head down on the kitchen floor. "She's just had a start and she may not know you just yet. Give her a minute before you give her a fright."

Tyler stopped dead in his tracks, his body going numb and his ears buzzing as he stared at his sister-in-law's body, still slumped toward the floor. He watched her slowly pull herself upright and when her bright green gaze met his wide eyes he felt his heart stop.

"Hello, Tyler. I hear it's been awhile." The words came out of Jane's mouth but they weren't hers. "I should have something eloquent and romantic to say right now but the only words that come to mind are anti-climactic such as "It's really good to see you"." She laughed and the sound squeezed Tyler's heart in some painful way that he didn't really understand.

When he could finally force breath back into his lungs, Tyler said the only words that he could coherently utter. "Hi, Karina."

18

Anna crept silently through the halls of the sanitarium, her eyes and ears on the alert for signs of the guards coming back. She paused at the end of the hallway to glance down at the tiny piece of paper in her hand with Iris's son's phone number on it. She quickly went over the numbers that she'd already committed to memory one last time, sending a tiny spark to turn the paper to ash in case she was caught to protect her friend. A wave of dizziness caught her, blurring her vision slightly as she dusted off her hands and slipped past the nurse's station unnoticed and out into the lobby where a telephone for family use awaited her in the corner of the room. Anna grabbed the corded phone and ducked down between the table and a potted plant, her fingers moving swiftly now that she had reached her goal. She stared at the dial pad as the numbers swam in her vision, the dizziness hitting more sharply than before.

"No, no, no," she muttered under her breath, willing the attack to stop long enough to allow her to make this one call. Her vision finally began to clear and she managed to hold the attack off long enough for her to dial the number before she was sucked off into oblivion, coming to on a worn kitchen floor. As she watched, the man she'd been trying to call burst into the room. *That's one helluva phone*, Anna thought, knowing now where she recognized him from and raising her eyes to meet his as his phone began to ring.

Tyler ignored his cell phone as it continued to ring, mentally cursing himself for not making the ring time shorter.

Anna looked down at her hands, curse words tumbling from her own lips as she recognized her sister's wedding band and it suddenly came to her who was on the other end of Tyler's ringing phone. "Answer the phone, Tyler." He remained rigid, still staring at her with wide, haunted eyes. "It's Jane! Tyler, answer the damn phone!" She lurched to her feet, ripping the ringing phone from Tyler's claw-like grip and answering it herself. "Jane! Don't hang up. Can you hear me?"

Anna's own voice floated back to her over the static-laden line. "Kari? Where am I?"

"You don't have a lot of time so listen carefully. You're in the sanitarium in Terrebonne parish. You're not supposed to be out of your room so get back as quickly as possible. We'll come to get you as soon as I frisk the statue of Tyler you left with me for his car keys. Get out of that room now. Take the first two lefts and find room 103. Iris will explain everything."

"My mother-in-law? She's in the sanitarium?"

Anna raised her gaze to meet Tyler's, knowing he heard the question. "You had to meet sometime. She's really very nice and has helped me get control over whatever this is inside of me." She was about to end the call when she heard scuffling on the other end of the phone. "Jane!" Her only response was a disconnected buzzing. Anna pocketed the phone and shook Tyler, trying illicit some response. "Tyler, we have to go. We have to get Jane and your mom and I don't know where the hell we are." Tyler remained mute, staring at her like she was the only thing that his glazed over eyes could focus on. Anna started searching his pockets, looking for keys. Tyler silently reached into a jacket pocket and held the car keys out to her. Anna took them, looking to Mama Cecile for an answer as he left the house.

Cecile shook her head as she gathered her supplies and drew Anna toward the front door. "He doesn't know what to make of you, child. Your death, it hurt him something awful. The things we want, they're always a mite different from what we thought when we get them. I know how to get to the sanitarium. I'll go with you and help get your sister out of this mess." Cecile paused at the threshold of the front door, allowing Anna to exit first and enter Tyler's wrath.

"How could you do this to us? To me?" Tyler snarled, shoving Anna up against the side of the rental car. "You made the decision to die and you just left us with it! Do you know what that did to your sister, to me? Do you even care? I tortured myself for a year, looking for you, trying to find a way to bring you back and you were here the whole fucking time! When we started looking for you we assumed that you didn't remember, didn't know who you were because if you had you'd have come home. But you knew me. The second you saw me you knew me!" Tyler snarled an inch from her face, his hands clamped painfully on her upper arms, holding her in place.

"I missed you too, Tyler. But you have to realize that Karina did die. My name is Anna now."

"Oh, don't give me that shit. You're Karina in a different body. Right now you're in another different body so really that should have no effect whatsoever on your identity. You're Karina, you've been

Karina. Is that why you didn't call, come by, let anyone know you were still alive? You didn't want to be Karina anymore? You want to be Anna in a sanitarium?"

"No! I didn't know you until I switched into Jane's body. Don't you think that if I had, I wouldn't have gone through hell to find you, to let you know I was okay? Even when I didn't know who you were I dreamed about you, had visions. I had no idea you were real, even when I saw you in the bookstore, I didn't recognize you for you" she finished softly, not daring to move.

Tyler quickly closed the gap between them, his kiss almost angry and his hands possessive as he jerked her against him. Anna wrapped her arms around him, her tongue sliding against his and pulling him deeper into her embrace. Tyler lost his self-control, his grip on reality, everything but the sure knowledge that he was finally able to touch the woman that haunted his dreams.

She finally pulled back from him, placing her hands on his chest to both hold him off and steady herself. "I've wanted to do that for a long time."

"You wanted to do that, huh?" he smiled. "Does that mean I can call you Karina instead of Anna?"

"Call me whatever you want as long as you kiss me like that again." Her eyes slid shut as she reached out, pulling his mouth back to hers. *Karina.* She tested the name in her mind and felt the thought vibrate back to her through Tyler's body. Despite her enjoyment in the moment, she still felt unease at the idea of resuming her former life so easily. She knew the name, she now had the return of her memories, but Anna felt so much separated from the person she was by the one she'd become. Tyler's hands at her waist brought her back to the moment and the realization that she should have not so easily forgotten. She broke the kiss, placing her fingers on his lips to keep

Tyler from reclaiming her mouth. "I can't take advantage of having Jane's body."

A stunned look crossed Tyler's face as he took a single step back. "Shit, I forgot. With your eyes you look…" his voice trailed off as if he were unable or unwilling to complete the sentence.

"I look just like I used to look," Anna finished for him. "For the time being, please just call me Anna. We'll work out the rest later. Right now we have to go. The guards found Jane while we were talking. It's not safe for her there, not in my body." She slid out of his arms and unlocked the car doors. Tyler stepped to the car and slid into the passenger seat with Cecile behind him without another word.

Mama Cecile reached forward, patting his shoulder comfortingly. "For what it's worth, she didn't know you 'til she saw you with her own two eyes." Tyler mulled the words over in his head silently as Anna started the car and drove down the dark road, following Cecile's directions.

"Get the absolute fuck off of me!" Jane screamed, attempting to physically shove the two orderlies restraining her. When that didn't work, she shoved outward with the power in her sister's new body, fire bursting from every part of her, engulfing the room in flames that tore screams from the mouths of her victims and temporarily blinded her. Jane stepped back from the damage she had caused in horror, the flames receding with her retreat. The men who had been restraining her were covered in second and third degree burns. One of them was laying on his back, mewling pitifully and clawing at his empty eye sockets, the gooey remains of his eyeballs oozing down his cheeks in a bloody ruin. Jane knew that she should find an exit, she should run, but she couldn't stop staring at the terror her touch had wrought, wondering if this was what her sister had to live with every day that she was in this body. An alarm sounded, snapping Jane out of her thoughts. She turned to run and fell right into the waiting arms of two men in fire retardant suits. She screamed in vain, feeling the flames begin to creep up again, hovering just underneath the surface of her skin. A young male doctor appeared beside them, syringe in hand.

"Anna, calm down!" He injected her with the drug and Jane almost immediately felt calmer.

"I can't make it stop," she heard herself say in someone else's voice as the body she was in fell limp with the effects of the drug.

"Don't worry, Anna. I'll help you make it stop."

"But I'm not Anna," Jane protested weakly as she lost consciousness.

"Drew, thank you for coming in. I apologize for calling at such a late hour but we really must discuss Anna's condition immediately. I'm afraid there's been an incident." Dr. Hawthorn stopped pacing and stepped behind the desk in his office at the asylum. He caught his reflection in the cheap mirror hanging on the opposite wall and sighed as he met the weary brown eyes staring back at him from his pasty wrinkled face and wondered when he'd begun to look so old. The doctor broke away from his own reflection and looked down at the man seated in a guest chair across the desk.

"You sounded upset over the phone. What has my beloved wife done now?" Drew rubbed his eyes tiredly, his irritation at being summoned to the institution clear in his voice and expression. Why he couldn't get rid of the blasted woman once and for all was beyond him. He thought that once she was committed it would be a fitting end at least in this lifetime for the bitch who'd sent him to hell once already.

"Anna's condition is worse than we previously anticipated."

"How can it be worse?" Drew held up his hands so that the doctor could see the burn scars forming on his pale flesh.

"She is not responding to medication. Last night she attempted to escape and burned two of my orderlies so badly that they've been transferred to the intensive care burn unit in New Orleans. One of them lost his eyes. Her condition is advancing rapidly and is increasingly unstable. We quite frankly are not equipped to continue treating her without taking very drastic measures to ensure the safety of everyone at this institution. Rather than take drastic measures to secure everyone else we would like to take drastic measures to reduce the threat that your wife represents. I hate to be the bearer of bad news, but it's either this or you will have to make other arrangements for Anna's continued treatment. I'd like your permission for Dr. Williams to run some rather invasive tests on Anna to determine the full extent of her malady."

"And if you find what you're looking for?" Drew reached for the documents that the doctor pushed across the desk in his direction.

"Then I'd like for you to consider allowing us to perform electroshock therapy to remove the disease from your wife's brain. I warn you though it may have other, unforeseen effects on her including some loss of memory."

Drew smiled grimly as he signed the documents. "Be my guest."

"Good morning."

Jane opened her eyes carefully, afraid of what she might see and still feeling the effects of the drug from the night before. "Where am I and what time is it?"

"It's just before dawn and you're in our room at the sanitarium. What happened last night? When the orderlies brought you in they were terrified, couldn't get their hands off you fast enough. What did you do to them?"

"To those two? Nothing that I'm aware of. There were two others that didn't appear to be so lucky." Jane slowly pushed into a sitting position, her vision swimming as she took in the sparse, drab surroundings and the small woman sitting on the bed across from her, lit by a dim lamp on the bedside table. "Iris?"

Iris moved closer, her keen eyes examining every minute detail of her roommate's face. "You hold her energy but you are not Anna. What have you done with her?"

"She's in my body with your son, Tyler."

"How do you know my boy?"

"I'm his sister-in-law. My name is Jane Stateton. I married Jared nearly two years ago."

Iris shook her head in denial, moving back from the woman in Anna's body. "Jared would never marry. His heart's too broken."

"He spent a long time waiting for me. I'm sorry for whatever heartache it caused you and your family," Jane replied softly.

"James," Iris almost whispered the word, her voice fearful. "What has my son done that has you standing here now?"

"He saved me from Purgatory. Please don't be afraid. I won't hurt you."

"I don't fear you hurting me, child. I fear what you've become. This isn't natural, you being here."

"I am what he is. But you already know that, don't you?"

Iris nodded unable to answer. She walked over to the bed and tentatively sat, gripping Jane's chin in her hands and tilting the other woman's face to the lamp light. She gasped as Jane's eyes changed color, releasing her before retreating back to the other side of the room. "Well, now I've seen everything."

Jane allowed a moment to pass before breaking the uncomfortable silence. "I'm not sure how long I'm here for, so I need you to tell me everything. How bad is it?"

"The situation? It's catastrophic. You nearly killed two men last night, or Anna did. It doesn't matter. What's important is that they'll retaliate against whoever is in that body. You can't escape."

"Can't I just use her powers and blast through a wall or something?"

"I honestly don't know. I've never seen Anna do such a thing."

"How does she control it? I feel it burning through me all of the time. Last night, I couldn't focus it, it just came out." Jane stared at her sister's hands uncomprehending.

"It's taken her a lot of practice to harness the power within. It has a will of its own. Hers must be stronger to control the fire."

"Well I need a crash course because if we don't swap bodies soon this one will turn into a bomb if I can't harness the power within it." Jane met Iris's horrified stare with determination so strong that it radiated from her borrowed body. "I'm not too keen on dying today. How about you?"

19

"How the fuck do we get her out?" Jared slammed the door on his rental car and stalking across the almost vacant parking lot to where Tyler waited with Anna and Cecile.

"Well, the facility opens in ten minutes and visiting hours start at ten. We have until about two to get in there, get her out and get Anna to Olympus. My idea was to wait until then to walk in and legally walk back out with her then have Cecile switch them back before your wife explodes the place. But I'm sure your jail break scenario will be much more effective, particularly when it lands us all in jail." Tyler crossed his arms and leaned against the front fender of his rented Prius.

"Stay out of my head," Jared growled.

"Oh if only I could. For the moment Jane's fine. I'll know the second that she's not. Actually you'll know it and I'll know it because we both can read her thoughts. We have," Tyler consulted his watch, "another six minutes before we can go in there and request to see her. It leaves us plenty of time to go in there, get her out and swap them back. You didn't have to come here. It was unexpected but we've got this under control."

"You call this under control? If we have the timing right, which knowing our sister is a huge if, we are still running out of time. What happens when we do get her out? Can Karina, Anna, whatever she wants to be called, control the phoenix?"

"That's what I am? Iris was right. I can't believe Danalia turned me into a fucking phoenix." Anna fought to control her breathing and her rising anger.

Jared turned his attention to the woman in his wife's body. "You didn't know?" He took her silence for an answer and turned back to his brother. "How can she hope to control this thing in a few hours when she didn't even know what it was until now?"

Tyler shrugged, glancing at Anna. "She says she can control it and I believe her."

Jared shook his head, a grim look marring his face. "You're a fool."

"He's not a fool, he's right. I've been working to harness the power inside myself. I can do this," Anna protested.

Jared walked over and grabbed Anna by her arms, forcing her to meet his eyes. "Do you know what will happen to you if you're wrong? What you've experienced so far is just a taste of your powers as a phoenix. In a few hours the training wheels come off and your full powers will be unleashed. If Jane is still in your body and she can't control it, that body will explode and take everything and everyone in

240

the vicinity with it. If you're in that body and you can't control it you will die. You will die violently and you will take a lot of people with you. Do you understand?" Anna nodded silently, prompting Jared to continue. "Now I want you to tell me that you can control this thing because I will not lose my wife again. Make me believe it or so help me by whatever God is out there I will have Cecile switch you back and slit your throat myself."

"I can control it, Jared." Anna's voice was firm, her gaze unwavering from the intense stare in his blue eyes.

He searched her eyes, looking for the truth behind her words. "I hope you're right. Because otherwise we all die today." Jared walked away, the frustration radiating off of his body.

"J, this will be fine. Cecile can switch them back in a few minutes, Anna can control her little power burst and we'll all go home," Tyler pleaded with his brother for understanding.

"This is not fine! None of this is fine!" Jared roared. "I never should've let her get on that plane. I shouldn't have trusted you to be able to handle this."

"You forget that you're not my keeper, brother. You are no better equipped to deal with this situation than I am. If it had been up to you we would've abandoned this quest and you would've let Anna burn, without her memories, without any idea of what was happening to her. Have you also forgotten that our mother is in there? That we owe it to her to get her the hell out and in one piece?"

"She is not my mother," Jared ground out through clenched teeth.

"Oh yes, she is. For the next dozen decades or so, she is your mother and mine. Don't be a jerk just because no one asked your permission before trying to save one of the very few family members that we have left. You don't get to push everyone else away because they dare to have their own thoughts. Your approval is not necessary to our survival. Your respect should be, but do any of us, even your precious wife, have even that?"

"Respect must be earned, not handed out like alms to the poor. If you or anyone else wants my respect, do something to earn it. Don't keep fucking up and expecting me to clean up the mess."

"When have I ever done anything without you, Jared? Anything that you didn't approve of? Have I ever stabbed you in the back, done anything other than support you? No! You have no right to speak to me as if I was in need of your protection. I've lived just as long as you, been through the exact same things and do not need you to clean up any mess for me, particularly one that you made yourself! I had nothing to do with this! I am just trying to right the wrongs that your actions caused." Tyler stepped up to his brother, meeting his angry expression with one of his own. "You did this! You put us in this position. And now because of you the woman I care about may die a second time. Don't you dare pretend that you are the innocent victim in all of this because the only innocent here is standing there telling you that she can handle this. Now you figure out a way to handle it and keep your damn voice down," he hissed. "We have to go in calm and without a police escort."

"I trusted you with my wife!" Jared hissed, pushing up into his brother's face. "You screwed it up so badly that we all may die. How is any of this going to be okay?"

"No one but you has any plans to die today." Tyler shoved his brother back. "This is not my fault. Even if the worst happens today and we all die in a few hours, so what? It's not like that hasn't ever happened to anyone in this group repeatedly. We die so much it's like a fricking hobby. At least if we all get blown to hell then this mess will finally be over, we can start over and thank whatever God is out there I can do it without you. The amount of dramatic insanity that you've dumped on me in the last three decades is astounding."

"Now? You're going to bring that up now?" Jared snarled.

"Why not?" Tyler glanced down at his wristwatch. "According to you we could die at any moment so now sounds like about as good a time as any."

"Why is being my brother such a burden for you? You weren't this much of a prick when we were being burned at the stake as heretics. If you want to run to the ends of the earth or back to Olympus to escape me, no one's stopping you."

"Because it's all about you, isn't it Jared. It's always all about you. Have you ever once asked what I want, thought that maybe I thought the decisions you were making for us were shit? No! You don't think, not past what you want when you want it. You're an egomaniacal sociopath. In your epic quest to make Jane love you, you've killed numerous people and now you're about to kill Jane and her sister twice. It should be impossible but not for the great Anyasis for whom the laws of physics do not apply. Do you even love her? Or is it just that she was the one thing that you couldn't have?"

"We're gods, Tyler!" Jared struggled to keep his temper in check. "None of the rules of humans apply to us or our kind. You are my brother. We have always had each other's backs. What is it about the last two years that has changed you so completely?"

"The difference is that I do not want your life. I don't want the life you've chosen for me. And when I found one person that did make me happy, she died. She died to save your wife, your happiness. I'm tired of this. I'm tired of all of it. I want to get Jane and Iris out of here, I want to have Anna back in her body and I want to leave this place. I get that we're all tied together but I don't have to live with you and Jane and keep repeating this cycle over and over again. This can't be all that my life is about."

Anna stepped between the two brothers, pushing them apart. "You're both children. It's no wonder Jane feels like she has to act without consulting either of you. You're both irresponsible, selfish assholes. If you want to fight, work it out later if we're all still here. Otherwise shut the fuck up and pay attention because unlike the two of you, Cecile and I have a plan."

"What are you doing?" Jane demanded as two orderlies came in to get her with the same young doctor from the night before. Iris stepped in front of her and was promptly moved aside by one of the orderlies as the other grabbed Jane, hauling her from her bed.

"We have to take you in for tests and treatments, Anna," Dr. Williams explained calmly in an even tone. "We're going to get rid of this. You'll feel better very, very soon." He stepped up despite Iris's protests and sank another syringe of drugs into Jane's arm. The two orderlies held her still, waiting for the drugs to take effect. Jane continued to struggle against her captors, though her arms grew progressively weaker with each passing second. When they began pulling her out into the hall, she realized that most of her struggling was occurring in her head rather than against the strong hands that held her against her will.

"Where are you taking me?" Jane felt the drugs making her system weak and her eyesight fuzzy as she was shoved unceremoniously into a wheelchair and propelled down the hallway.

"Anna, you are a danger to yourself and to everyone around you. Obviously either you cannot control what's going on with you or you choose not to. No matter which one it is, we at this institution are tasked with making sure that you cannot hurt anyone again, including yourself. Did you know that your little stunt last night may have killed two people?"

"That orderly's eyes. Are his eyes okay?" Jane whispered, the memories floating back through her fogged mind like ghosts. She fought to sense anything past the sedatives working their way through her system.

Dr. Williams signaled for the orderly pushing the chair to stop. He knelt down in front of Jane, his dark eyes meeting her drugged gaze. "He's blind. By the time that we found him there was nothing left of his face. The doctors expect him to die from his injuries, injuries that you inflicted. Do you see how serious this is now, Anna? You were brought here because you injured your husband, Andrew. Now you may have killed two people trying to escape. The district attorney will press charges. If you want to avoid jail you will let us help you." He stood and motioned for the orderly to continue down the hall. The doctor walked companionably beside Jane.

"Where is my husband now? Why isn't Andrew here to see the fruits of his good work?" Jane searched inside herself, locating the drugs nestling in her blood and using the fire element she held inside herself to burn it off, eradicating it like the unwanted pest it was. She fought very hard to remain still, keeping her breathing and heartbeat at a steady pace. "What are you going to do to me?" Jane pretended to fight through the dizziness long enough to glare up at him for an answer.

"We're going to use an antiquated procedure to shut down the diseased parts of your brain. It will give you a reboot, to put it simply. Possibly you will have another chance at life if we can prove to the authorities that you are no longer capable of harming anyone. Maybe your husband will even reconsider committing you."

"Is he here? Can I see him?"

"Yes, he's here, Anna. You can see him after we run our tests."

"Come on, doc. We both know that you're not planning on running any tests. I'd be willing to bet that anything you have planned for me is also illegal or you wouldn't be so hesitant to fill me in. So why don't you just drop the nice guy act and level with me. We both know you're not my friend. Friends don't shoot each other in the arm with drug cocktails."

"You misunderstand me completely, Anna. You and I are friends. In fact, you may be my favorite patient of all time, if I can harness the power residing in that precious little body of yours. I want to figure it out, reproduce it and turn it off." They came to a halt in front of a heavy metal door with a small pane of glass about shoulder height. The doctor opened it and their small processional continued inside. The orderly left them and Dr. Williams locked the door behind him. "And there most certainly are tests." He stepped over to a small surgical table and picked up a scalpel. "You just may not like them very much which is why we needed the drugs. I know that you're powerful on a different level than us mere normal humans, but what I gave you should keep you compliant. At least for a while." He smiled at her as he walked over to a small surgical table and picked up a scalpel. "You just may not fully appreciate my methods yet." He grabbed Jane's forearm and made a long slash across it, watching as small sparks leapt up from the split flesh. Jane felt the phoenix rising to protect its host and she struggled to keep it under control, just below the surface. If the phoenix rose now, Jane didn't know that she could rein it in, even with her added destroyer powers. "Oh, Anna, you're going to make me famous."

"Can anyone feel Jane?" Jared uttered the sentence for about the tenth time in as many minutes. Tyler fought the urge to grind his teeth in irritation, instead shooting a glance in Anna's direction, silently mouthing *Your turn.*

Anna rolled her eyes and answered Jared patiently. "No. Neither of us can feel Jane or sense what she's thinking. Since she's bound to you, you'll probably be the first to know when she's back online. They probably have her drugged which is why Cecile is working very hard to switch us back so that I can control the phoenix if she feels threatened."

"How much longer is this going to take?" Jared began pacing circles around the car.

Cecile barely glanced up from her herbs. "It takes as long as it takes. You acting like a child ain't gonna help things none. Relax. I'm not gonna let my child die twice over this supernatural bullshit. Not on my watch."

Jane drew in a breath through clenched teeth as the doctor made another experimental cut across her midsection. "Come on, doc. We both know that this is a losing proposition for you. That's what, your twelfth cut? I'm not giving you what you want, you can't bleed me out, you can't maim me. How would you explain making fleshy little ribbons out of my skin as therapy?" When he didn't answer, Jane just continued speaking as if they were having a conversation. "Tired of cutting? Oh, try the blowtorch next, I dare you!" She laughed maniacally, flexing her hands against the restraints binding her to the cold steel table. "Trying to burn the person who's flame retardant should keep you occupied for a while."

The doctor picked up and lit the small blowtorch that Jane had seen on the floor, holding it close enough to her that Jane could feel the skin on her forehead warming from the outside rather than from within. "You're not indestructible, Anna. You will give me what I want." He inched the blue-white flame closer to her eyes.

Jane burst into laughter. "There's only one thing that can destroy me, doc, and you're not it." She smiled, holding his gaze as she felt the restraints around her upper body disintegrate to ash. The phoenix melded with her destroyer and the two began to rise within her slowly. Her hands came up quickly, grabbing Dr. Williams around the throat and pinning his head to the table below her feet with one hand while the other ripped the blowtorch away from him and tossed it harmlessly against the far wall. "I am much harder to kill than you are. You think I can't heal these wounds? That I won't break you into a million pieces with my bare hands?" She leaned over to whisper sweetly in his ear as she ground his face into the unforgiving metal, ignoring the pain in her arms and stomach where the cuts were slowly beginning to knit themselves together. The doctor squeaked in protest as his eyeglasses broke and the pieces began to work their way into the softness of his face. "I am the destroyer, you idiotic, egotistical mortal and I am in the body of a phoenix. If it continued to amuse me I would hold the flames under my skin just to piss you off. As it is I'm in a bit of a time crunch, which means that I do not have time for your particular brand of idiocy." Jane increased the pressure, shoving his skull into the metal table and sharp fragments of his glasses.

"Wait! Wait! If you hurt me, I'll scream and you'll never be able to get out of here, Anna. Just work with me. Please, Anna!" he pleaded for his life as she laughed.

"Haven't you been paying attention?" Jane heard the cold, empty anger in her voice but did nothing to quell it. She leaned over, placing her mouth right next to his ear, enjoying that she could see his pulse jump in his pasty, sweaty neck in between her fingers. "Anna's not here right now," Jane whispered sweetly, relishing the wide-eyed terror that her words brought to the surface.

"Who am I talking to? I'm a doctor, you can trust me. I can help you get out of here!"

Jane picked him up by the throat with one hand as if he weighed nothing. She regarded him with cold eyes, ignoring his gasp as he came face to face with her hair flaming with energy and wind from another plane and her jet black irises. "Also not schizophrenic," she commented blandly. "You bore me." She felt the energy in her skin spread down her body, burning away the last of her restraint. She allowed enough heat to escape through her fingertips that it caused the good doctor to whimper softly in pain. "Oh, did that hurt? Don't scream. If you try, I'll melt your vocal chords. So tell me, doc, what were you going to do to me?"

"E-electroshock therapy," he stammered, struggling to free himself. His breath wheezed as Jane swung her legs over the side of the table and stood, hoisting Dr. Williams high enough in the air that his dangling feet barely scraped the floor.

"And why were you going to do that?"

"At a high enough voltage it would reset the neurotransmitters in your brain. I could stop you from burning things."

"Or you could turn me into a vegetable."

"That was a possibility. Your husband signed the release papers this morning." He paused. "How do you do it? What causes the flames?"

Jane pulled his head down close to her mouth to make sure that he could hear her, bending his head at a harsh angle. "I am not Anna, doc. My Greek name is Santiranika. I am the bringer of death, destroyer of worlds. You should count yourself lucky that you won't live long enough to see what my wrath really looks like." She touched her index finger lightly to his temple and felt the electricity slip from her body into his brain. Jane watched his body jerk with the electric current for a full minute before she withdrew, allowing his limp body to slump to the floor. "Don't fuck with a goddess, doc." She kicked him aside, barely noticing as his body flew across the room, his head crashing into the wall with a sickening crunch. Jane stepped out of the room, easily tossing aside the orderlies who attempted to stop her. She wound her way through the hospital back to her sister's ward. She located Iris in the common room.

The older woman gasped at the still healing wounds dripping blood down her roommate's arms. "Oh, my God, Anna! How did you get out?"

"Gave the doctor a taste of his own medicine." Jane ignored the stunned glances of the other patients as she grabbed Iris by the arm and steered her toward the door. "Grab your photo album if you want it, but be quick about it. We're getting out of here. Now."

"You're still not Anna."

"Nope." Jane glanced around the hallway for anyone who might attempt to bar their escape. She felt the phoenix attempt to surge to the surface and shoved it down deep, trying to wrench control away from the alien thing.

Iris darted into their shared room, emerging a moment later with the small book clutched tightly to her chest. "Let's go."

Tyler opened his eyes as his brother stepped around Cecile, walking toward the sanitarium's entrance. "Where do you think you're going?"

"I'm done waiting. If we can walk out with Karina in that body, we can walk out with Jane in it. I'm not leaving her in there any longer."

"Give it a few more minutes."

"Time's almost up, Tyler. I've given it nearly two hours and Cecile hasn't been able to switch them back. Get out of my way, brother. I'm going to get my wife."

Tyler fell into step beside his brother, leaving Anna to watch over Cecile. "This is not one of your better ideas."

"Have you got a better one?" Jared snarled as they crossed the parking lot.

"Nope."

Jane inwardly groaned as she felt the internal clock ticking down the seconds of her sister's life speed up in its final moments. "Damnit," she muttered as she and Iris rounded the corner into the waiting room, the same one where she had nearly barbequed two men the night before. "Iris, in a minute I'm going to tell you to make a run for it because I might spontaneously combust. As soon as we clear the lobby I need you to move as fast as you can to as far away from me as you can get. Tyler and Jared are in the parking lot. I can feel them out there so I know they'll be close to the building. They can't feel me because if I let them in I might not be able to protect them if I explode. You need to get to them and get as far away from this place as possible. Do you understand?" Iris nodded as they pushed through the double doors and Jane met the eyes of Anna's husband, Andrew. She saw a spark inside of him that she recognized from her past and the sudden blinding rush fueled by the rise of the phoenix within her left her nearly breathless. She pushed Iris in front of her to the entrance doors. "Go. Get Jared and Tyler away from the building." Iris darted out of the doors as Jane and Andrew approached each other. "Hello, Zane."

"You bitch," Drew snarled. "I knew you were in there."

"What idiot let you crawl out of hell? I thought you were destroyed."

"Apparently souls aren't that easy to destroy. So instead I spent a year being tortured in Purgatory. The things they did to me…well, you would probably enjoy it. You know what kept me from going crazy? The idea that I would get out of there, come back and fuck up your fairytale. So you can imagine how overjoyed I was to see you pop in. Well, I thought it was you. Turned out to be Karina, not that it matters. One of you is really just as good as the other because at the end of the day the two of you always manage to stick together. When I found out that she got an express ride back topside I grabbed on and pulled myself up with her. Oh I was so happy that we ended up together. She needed someone to guide her when she woke up without a memory. I was only too happy to help her out. After all, we were family until you both sent that whore Sabina to rip my heart out. Who knew you were marrying into a family of cold-blooded psychopaths, Jane."

"At least they're an upgrade from spending eternity with you."

"You forget your place, Janey. I'm legally responsible for that pretty little body you're in. And I think it's time you went back to the doctor and took your treatment like a good little girl before I hunt down Karina and continue torturing her. If you're in her body, I'd be willing to be that she's in yours and human now, since you've got all the power right?" He took a step closer. "Isn't that how it works with you, Janey? You control everyone, you control everything, you get to hold all the cards and be mistress of the universe." Andrew's face turned ugly and Jane could see Zane's black soul shining through the mask.

"You will never touch Karina. Even if she is human she's in the company of a hoodoo priestess and two Greek gods. You'll never get close enough to think about laying a hand on my sister ever again." The phoenix pushed at the boundaries of her body and for once, Jane was glad. If she was going to die here, she at least knew that Zane's undeserved second chance at life would be destroyed with her.

"I will get near her because your little gods will never see me coming. I will take her and I'll torture her in front of you slowly, painfully and make sure that her spirit is truly gone before I even think about letting her die. That is your choice, Jane. You or her. Personally I would rather watch you burn, you bitch. And afterwards, when your brain's Jello and you can't do anything about it, I'm going to spend the rest of the time we have left together making you as miserable as you've made me the last millennia."

Jane rolled her eyes. "And if you've turned this body into a vegetable? What then?"

"You'd still be trapped and I'd still torture you. I kind of hope you can't fight back. Watching the fury enter those eyes of yours will be better than the best orgasm. You know, your old body was good, but this one's more my taste. Darker, fuller, sexier." His gaze slid up her borrowed body in a way that made Jane immediately want a shower in bleach and Lysol. "I would definitely enjoy you being helpless for once."

Jane sighed with impatience, trying to keep him in place until the phoenix fully appeared. "Are you done with your little villain's speech? I'm kind of on a timeline here."

"Trying to put Karina back in? I don't think so." Drew grabbed her arm, attempting to hold her in place.

Jane lost what little patience she had left and grabbed his injured arms, tossing him across the room. "Will you never stop being a douchebag?"

He sat up, stunned at her sudden strength. "What are you?"

Jane smiled at him as the ticking stopped and she knew that her time was up. "Pay attention. You're about to find out."

An evil sneer crossed his face as he stood and advanced on his former soul-mate. "You might be strong, but you're not the only one who picked up a few tricks in the last year." Drew's eyes glowed red, his skin growing darker as black magic binding runes flowed down his arms and up his neck to color his face.

Jane laughed at the sheer perfection of the situation. "You're a demon? That's your trump card? Really? Instead of being destroyed you were passed off to the devil as a minion. You're Satan's bitch boy for eternity and I'm supposed to be impressed?" Jane felt the full power of her sister's phoenix being to flow through her borrowed body, greeting and mingling with her destroyer like old friends. The two powers wrapped around each other, melding into one perfect beast. Jane smiled at the sudden knowledge that she could wield them, that they were one. "I am the host to two mythical beings. A god. You aren't worthy to be the scum under my shoes, you arrogant prick."

"Oh yeah?" Drew smirked, taking a swaggering step forward. "You're sweating and shaking, Destroyer. Doesn't look like that body can hold you much longer." He stopped a step away from touching her, pushing his face up close to her, his hands clasped innocently behind his back. "You may want to take me out but you can't. Just like last time, you don't have it in you. And now I'm protected and you're dying," he whispered.

"I'm not dying. I'm a true immortal. You, though, you can die. I can send you right back to the hole in the ground that you crawled out of and seal your tomb. You can spend eternity shoved up Satan's ass getting tortured with a pitchfork. And the laughter you hear? That will be mine. I intend to make sure that you understand when I kill you that you belong to me. I can destroy you, bring you back and kill you all over again. Because no matter how special you think you are, no matter what connections you think you have, Zane, I am the destroyer. You live at my whim; you breathe because I allow it. And when you forget that I'll be only more than happy to remind you. Because if you think that your existence was linked to me before, you know absolutely nothing. Now your existence is tied to me. Mine is not tied to you. And if you think for a second that anyone else will step in to save you, you're dead wrong. How does it feel to know that even God has given up on you?" Jane felt the heat start to spread through her borrowed body and she welcomed it, feeling the intertwined powers of her destroyer and her sister's phoenix rising together. She reached out and grabbed Zane by the throat, delighting at the startled look in his eyes when the flames arced down her arm to his skin. "You've never been burned alive, have you? How do you feel about it now?" Jane felt the huge power burst lurking just below the surface and pushed it outward, letting go of everything she'd ever held back and embracing the power inside of her. In the second before she felt it take her over, Jane felt her eyes turn sea green and thought of Jared's face. She felt her power seek him out, surround him, just before everything burst out of her in a violent wave. Even as everything around her started to burn away, Jane knew that nothing would ever feel as good as that moment. Even as the fire burned through her and out of her control, Jane's last thought was not for the man standing before her, his skin bubbling red and flaking away as he screamed, it was regret for the two men that might burn with her.

Tyler saw his human mother clear the building just as the clock ticking down the remaining seconds of Karina's life stopped in his head. He turned back to look at Anna, wishing that she could hear all of the things he'd left unsaid between them. He had enough time to take one last look at her eyes in Jane's face before Iris collided with him and Jared and the heat washed across his face, the fire blocking everything else from his sight.

It took a few moments for Tyler to hear the screaming, to realize that despite the carnage surrounding him, he was still alive. He heard his brother's horse screams for his wife. He heard Anna as she ran toward him, even though everything sounded far away, as if his senses had been dulled by the blast. Tyler watched the tears fall from her eyes when she realized that he was still breathing. He saw his hand reach out to wipe them away, silently marveling that anyone would feel such a loss at the idea that he was gone. He crushed her to him, not caring that they were both covered in ashes and soot or that the probability that one or both of them was injured was high. Tyler just wanted to make the sadness leave Anna's eyes. It took him awhile to realize what had happened, to take a good look at his surroundings. When he finally did look up, Tyler realized that there was nothing but devastation surrounding them.

Where the hospital had been there was nothing but a charred ruin remaining. A crater had been blasted through the cement foundation that extended to cover half of the parking lot and the swamp surrounding the area. Anna pulled away from him and went to help Iris up from where she had fallen at the edge of the crater. The older woman stumbled to her feet with Anna's help. Tyler noticed her clutching a small leather-bound book to her chest and was surprised to recognize it as the album of photographs she had taken of him and his brother over the years. It dawned on him then how much he and Jared must mean to Iris for her to go to an institution for her beliefs and then for the only thing for her to salvage in the face of total destruction was their family photo album. If they all lived through this, he vowed to make an effort to make Iris a part of their family. He looked to his left and saw Jared struggling to right himself. His brother had blood oozing out of his ears and a cut on his head. His hands were burned and raw. Tyler heard Jared screaming for Jane but he didn't think Jared could hear his own voice. Tyler grabbed his brother just before Jared face-planted into a pile of upturned earth and concrete. Jared's weight dragged them both to the ground and it was then that Tyler realized the explosion had taken more than his brother's hearing. Where his eyes used to be there was nothing but blacken, bloody holes that oozed a clear liquid Tyler couldn't help but think was probably what little remained of his once blue eyes. Tyler couldn't understand why he had been so shielded from the blast when his brother had taken it full force. And then he saw her.

Like the metaphorical phoenix rising from the ashes, Jane stood among the ruins, still in her sister's body and completely unharmed. Her bright, flame red hair flared around her head in an otherworldly wind and he watched her toss away what looked like the remains of a human skull. As she stepped out of the wreckage, Tyler watched in awe as the hospital and the area around it began to rebuild, seemingly of its own volition. Jane stopped, watching as the skull that she had tossed to the pavement began to rebuild into a human body and was more than a little surprised when he saw Zane standing there, whole and alive.

Jane approached Zane with a languid walk, each step she took silently proclaiming that she owned this area and everyone in it better than any words ever could. Tyler felt Zane's fear and the sensation kept both men rooted to the spot. Jane stepped over to where Zane knelt, breathing heavily, and grabbed him by his throat, hauling him to his feet. Her voice reverberated through Tyler's head making it impossible for him to not hear her words to Zane. "You will not approach me or my family again. You will understand that you live only as long as I allow it. You will live in a manner that I dictate. If you think to defy me, I will turn you to ash. If you cease to amuse me, I will turn you to ash. If you annoy me in any way, I will turn you to ash, bring you back and watch the skin melt off of your face while you scream because I enjoy it." Jane gripped his throat with one hand and took his left arm in the other, pulling the appendage up in front of his eyes and burning it to ash while he watched, too afraid to even scream. She released him and the arm grew back almost immediately. "Do not cross me, Zane. Do not make a spectacle of yourself. Spend your life in this wasted body and live a simple life. Nothing else will be tolerated. Do not run because no matter what plane you hide on and in what guise, I will find you. And I will be very displeased. Blink once if you understand me." Zane's wide eyes closed and then very slowly reopened. "Good. Leave this place and never cross my path again." With a wave of her hand Jane made Zane disappear. Tyler was very sure that he didn't want to find out where the other man had gone.

He watched his sister-in-law, his soul-mate, walk across the devastated ground, the hospital rebuilding itself, grass replanting and people pulled back into being seemingly from nothing in her wake. She reached them, the residents and workers of the asylum going about their day as if nothing out of the ordinary had happened. People who had been reduced to gray dust only moments earlier were walking around as the walls of the asylum rose around them as if nothing had happened. Tyler fought the urge to back away as she approached them, turning his attention instead to his brother who was still lying on the ground, whimpering in pain as his eyelids vainly tried to clear grim from his ruined eyes.

Jane knelt down beside her husband in the rubble. Her detached gaze took in his ruined face, his burned hands and she was puzzled by the tears that fell out of her own as. As the tears slid down her cheeks to fall on her husband's ruined body, Jane remembered her last thought before the explosion and began to cry at the idea that she would never again be able to look into his blue eyes, never feel his arms around her without also feeling the scars that the burns caused. Before she felt fully returned to herself, the idea of killing him so that he would soon be allowed to return to this world crossed her mind briefly. Her saner senses prevailed, allowing her repressed emotions to come back full force, nearly taking her breath away with their intensity. As her tears cascaded onto his skin, the ruined flesh began to knit itself together again. Jane ran her fingers over his closed eyelids, across his cut temple and over his ears. Everywhere that she touched healed as soon as her fingers moved away. Jared opened his eyes and blinked up at her, his aqua eyes brighter when built from her memories of them.

"Jane?" Jared sat up and grabbed her, hugging her to him unaware of any pain if he felt it at all. Jane hugged him and Tyler watched warily as her personality began to return to her eyes. He blinked and her body reformed, melting to her normal form. Tyler glanced back at Anna, watching in terror as she bent over and began screaming. He watched helplessly as she burned from the inside out, reforming in Anna's body.

She caught him watching her and held out a hand to stop Tyler from advancing as she gasped for breath. "Don't! I'm okay."

Tyler caught himself just before he touched her. "Which one are you?"

Anna laughed despite the pain it caused her and straightened, reaching out to him. "Which one do you love?" She wound her hand through the short hair at the nape of his neck and pulled Tyler's mouth to hers.

Tyler pulled her body against his, swallowing the little moan that came from deep in her throat as she opened for him. He fought the urge to show her with his lips, his tongue just how deeply his desire for her ran. He broke the kiss too soon for either of their liking, knowing that it was foolish to try to continue here. As he pulled away, he saw the promise in her eyes and knew with absolute certainty that their exploration of each other was far from over. "You know, I never said I love you," he smiled lazily, staring into the hazel green eyes that he had sought for almost a year.

Anna smiled and released him, taking a step back. "You didn't have to."

Jane stood, pulling Jared up with her. "Are you okay?"

Jared looked down watching the pavement reform under him, closing the edges of what had only moments ago been a crater. "No, I'm not. But I will be once we figure out what the hell just happened here."

"Karina, I mean Anna's, phoenix powers." Jane looked at her sister for the first time in her new body. "What do you want to be called? This is getting confusing."

"Either really works. Karina is fine. I was using Anna because I thought it would be easier since I'm in her body. She died and I guess I just kind of took her body." She shrugged. "Guess I'll either have to legally change my name back to Karina though or get used to

259

seeing Anna on my driver's license. For simplicity I guess we can go with Karina."

"What is your last name?" Tyler's curiosity got the better of him.

"Matthews. Why?"

"Danalia told us your name was Anna Molly."

"Like the song?" she wrinkled her nose in distaste.

"Like "anomaly" so yeah, I guess." Tyler shrugged.

"Huh. I guess that explains the "M" initial for a middle name." Karina walked over to where Iris was standing with Cecile a little apart from the group. "Are you okay?"

"Fine, dear, just fine. So I guess you got your memory back?" Karina nodded affirmatively. "And you really do know my boys."

"Yes, ma'am, I do." Karina snuck a quick glance at Tyler. "I told you your sons would get us out."

"They didn't come for me." Iris smiled at the younger woman, gently touching her cheek. "I don't pay it no nevermind though. We're all free."

"Why were you in there?" The question came from Jared as he hesitantly approached the woman who had raised him.

"I didn't do as you told me. I stayed in one place too long. Made folks nervous, then scared and paranoid. One day I said the wrong thing to the wrong person and they locked me in here. Had me on drugs and used me like a lab rat for a few years. Once they finally let me sober up, there wasn't nothing to go back too." Iris shrugged, her shoulders still stiff as she clutched her book tightly to her chest.

"You should've called or sent a carrier pigeon or something." Tyler hugged her, forcing some of the tension out of her body. "We would've come for you. We wouldn't have let them hurt you."

"I couldn't get you boys involved. Wasn't sure you wanted to be," Iris admitted, her cheeks growing pink at her blatant honestly.

"Mom!" Tyler rolled his eyes as he released her. "You're coming back home with us."

"No, she not," Cecile spoke up. "Your momma is one a' mine and I'm keepin' her. She gone stay with me an' that's it. None of this foolishness about her goin' to California. You ain't gon' be there anyway. You boys gots another home you need to be seein to. Iris already done her part. Now it's your turn. Before you go to your real home though we gotta get that thing outta my girl before she blows the whole place up again."

"Jane still has the phoenix?" Jared turned to look at his wife who was still looking at their surroundings with that strangely blank but curious expression on her face.

"It likes me." Jane answered simply. "It's not like I told it to take up residence or anything."

"That thing don't like you, it likes your destroyer," Cecile pointed out.

Jane turned her head to look at the older woman. "What's the difference?"

Tyler and Jared exchanged a worried glance before Jared broke away to place an arm around his wife's shoulders. "Why don't we get out of here and then reassess the situation?"

"Why are you so worried? I'm fine." Jane smiled and the expression almost reached her eyes. "If I'm holding a destroyer, might as well add a phoenix to it." She got into the car between her husband

and Iris, watching from the backseat while Cecile slid behind the wheel, taking the keys from Jared. Jane looked up at her husband. "I really am fine. A little warm, but fine."

Jared kissed her forehead, catching Iris's worried glance over Jane's head. "I believe you. We just need to let Cecile check you out just in case."

As Jared's rental car pulled away, Tyler faced Karina, his hands balled and shoved in his pockets to avoid touching her. "We should probably follow them."

Karina tentatively bit her lower lip, her gaze dropping from Tyler's eyes to his mouth. "Uh-huh. We should definitely go. Somewhere."

Tyler laughed, forcing his body to shift away from her and toward the rental car. "Stop looking at me like that. You can't look at me like that."

"You know, I am really sick of people telling me what I can and should be doing. I want to look at you. I've waited a long time and even come back from the dead to look at you any way I like." She stepped between his body and the car, hooking her fingers through his belt loops and pulling him toward her.

Tyler sighed, bracing his hands on either side of her on the trunk of the car, locking his arms to keep space between them. He dipped his head so that he could meet her hazel eyes with his green ones. "We have to continue this but we have to do it later, somewhere else. We're in a parking lot and you're still dressed in patient's scrubs. Besides, we have to get your phoenix back and save your sister."

Karina's hands slid over his waistband and under the hem of his shirt. Tyler sucked in a deep breath when her hands touched his bare skin. "There's always something else to do, someone to save. Sometimes it's ok to take just a moment for ourselves, to take," she arched into him, making sure that everything from their knees to their necks touched, "something we want."

Tyler gave in. He kept his eyes open to watch her face, enjoying that she was bold enough to hold his gaze while his tongue traced her lips before coaxing them open, letting him deepened his exploration. With a sigh, Karina opened to him, her hands moving up his bare back underneath his shirt as her tongue slid over his, their lips crushing together. Tyler used one hand to cup her chin, the other to press her tighter against the front of his body. Karina trembled in his arms, her lips moving faster, more insistently against his. Tyler fought himself to not push his mouth too hard against hers, to contain how much he wanted to make this moment more than it could be in a parking lot in full view of anyone who cared to watch. He wanted her to only feel the barest edge of his desire because he knew that there was absolutely nothing that he could do more than this for hours at least. More than anything he wanted to take her back to the hotel, rip her clothes off and show her in every way possible that he'd thought of nothing but her for the last year, that he wanted her more than his next breath. He finally understood the madness that his brother had felt when Jane was taken away from him and the lengths that someone could go to in order to bring back someone they loved. Love. The word pinged around Tyler's brain, urging him on rather than dousing the fire that was threatening to consume him if he didn't allow it to be satisfied. He ran his fingers down her spine and felt her fingers knot in his t-shirt, straining the soft material. Karina moved frantically against him and he couldn't resist grabbing her hips with both hands, placing her body exactly where he wanted it most. They both groaned aloud at the intimate contact, desperate to touch what was hiding beneath too many clothes. Karina slid her hands into his dark blonde hair, sealing his lips against her so tightly that he could feel her teeth nip lightly on his bottom lip before her tongue continued its exploration of his mouth. Tyler pulled back reluctantly, holding his hands out to the side to keep from touching her again. "We have to go. We have to get to Cecile's…"

Karina pulled his mouth back to hers quickly before pushing him away and walking to the passenger side of the car, her eyes wide and lips swollen from his kiss. "You're right; we have to go. How far is it from here to Cecile's house?" She stepped back, as she opened the car door.

"About half an hour or so." Tyler took a deep breath and walked around to the driver's side, trying to steady himself before he got in the car with her. He took a cue from Jane and slowly counted to ten before opening the door and taking his seat behind the wheel.

"That's perfect."

"What is?"

"The drive time."

"Why?" Tyler closed the door and fastened his seat belt before starting the engine and backing out of the parking space.

"Because it give you just enough time to tell me in detail all of the things you want do to me when we're finally alone." Karina's seatbelt clicked into place and she smiled at him as the rental car pulled out onto the street.

20

"Jane, you have to give it up!" Tyler walked into Cecile's small house to hear his brother screaming at his sister-in-law, the sound echoing through his head.

"It doesn't want to leave me, Jared!" Jane shouted back. "I can handle this! Why don't you believe that I can handle this?"

"It's not you! The phoenix is not yours. It belongs with Karina. If you try to keep it, it's just going to keep trying to destroy you so that it can go back to her."

"What if I can do this for her? She can stay out of this. Karina can remain human!"

"No, she can't. We're not human, Jane. None of us are human. Our children will not be human. Karina doesn't have a chance to be human because she's not; she never has been. If you try to make her human you'll be taking a part of her away from her. You're denying her a part of herself. Would you want someone to take everything away from you that makes you special or different?"

"I wanted nothing but that for nine hundred and seventy-two years. Nothing but to be normal, to not have to look over my shoulder, to not die because of what we are. So yes, I would make that decision for her, for my sister."

"The phoenix is immortal."

"So am I! It can't kill me."

"That doesn't mean that it won't stop trying. Jane, you're not meant to hold all of this power. If you try it's just going to keep leaking out, keep finding a way to express itself. You blew up a town today."

"I put it back together. No one ever knew the difference."

"Jane, calm down. You're getting too hot." Concern brought Jared's voice down an octave.

Tyler stepped into the small kitchen followed closely by Karina who had been watching the argument unfold over his shoulder. "What happens when she overheats? Do we all need to run for cover again?"

"Don't tell me to calm down, Jared!" Jane shrieked just as she burst into flame in a blinding ball of light. Tyler pulled Karina back out of the room, ducking down and protecting her with his own body. The white-hot blast condensed at the spot where Jane had been standing. When Tyler stood and looked around the doorframe he saw that Cecile had not moved from her post by the stove where she was making tea and Jared hadn't budged from the spot where Tyler had last seen him standing less than six inches from Jane. Tyler looked for Jane. He didn't see her but he didn't feel the loss that would indicate her death. As he watched, Jane seemed to be pulled up through the floor, dramatically rising from the gray pile of ashes at her husband's feet. "What the fuck was that?" Tyler pushed Karina a bit further behind him.

Jared just sighed. "That's the fourth time she's done that since we got back. Apparently, if you piss her off enough, she combusts."

Karina stared at them. "But you're not hurt. At the hospital, she burned half your face off. How are you standing there now and not hurt?"

Jared shrugged. "I took cover the first time. Then Cecile noticed that Jane didn't even scorch the floor. It doesn't seem to affect anyone or anything other than Jane."

"And I can handle it." Jane glared angrily at her husband.

Jared turned to his wife. "Wasn't that little explosion supposed to chill you out?"

Iris looked at Cecile from the safe distance of the sitting area. "Are they always like this?"

Cecile shrugged in response. "Beats me. She showed up on my doorstep after forty some odd years with the other one."

Karina stepped closer to visually inspect her sister. "I never did that."

"The phoenix wasn't at full power inside of you either. I'm fine. It's just a little temperature fluctuation."

"When you turned into an elemental that was a little temperature fluctuation. This..." Karina shrugged helplessly, "this is unreal. You blew up the hospital and the swamp and the town. We nearly hit someone because he was reforming in the middle of the street as we drove by. I saw Jared's face earlier. Your powers stopped just short of melting his face off and you're bound to him. I can't imagine what this will do once it's allowed to grow." She stopped in front of her sister and met Jane's angry gaze. "This destroyer has put so much power in you, so much anger that you never had. Your fire element has bonded with it to make something different and it may work inside of you, I don't know. I do know that combining my phoenix with all of that fire already inside of you is too much. You can't stop it from leaking out. What happens when you combust in front of someone else, a mortal? Are you never going to leave the house again?" She took a breath but didn't wait for Jane's response before continuing. "You can't be everything for everyone. And I don't need you to do this for me. My phoenix and I, we know each other. There is nothing in me that it can hurt, nothing that it wants to hurt. You're already a destroyer and an elemental goddess in the making. Let me take this one."

"I can handle it. You don't need to go through this," Jane ground out through gritted teeth as she fought to not fall apart again.

"That fighting you're doing to control it? That's happening because it's trying to get out of you to get back to me. You can't keep it even if we both wanted you to. It can't destroy you because you're immortal but it will keep trying." Karina held out her hands to her sister. "Please, Jane. Don't do this to yourself. Let it go. Trust me, I can take it." Her hazel eyes met her sister's tortured gray gaze. "I choose this life, Jane. I chose it a long time ago. I want this."

Tears fell from Jane's eyes as her body tensed, waiting to explode again. "This hurts like hell. I can't let you take this."

"It doesn't affect me the same way that it does you." She forced Jane to take her hands and smiled sadly. "I'm sorry, sister, but I'm not giving you a choice." Karina reached up to touch her sister's face. Jane fell to her knees screaming while the phoenix traveled through her body and into Karina's like a glittering cloud of gold being inhaled. Tyler just stood there, rooted to the floor and stared, a bit in awe of the peaceful expression on Karina's face as the phoenix fill her.

When it was over, Jane put a hand to her chest, trying to calm her panting breath. "Fuck, that hurt." Her eyes were almost translucent from the pain as her gaze rose to meet her sister's. "A little warning next time?"

"You've been through worse." Karina pulled Jane to her feet. "Thank you for looking for me."

Jane hugged Karina. "I'm glad you're back. And I would say that you're welcome for finding you, but it wasn't me. Tyler was the one who knew that we should be looking. He figured out where you were. Cecile did the spell to switch our bodies. I was just the decoy."

"Iris helped me to realize what I am."

Tyler crossed the room and hugged his human mother tightly. "Thank you for saving her. I was afraid we wouldn't locate her in time and that she'd die alone, not understanding who or what she is. Thank you," he repeated softly, his head bowed against his mother's shoulder.

Iris wrapped her arms around him, stunned by his sudden display of affection. "You're welcome."

Jared approached Jane cautiously, sliding his arm around her shoulders and tucking his wife securely to his side when she didn't protest. "Please stop scaring the hell out of me," he whispered softly in her ear.

Jane smiled and patted his chest lovingly, leaning back to rest her head on his shoulder. "If I played it safe, we wouldn't be married so stop complaining and being a crotchety old man, Jer."

Jared smiled briefly and kissed the top of her head. "Now that the mission is accomplished, are you ready to go home?"

"I do believe that I have a book to finish and you have an album to work on."

"We also have a fight to finish and a lot of make-up sex to get to." Jared hid his smile in his wife's long dark hair.

"Let's just skip straight to the sex part." She kissed the spot on his neck that she knew made him shiver, nipping it lightly with her teeth before stepping away. "Kari, is there anything that we need to pick up, pack for you before we go home?"

Karina and Tyler exchanged a quick glance before Tyler cleared his throat, preparing to address the room. "Um, we're not going back to Los Angeles, at least not immediately."

Jared took a step forward, stopping when Jane grabbed his arm, cautioning him mentally to watch what he said and did. He took a breath, blinking slowly to give himself time to gather his thoughts before speaking. "What are your plans?"

Karina tucked her hand in Tyler's in a show of solidarity. She wouldn't admit even to herself that she enjoyed the slight contact a little more than was necessary given the situation. "We're going to stay here for a while. I need to readjust, decide what I want to do now. I love you, Jane, but I'm not really sure that going back to L. A. right now and trying to drop into a life that I left a year ago is the best idea. I'm still me, but in some ways I'm not the same anymore and I don't want to conform to someone else's idea of me before I decide for myself who I am now and what I want. Please don't be angry, Jane."

"I'm not angry. I'm surprised. Why stay here for this?"

"Because I want to spend some time with Iris, make sure that she's set up and taken care of," Tyler spoke up. He looked to Iris and Karina fought the urge to smile as she watched his usual fixed expression soften. "It's about time that someone takes care of you, Iris." She smiled her thanks and he turned back to continue addressing his brother. "You still have at least two weeks of pre-recording work to do on the new album with the songwriting and pre-production work. You don't need me for that. I'll be back in time to do my parts and record."

"You're not giving me a choice?"

"Jared, it's not your decision." Tyler squeezed Karina's hand and smiled into her warm green eyes. "Everything is different now."

Jared crossed his arms over his chest, narrowing his eyes at Tyler and Karina. "Not that it would surprise me, but are the two of you together now?"

"No," they answered in unison.

Karina laughed, stepping away from Tyler and reluctantly releasing his hand. "We're friends. We may want to see where things go with this, but we can't do this with the two of you looking over our shoulders all the time to see what we'll do."

"You know there are issues in the world other than your relationship. Or lack thereof," Jane amended jokingly. "I just don't want to lose you again." Her tone dropped, matching the serious tint of her eyes. "We just got you back. We haven't even had time to catch up. I don't know what happened to you the last year."

"Why do you need to know? So that you can feel bad about it, tell me that you're sorry, that you should've found me sooner?" Karina took a deep breath to calm her rapidly rising temper. "The last year is in the past. And I love you and don't want to seem ungrateful to you for coming out here for a week and trying to save my life but I'm fine. I don't need you to save me. Getting my memory back is great but the phoenix wasn't going to kill me. I already had it under control, thanks to Iris. If I go back to Los Angeles now, with you, that's all my life will ever be is about you. That was my life, it was my home and I made the ultimate sacrifice for it. You can't do more than give your life for someone else. I didn't make that deal with Sabina and Danalia for you

271

so that I could come back to the same life I had. I made it for me, because I want something different. I don't want things to go back to the way they were. I'll come back to L. A., eventually. Right now I've got to figure some things out before I decide how I want to move forward."

"Wow. Is that all? Sorry, Kari, I didn't realize that you were so unhappy. Don't worry, I won't try to take you home again or assume that you'd want to be with your family for longer than it takes to raise you from the dead." Jane glared at Tyler. "Try to block your thoughts when you're fucking my sister."

"Why, you never bother to block yours unless it's convenient," Tyler muttered under his breath.

Jane's eyes turned nearly black with the force of her anger. She pulled on a pair of sunglasses, barely noticing the heat that her hands transferred to the metal frames. She plastered a smile on her face, the dark shades hiding her irises and she hoped that she wasn't facing her mother-in-law and former teacher still looking like she wanted to rip someone to shreds with her fingernails. "Iris, it was nice to meet you. Mama Cecile, thank you for your help. Hopefully next time we meet it will be under better circumstances." Both women remained glued to the spot, barely daring to breathe until Jane stepped through the back door and out of earshot.

"Hopefully next time we meet you'll be in a better temper," Cecile commented quietly.

"Don't take it personally, it's been happening for weeks," Jared replied calmly. "She'll be fine." He heard a large cracking noise come from outside along with the unmistakable sound of a tree falling and winced. "I'm going to go try and stop her from killing anything else." He nodded to the room in general before rushing out after his wife.

Karina turned to Tyler, a mischievous glint in her eyes. "Why would you have to block your thoughts from Jane?"

Tyler sighed and rubbed the back of his neck, his eyes on the floor. "Because Jane's my soul-mate."

"Excuse me?"

Tyler shrugged helplessly. "When Sabina told me about your deal I assumed it would be you. It wasn't and that's why it took us so long to find you."

"That's…" Karina searched vainly for the right word.

"Strange," Iris finished for her.

"Thank you."

Tyler sighed. "There's a lot to catch you up on."

21

Four hours passed before Karina could begin grilling Tyler on what she'd missed in the past year. After Jane and Jared left, Tyler wanted to give them plenty of time to clear out before he and Karina went back to the hotel. They spent the time having luncheon with Iris and Cecile, attempting to dispel the disquiet that remained in Jane's wake. Tyler helped Iris get settled temporarily in Cecile's second bedroom, making plans the next day to start looking for a permanent residence. After leaving the two older women to their reminiscence, Tyler took Karina back to the house she had shared with Drew as Anna. It came as no surprise to her that her supposed husband had taken the few items they had of value and skipped town. After glancing through what was left to make sure there was nothing that she wanted, Karina took what little there was of personal effects and bagged them up for the trash. The rest she left along with her set of keys for the real estate agent she called to list the property immediately. After leaving the house, Karina and Tyler made a quick shopping trip for necessities before finally returning to his hotel. Now she was wearing nothing but a black tank-top and brightly patterned boyshort underwear, lounging across one of the two beds with a glass of wine, watching Tyler pick the toppings off the last slice of pizza sent up from room service over an hour ago. They were well into their second bottle of wine, past all of the food and Karina couldn't remember feeling this comfortable with anyone ever. Even if she was nearly naked. While Tyler idly munched on the remains of the food, Karina allowed her eyes to slide down his body, starting at his head, traveling down his naked, well-muscled torso, lingering on his hipbones before lifting where his shorts bunched just above his knees. She couldn't keep her eyes from lingering just a little too long on the well-defined indentions at his hips that were just visible over the waistband of his shorts. She wasn't sure what they were called but watching him lounge near her feet, Karina thought it was possibly the most erotic sight she'd ever seen.

"Stop thinking so hard or I'll start blushing," Tyler murmured, never looking up from his pizza.

"Do you never get tired of that, hearing what people think all the time?" Karina took another sip of her wine and tried very hard to not look as self-conscious as she felt.

"I would if I knew what it was like to not hear what other people were thinking. Probably." He pushed up off his side and reached across her legs for the wineglass he had left on the bedside table. "You're worried. What are you worried about?"

"Can't you just see inside my head?" Karina teased, nudging his arm playfully with her foot.

Tyler caught her foot and pulled it into his lap along with the other one. "I could but I'd rather you tell me."

"I'm having a hard time with something," she admitted, gulping down more wine and hoping that it gave her more courage.

"With this?" He gestured to their shared room.

"No!" Karina laughed. "This feels normal. This," she gestured up and down her body with her free hand, "feels weird. I'm having a bit of a girly moment where I'm not sure if you like me in this body as well as you liked the other one."

Tyler fell over onto his back laughing. "I'm sorry! I know that was serious but if that's the thing you're worried about, we have a lot less problems to figure out than I thought. You think that it matters to me what body you're in? Does it matter to you what I look like?"

"Oh quit playing the humble card with me! You're wasting it." Karina half-heartedly tossed a bed pillow at his head. "You look hot and you know it. And you look the same no matter what lifetime it is. Your parents are gods, for Christ's sake! No, I don't particularly care, but yes, I am enjoying the view. However, while you aged one year, which is like a minute for you, I changed ethnicities and gained three cup sizes." She grimaced at her chest.

"You also grew an ass," Tyler commented smiling. "You're gorgeous. If you're happy in this body, then I want you exactly like this. You'll get used to seeing yourself in the mirror in a few days. The weirdness will pass when you let it." He sat up and began pulling her long dark auburn curls through his fingers. "I am glad that your hair tamed down a bit. It was pretty bright when Jane was riding the phoenix high."

"I've only noticed it turn bright red like that when the phoenix's powers are being used. Otherwise it seems to stay darker, though I have noticed a few changes, like the red and gold highlights."

"It suits you," he murmured before pulling back slightly. "If waking up in a different body freaks you out, just think about going to sleep as an old man and waking up as a child. That was always fun." His hand fell from her hair to touch the olive skin of her bare shoulder.

"You won't have to now. You're soul-mated to a true immortal. You won't die now." Karina leaned into his hand as it slid from her shoulder to his hand.

"Maybe, maybe not. But doesn't life lose some of its mystery if you know you'll live forever?"

Karina laughed. "You'll live forever technically regardless. You just have to decide if you're all right being Tyler Stateton forever." She picked up the room service platter and placed it on the nearby cart, turning back around to refill their wineglasses with the remainder of the bottle.

"I won't be Tyler forever. At some point he'll have to disappear from public view and I'll have to leave home for a while. I already look a little younger than my age. If this is where I'm stuck forever, just like this, then I won't be able to live in one place for every long."

"We'll have to master the art of creating a new identity." Karina settled back on the bed with her wine, sitting Indian-style near the foot of the bed while Tyler stretched out, his upper body reclining against the padded headboard. "I won't age anymore either. It's kind of sad."

He laughed, taking a swallow of his wine before returning the glass to the bedside table. "You're sad that you won't get sick or grow old and you probably won't die, at least not for a few thousand years."

"I don't think I've ever had the opportunity to be immortal before. I mean, it sounds great in theory, but in practice..." She shook her head negatively. "You're partially immortal but at least you know what it's like for a human to live. You know that you'll grow old.

You know what it's like to live and die alongside someone you love. I gave that up for the opportunity to live alongside the people I love but I'm frozen. There's not death, no aging, no nothing in my future but potentially living long enough to see everything I love die. I won't even be able to keep you. You'll die eventually too if being bound to Jane doesn't make you truly immortal." Karina reached across the space between them, entwining her fingers with his and examining how his hand looked against hers.

Tyler smiled, holding her hand more tightly. "I think you give your humanity too much credit. You forget that you're a phoenix. How many times will the people who love you watch you die, hoping that you'll come back, wondering which time will be the last before another phoenix takes your place? You're the first of your kind in almost a thousand years. You're rare, an endangered species. You're going to have to be more careful now than you were as a human." He slid closer to him, still maintaining his relaxed position and a space between them. "And you're wrong about a couple of things. First, I've never lived and died with anyone I loved other than my brother. And two," he ticked his points off on the fingers of his free hand, "I might not die. This life, this incarnation, this is my big adventure. Because I don't know. I don't know if I'll become immortal by association or if I'll live and die like I've always done. And then there's the third option where I don't have a life after this time. It's a little scary but at the same time it's a little exhilarating. This gives me the freedom to do what I want to do, anything that I want. And Jared can't make me feel guilty about it because he gets to live forever with the love of his life. Hell, when the world ends Jane, as the destroyer, will probably be the one tasked with making this plane of existence burn. I've never had that; I won't have that. There's never been anyone who would make the world burn for me."

"I can start setting things on fire, if that will make you feel better," Karina joked, laughing weakly to break the sudden tension in the room.

"I don't think that would help, but thanks for the thought." He smiled shyly.

"Can I ask you a personal question?"

"Do you really need to ask that?" Tyler laughed.

"Fine. How have you never been in love? Why don't you have any children?" Karina released his hand and shifted on the bed so that she could better look at him.

"I didn't say that I've never been in love." Tyler pushed further up on the pillows. "I have never had children. It's a part of our curse; we can't have children until we're mated."

"No offense, but that sounds awfully conservative for your people."

"It is. The thing is that our father is a direct descendent of the titans. He wanted to keep our bloodline pure, avoid the issues that come from creating half-bloods. So this way, any children that we do have must be the product of two gods because the curse isn't lifted until our mate has accepted his or her god-like powers."

"Which brings up another interesting question. What if one of you mated with another guy?"

"Do you really think that would be a problem?" Tyler raised an eyebrow in her direction. "Lack of a vagina hasn't ever stopped our people from reproducing in the past. I don't think it would be a problem now. As it is we're currently both straight, but we're not narrow-minded enough to think that's the only way to be or to have limited our previous romantic interests to one sex or another. You never know who you're meant to be with. Why limit your options of people to love?"

"I guess I just never thought of you that way."

"When I love one person, I'm with that person. When I'm not, I don't see the big deal in exploring yourself and your options."

"Tell me about when you were in love."

"Which time?" he teased.

"The best time. The time that you thought she might be the one that you can't live without."

Tyler lowered his eyes and examined a scar crossing his left palm as he weighed his words carefully, rubbing the spot as if he could concentrate and make it vanish from existence. "I've loved people, but I've also known when it was time to let them go, even if the decision was taken out of my hands. I've only ever offered my blood, my life, to one other person. And I was too late to save her." His eyes darted up to meet hers just for a second before he went back to examining his hand.

"I'm sorry that it didn't work, Tyler. In that last second I really wanted it to. I wasn't ready to die. But I had to, to save you. To save all of us one of us had to make that kind of sacrifice. I picked the only one that I could live with and that was me."

"Yeah, but did it ever occur to you in that year before that it might not be a sacrifice the rest of us could live with?"

"Why do you think I didn't tell anyone? I didn't want anyone to try to talk me out of it or to try and break some rule to get me out of it. I made my decision and I wanted to do it for my family. For the future that I might be able to have now that wasn't possible before. I did what I could to try to make it easier. I tried to keep my distance so it wouldn't be so hard on you when I was gone."

"I assumed as much. Just for the record, so you know, it didn't help."

"Are you so sure about that? I've watched you become more of yourself, your true self, these last few days than you ever were before. If things had been different, would you still be here with me and Iris or would you be in Los Angeles following Jared's lead? You've always been there for him, always doing what he wanted, what was best for everyone but you. Like you owed him something. You don't owe anyone else your life. So what do you really want right now? Fuck everyone else and their agendas. What do you really want for you?"

"I wanted you."

Karina reached across the room service tray and picked up a knife, slashing her left palm open. "Do you still?" She offered the knife and her bleeding hand to him. "If that's what you really want, it's yours. Come and take it."

He shook his head, refusing to look at her. "You don't mean that."

"Look in my eyes and tell me that I don't mean it." Karina moved closer and leveled her gaze to meet his. "Whatever you want, Tyler, stop worrying about what other people think, stop waiting for permission, stop thinking about the consequences and just take it. Right now, in this moment, you can do whatever you want. If you want my blood, you can have it. If you want immortality, I'll give it to you. If you want me, I'm right here and I wanted you a long time before you almost kissed me in that elevator. Anything that happens after right now is because you choose it. So what do you want?"

Tyler smiled and moved closer, grasping her bleeding hand and bringing it up to his mouth. He placed a kiss on her palm before taking his shirt from the side of the bed and wrapping the soft cotton around her wound. "I appreciate the offer and one day I may want to take you up on it. Right now I'm enjoying not knowing." He reached up and pushed one long curl back behind her ear. His hand slid to the back of her neck, tangling in her hair as he gently guided her mouth to his. Tyler's lips slid softly, hesitantly against hers. He pulled back far too soon, his eyes searching hers for a reaction.

Unconsciously, Karina's hand fell to his waist and pulled him closer. She smiled into his worried face. "Is that all you've got?" Karina slid her other hand up to wind into his short dark blonde hair, tugging his mouth back to hers. She sighed as she felt herself falling deeper into the kiss, some part of her surrendering to Tyler's caress. He pushed her back on to the bed, covering her body with his own and settling between her thighs.

Karina's frantic brain tried to slow, to process the nearly paralyzing tidal wave of emotions that she was feeling and think about the consequences if they took this a step further. She sighed as his tongue touched hers and quickly decided she didn't care, each moment that she spent in his arms feeling better than the last. Her eyes fluttered open for a second, enough to give him pause and make him pull back from her mouth. Karina didn't care that he heard the involuntary groan that escaped her, secretly hoping that it would give him encouragement to continue his exploration of her mouth.

"Do you want me to stop?" Tyler's voice was low, stretched taunt with desire, his lips hovering just far enough away that he was unreachable from her current position. Unable to even articulate an answer, Karina rose up to meet him, capturing his lips with her but keeping her eyes open so that he could see the naked hunger lingering there.

"I don't want you to hold back," she whispered against his neck before devouring his mouth as if she were starving, as if he was her only link to a cool oasis in a parched desert. His body crashed back into her, his lips mimicking what he would do to her without the hindrance of clothing between them.

Tyler smiled against her lips, pulling her closer and ripping the tank top from her body. "Now we're even."

"Oh we're not even close to even yet." Karina's hands slid down his back as she pulled him to her as she started to slowly burn the rest of their clothes away. "Hope you don't mind. I'm impatient."

"I like the way you think." Tyler's smile turned to a grin as he captured her full lips with his, his day old stubble scraping across her skin. Karina shuddered with pleasure as he slid into her, feeling all of her pent-up energy release as he touched her body in the way that she wanted him most. She fought to keep her eyes open as they moved together, every gasp and intake of heated breath pushing them both closer to the edge. "Look at me," Tyler commanded, one hand supporting his weight while the other guided her gaze back to his. "I want you to see me, I want you to know exactly what you do to me." Karina swallowed hard as she kept the intimate contact, felt her body contract around his. She fought the urge not to scream as the release she was seeking spiraled into her and she watched Tyler groan through his own release, burying his head in her neck as the pleasure caused him to grit his teeth and he fought the urge to bite her. Her fingernails dug into his lower back and she laughed in the aftermath of their passion, startling Tyler from his relaxed pose. "What's so funny?"

Karina smiled before she pulled his gorgeously full lips back to hers. "I just noticed what a truly sexy ass you have."

Tyler woke up the next morning and smiled when he saw the woman sleeping peacefully in his arms. He couldn't believe that for however brief a moment, the beautiful creature lying there was his. He leaned over and kissed her forehead, not wanting to wake her but enjoying that he was finally able to do such a simple thing. She stirred but refused to open her eyes.

"That's the best night's sleep that I've had in a very long time," Karina murmured, kissing his chest before finally opening her eyes to look up at him. "How do you feel?"

Tyler chuckled, sliding down further on the bed so that her head rested on his shoulder and her lips were within kissing distance. "Shouldn't I be asking you that?"

Karina bit her lower lip and shook her head. "Absolutely not. You've given me a life. For that I am eternally grateful."

"Have you thought about what you want to do with that life yet?"

She smiled and nodded enthusiastically. "I want to spend as much of it as I can right here."

He pulled her cut hand onto his chest and carefully unwound the makeshift bandage his shirt had created. An ugly mark still showed but it was far more healed than it would have been were she still a human. "Do you still want to be bound?"

"Do you?"

"Not really. At least not yet. I want to just enjoy this, live our lives, without knowing what happens next. It's kind of nice actually. And it means that I'll never take holding you in my arms for granted again. My biggest regret is not staying with you that night, not seeing where things would have gone if I hadn't been so worried about everything else that had nothing to do with who you and I are to each other."

"And who is that?"

"I don't know. But I intend to have one helluva good time finding out." Tyler grinned and pulled her deeper into his embrace.

When they finally came up for air, Karina laughed, pushing away from him playfully. "You know, we still have to meet your mother in a few hours and I'm pretty sure that she won't appreciate finding us naked."

Tyler sighed, allowing her to pull away and feeling cold the instant that her warm body slid from the bed. "Do you think that we should try to take her back to Los Angeles?"

"Do you even want to go back to Los Angeles?" Karina's words barely registered in his passion dazed mind as he watched her sashay to the bathroom.

"At this particular moment, no. But it is a reality that we'll eventually have to deal with." He unwrapped his legs from the tangled sheets and followed her into the adjoining room.

"I think we should honor her wish to stay here with Cecile. I want to make sure that she has a house, that's she's comfortable, that she has everything she needs before we leave."

Karina laughed as he entered the room and his hungry gaze watched as she bent over the bathtub to turn on the water for a shower. "Wow you're easy."

"You have no idea." His arms wrapped around her from behind, pulling her back against his body so that she could feel just how happy he was to have woken up beside her.

"Back to the subject at hand," she pushed him away and stepped under the warm spray, "to make her comfortable we really just need to find out what she wants and get a metal detector."

"A metal detector?" the words were garbled around the toothbrush hanging from Tyler's mouth. "Why?"

"Apparently she has a literal pot of gold buried in Cecile's backyard. We just have to help her find it."

"Seriously?"

Karina laughed at his expression, jerking the shower curtain closed and obscuring his view of her naked body in the mirror. "Get dressed and we'll go find out."

22

"I can't believe it's already been two weeks," Karina groaned as she directed her new car up the familiar off ramp to the main road that led to her former, and she assumed new, home.

"It's been two weeks and three days," Tyler corrected her, barely looking up from the message he was replying to on his cellphone. "We were lazy. Jared's been asking me when we were coming back for a week. If I didn't know any better, I'd say he missed me."

Karina's eyes cut over to where he was sitting in the passenger seat for a brief moment before returning to the road ahead of her as she guided the car on to the main road. "You know that he missed you. I love you but the two of you are so co-dependent I can barely believe that you've been apart this long." She rolled her hazel eyes hidden behind a borrowed pair of Tyler's sunglasses in deference to the blinding southern California sun.

"We've been a part for longer." Tyler glanced up. "I guess I should text him so that he knows we're coming since Jane's got the shields between us in full effect."

"That really bugs you, doesn't it?"

"It is what it is. I'm assuming that she doesn't want to see us having sex almost as much as I don't want to see her and Jared. Though I may never get used to hearing you say you love me." His grin was contagious and Karina felt its effects long before she knew that a similar smile had already blossomed on her face. "It's still fun to say it and know that you feel the same way."

"I love you. There, I said it."

Karina couldn't help the laughter that tumbled from her lips. "I already knew it."

"Yeah, but it took me a long time to realize that it was true and a lot longer to be able to admit it to myself, little less say it out loud. Just let me enjoy the moment, okay?"

Karina continued to giggle. "So how are we going to work this when we get back? Are we together, are we sleeping in the same room, what are we going to tell Jared and Jane?"

"Are you asking enough questions?" Tyler teased, interrupting her. "How about we see how it goes? I don't feel like we really owe them any explanations. We're figuring things out, seeing how it goes. Would you be more comfortable in your own room or with me?"

"Are you really going to leave me alone?"

"After last time, not a chance in hell unless you don't want me there. I was just thinking that if you want your own space, or the option to go to it, I'll only argue with you a little bit. Then I'll just make you give me a drawer so that I don't have to do a walk of shame every morning across the house."

"Oh, I might enjoy watching that. Sexy naked man slightly embarrassed walking across the living room every morning? I could get used to that," she teased, glancing over to see his expression as she turned off onto the private road that led to the house.

"Haha, very funny," he commented as they wound further up the mountain. They drove in silence for several minutes before Tyler finally broke the comfortable silence in a way that he deeply wished wasn't going to be as awkward as he felt that it was going to be. There were things that he had been hiding from Karina, things that he thought might spoil their limited amount of private time together. He watched her out of the corner of his eye, delighting in her obvious happiness and worried that the words that were going to come out of his mouth next would ruin it, even momentarily. Two nights after they had first spent the night together he had a vision, one that was too terrifying to be a dream and too real for him to not think that it was borne of Jane's power of foresight transferring over to him. He'd pushed it to the back of his mind but now that they were almost home, there was no way that he could hide what he'd seen from her any longer. She had to know and he had to man up and tell her before they reached the house and his brother's prying ears.

"Karina." Tyler put a hand on her arm, neither of them sure if it was for caution or for comfort. "There are some things you need to know before we get to the house."

"Okay." Startled by the sudden seriousness in his tone, Karina pulled the car into the overlook, parking in full view of the valley between mountains leading to the bright blue waters of the Pacific in the distance, the water a hazy gray blue under the bright cloudless sky. Rather than concentrating on the breathtaking view, Karina turned sideways in the driver's seat to meet Tyler's gaze. "I figured there was something you weren't telling me."

He took one of her hands in both of his, staring down as their fingers wrapped around each other's. Tyler thought about how perfect the last few days had been, away from everything and everyone that caused their lives to be a little more than ordinary. Being ordinary for a little while had been nice, peaceful and he felt guilty in these last few moments together that he was potentially going to ruin it for both of them. Tyler took a deep breath. The bubble they'd placed themselves in had to pop sometime, he reasoned. He just didn't want to be the person to do it, he realized with a start. "You already know that Jane's becoming the destroyer and she doesn't really have a handle on it yet. She's going to have to be brought to Olympus soon for training. Danalia will help her in the beginning but there's only so much that she can do before she risks crossing our father or grandfather, something that she would never do, not even for us. I think that despite whatever differences we may have between us and Jared and Jane and whatever our relationship to each other may be, these things coming will trump all of that and I don't want you to feel blindsided or that I ever kept anything from you. It's very important to me that you know that there are no secrets between us. You were always my friend first and you know the good, the bad and everything in between that I'd rather forget. I'd like to feel like I know the same about you and that whatever we are, we're good with finding out together and not putting a label on it until we're sure about where it's going."

Karina shut off the engine and turned sideways in the driver's seat to stare openly at him. "That's what we agreed on and you pretty much know everything about me so I'm not sure where you're going with this. What are you not telling me, Tyler?"

Tyler took a deep breath to steady his nerves and turned so that he could meet her hazel gaze head-on. "There's a war coming and I don't know what our part in it will be. I don't know that we'll all survive it."

"Since when are you psychic? You can't know what's coming. The future isn't decided; it's predicated by the choices we make now and days, weeks, years from now. It changes all the time."

"Not always," he shook his head sadly. "Sometimes it just is."

"How do you know this?" She reached across the center console and gripped his chin, forcing him to meet her eyes. "Did this come from your father or one of the oracles?"

Tyler shook his head negatively. "I saw it."

"How?" Karina demanded, refusing to back down or let him go.

"Jane's foresight."

"Jane's foresight has always been subjective and extremely limited. It can't be directed and it can't be used to see anything further than about five minutes into the future. And she hasn't been able to use it since she became an elemental when she met Jared. That was years ago. How could you possibly get anything from it now?"

"When your deal with Sabina misfired and caused us to be soul-mates, some of her powers came to me. I'm sure she got a replica of some of mine. Her foresight is a lot more powerful inside of me than it was in her. I can direct it. I can see things years from now. And I see all of the possibilities, not just one. If there's a common thread between them, that thing more than likely won't change no matter what decisions are made. It just may take longer to get there. Some things never change."

"I don't doubt you, but you said it may happen. That leaves the probability that nothing will happen. The future hasn't happened yet so it can change."

"In the futures I saw our family defied the gods and they force Jane to destroy the world. We don't all survive."

"Easy solution. We don't defy the gods. Simple, easy, done." Karina squeezed his hand. "You have nothing to worry about."

Tyler shook his head negatively, refusing to meet her eyes. "To do that you're asking for something none of us will agree to part with."

"It can't be worse than all of us dying and destroying the world in the process. If there is no world there's nowhere for us to exist as immortals anyway. Anyone who lives will die anyway."

Tyler laughed. "The way you see things is so linear. The destruction of this world is inevitable but it's already been destroyed, reborn and everything else you can imagine. This reality, it's only one. There are so many more, so many different planes of existence. They blink in and out of being every day and most people never notice. There are a thousand different incarnations of you. Every choice that every person makes has the potential to create an entirely new state of being. Occasionally one plane may be dependent on another, sometimes they blink out of existence when someone dies or they collide when a person makes a similar decision that causes two different realities to meld. In some planes we may be human, we may not know each other, you may not know Jane or Jane may not exist. What would happen to us if just this world, just this one plane died? We could go live in a different one, have different lives. Maybe have the same life. What I'm talking about, this war, it would destroy everything. Not just this plane, not just this version of the world, not just this world. The whole thing would go up in flames. And without anyone to create a new plane, the only one that would exist, if any survived, would be Olympus and only because I'm not sure that Jane can wipe out what's left of it."

"They Olympians are not the only gods out there. Nor do I for a second believe that they're the most powerful. If I did, I would also have to believe that we're potentially some of the most powerful beings on earth and I don't. Not when we can still be hurt, still be hunted, still die. This war does not have to happen. And even if it does, it doesn't have to involve us." Karina leaned across the center console and kissed him, attempting to banish the dark thoughts from his mind. "We just got our lives back. Don't waste it by worrying about what might happen." Karina's hands slid inside of his shirt, plucking the buttons on the black dress shirt open to expose his bare chest. She pulled him closer to her to place her mouth against the hollow just under his ear. She balanced on one hand, using the other to reach up and massage down the other side of his neck, her teeth nipping his skin in time with every stroke of her thumb.

"Kari, this is serious," Tyler breathed, pulling her closer instead of pushing her away.

"So's everything. So what? There's no ticking clock forcing us to get back any time soon. We're on a private road, we've got a gorgeous view." She slid across the arm rest to straddle his lap, reaching down the side of the seat to let the backrest down. "And I don't believe we've christened this car yet." She smiled, looping her arms around his neck. "You game?"

Tyler smiled, crushing her lips to his and grinding her hips down against his, feeling some of the dark cloud dissipating at her touch. He slid his tongue into her open mouth, briefly tangling with hers before angling up to draw tight little circles on the roof of her mouth. He felt her hands between their upper bodies, confidently unbuttoning the rest of his shirt. He grabbed her hands and groaned in pain as he gently pushed her back. "I have to finish telling you about this before we go back. I don't want Jane or Jared to hear, not yet."

Karina shoved their joined hands into the seat above his head and claimed his mouth, her tongue thrusting in between his lips and licking its way back to the border of their joined open mouths. She could taste his arousal and met his groan with a more insistent kiss, refusing to hide her need for him. She dragged her lips from his to kiss a path across his jawline to his ear. "What could we possibly do that would cause the collapse of every plane of existence?" Her hand slid down between them to unbutton his jeans and caress his freed erection, making his body arch into her touch and his eyes flutter closed at the surge of arousal. "Tell me whatever it is quickly because I fully intend to take advantage of the fact that I'm wearing a skirt and you're going commando," she whispered, her lips against his ear and her quick breath a warm caress on his cheek.

"Jane's baby. She gets pregnant and the Olympians will want her to turn the baby over to them." Tyler captured her mouth with his, ending the rushed explanation.

Karina pulled back to lean against the dashboard, her skirt pulled up so that she could straddle his legs. She smiled at the obvious pleasure on his face as she continued to stroke him, gently massaging his balls before working her hand up his long, thick shaft to circle the tip with her thumb and slide back down. "Do you know what a contradiction it is for a destroyer to give birth? I don't think we have anything to worry about right now."

"You're probably right. She's not even fully immortal yet," Tyler gasped out, his green eyes rolling back and his hands gripping the sides of the seat to fight the urge to thrust his hips up into her hands. "I can't think while you're doing that."

"I don't want you thinking. I want you to know how much I enjoy touching you." Karina smiled as she watched his eyes drift closed for a moment. Tyler felt his flesh quiver in her hands and he fought to keep from surging and exploding all over the car. "You have no idea how much I get off from touching you like this."

He smiled, his eyes opening lazily as his hand snaked up her thigh and brushed his fingers across her lace panties. "Oh really? Let's see just how much you enjoy it."

Karina felt her knees open wider to give him better access, allowing a moan to escape her throat as his fingers pushed her underwear out of the way, barely brushing against the place she craved his touch most. He slid two fingers inside of her and smiled when she moved against his hand. "Hhhmm, so you really do like it when I do this. How about this?" His thumb moved up to circle other swollen, sensitive places while his eyes watched her knowingly. Her hands unconsciously moved away from him to grip his jean-clad thighs, her body moving against his hand trying to take his fingers deeper inside of her. Tyler found that spot inside of her he knew would make her scream and feathered his fingers against it, enjoying watching her hips quicken their pace and her eyes close in ecstasy. "Keep going, baby," he murmured, thrusting his fingers inside of her harder. Karina moaned, feeling herself falling over the edge and everything shatter into sharp, shiny pieces before she slumped against Tyler's chest, attempting to force her ragged breathing back under control and failing as she inhaled the sharp scent trailing off of his overheated skin. She took another ragged breath and smiled against his neck. "Your turn."

Tyler drove the car into the driveway, parking behind Jane's Mustang. He shut off the engine, glancing sideways at Karina as she finished reapplying her lip gloss and fluffing up her dark loose curls. He watched the sunlight glint over the bright fire red and burnished gold strands that wove through the natural dark chocolate and bronze of her hair. He tucked a wayward lock behind her ear and smiled. "Are you ready?"

She glanced over at him and grinned. "No, I want to drag you into the backseat and repeat the last ninety minutes until one of us breaks. I just happen to know that when we're finally allowed to get to it, there's a bed in a soundproofed room waiting on us."

"And a fur rug and a sofa and a fireplace and a very large soaking bathtub." Tyler leaned over and kissed her, his hand sliding down from cradling her face to sliding between her breasts before stopping to grip her hip as his tongue tangled with hers.

Karina moaned into his mouth, pulling his mouth tighter against hers for a brief moment before letting him go and opening her car door. "I say that we say our hellos quickly and move on to the bedroom."

Tyler smiled as she stood, straightening her full burgundy skirt and white tank top. He got out of the car, walking around to the back of the car to retrieve their suitcases before meeting her at the passenger side. "I like this plan." He extended his free hand to her, waiting expectantly.

Karina hesitated only for a moment, reaching out to twine her fingers with his and pull him towards the front door. "You know that they know what we were doing." She pulled him to her, trapping her own body between him and the front door of the house. Her hands came up to caress his face, her fingers sliding from his eyebrows down to his nose and then lips before settling on his shoulders as she rose up on her toes to kiss him passionately. Tyler's free hand wrapped around Karina's waist, pulling her tighter against him. She pulled away far too soon for his liking, giggling as he reached behind her to open the door. They fell through the open doorway together, laughing, until Tyler glanced into the living room. He sobered up quickly, dropping their bags in the entryway and pushing Karina behind him.

"What are you doing?" She fought to see over his shoulder.

"What the hell is going on?" Tyler ground out, taking in his brother's grim expression and Jane's blanched face. They both sat stiffly in their chairs opposite Danalia who was lounging comfortably on the sofa. She languidly drew to her feet, smiling and clapping her hands together happily at their arrival. "Finally! I'm so glad you've arrived. You know how I hate languishing in the mortal realm."

Karina peeked around Tyler's shoulder. "Who is that and why am I standing behind you?"

"That's my half-sister Danalia. She's the one who made you her pet phoenix science project."

Karina slipped around Tyler and down the two shallow stairs into the living room. "I didn't know what you look like, I just knew the name. You did this to me?"

Danalia smiled, holding out her arms in warm welcome as they approached each other. "My beautiful little firebird. You came out so much better than I could have ever hoped. I had almost lost hope for you until Anyasis and Jane came to me to ask for you to be brought into your full powers. What a delight it was to learn that you were already well on your way to achieving them yourself before the time of the deadline approached." She reached out and wrapped one of the other woman's long locks of hair around her hand, leaving a few blossoming dark purple star shaped flowers behind when she withdrew. "You are one of my finest creations, Anna Molly. I'm so glad you survived."

"My name is Karina." She batted away the other woman's hands, knocking the flowers out of her hair. "And I survived no thanks to you. You could've at least left me with a memory of something to warn me that I could combust at any moment," Karina grumped. "Why are you here?"

"I came to see you, of course."

"You've seen me. Now please leave. You're making my family uncomfortable."

"Though this is my family, I came here for you. For you and your mate," Danalia shrugged nonchalantly meeting Tyler's green eyes. He shifted his gaze to Jared's, reaching through his connections to Jane and his brother to try and discern what was going on. All of his mental probing met a virtual brick wall. They were shielding against him like crazy and he didn't know why. Danalia noticed his curiosity and dismissed it with a wave of her hand. "I asked them to shut you out. I don't want them to ruin my surprise."

"Surprise?" Tyler echoed hollowly, silently begging one of them to clue him in before Danalia got around to making her big reveal. Jared glanced at Danalia, then to Karina before returning to hold his brother's look as he allowed his shields to slip ever so slightly. Tyler gasped when he saw his sister's true intentions, fighting the urge to grip his chest over his heart at the sudden pain. His panicked gaze slipped quickly to Karina before going to Jane's, allowing the calm she was forcing upon herself to slip over them.

"Danalia, allow them through the door. They've been away for a while and I would like to greet my brother properly. I'm sure my wife would like to greet her sister as well." Jared approached them cautiously.

Danalia stepped aside immediately. "Of course! Greet your family. I can wait a few days but we will have to leave soon." With that Danalia disappeared, leaving them to their own devices momentarily.

Karina took a deep breath, stepping further into the room and hugging Jane who stood and rushed over to her. "What the hell was that all about?"

Jane hugged her sister, allowing the tears she'd been holding back to slip from her eyes. "I love you and I'm so glad you're home. But you have to run."

"Run? Why? What the hell, Jane?"

Tyler grabbed Karina, pulling her protectively to his side. "Don't worry about it," he murmured into her hair. "We'll figure out a way to fix this."

Jared shook his head negatively. "We'll try to find a way to fix this but in the meantime Jane's right. The two of you have got to get out of here. Move quickly and change places a lot. It won't last forever but it'll buy us some time."

Karina spun around to face Tyler. "What are they talking about? Why do we have to go anywhere?"

"I was wrong. I'm so sorry. Danalia is here to take us to Olympus. She thinks we're mated."

"Why the hell would she think that?" Karina demanded, crossing her arms over her chest and stepping back beside Jane.

Jared took a step toward Karina, reaching out to gingerly touch her flat stomach. "I'm sorry to be intrusive but I need to see if Danalia is right…" he allowed his voice to trail off as he touched her.

"Oh, God." Karina felt her heart sink as she glanced back at Tyler.

Jane hugged her. "It'll be okay."

"But we're not…I mean, we can't…" Karina sank to the floor, her head in her hands. "It's not possible. You have to be mated before that's even a consideration. I'm not a goddess. It's not possible."

"We're magnets for the impossible, Kari." Tyler sat down beside her, wrapping an arm around her shoulders. "We'll figure this out."

"Are we…?" her voice trailed off, the fear overriding her ability to speak. Tyler looked to Jared for confirmation before nodding affirmatively. "Did you look? Did it change? What do they want from us?" Karina whispered frantically, her hands wrapping around her stomach to protect herself from whatever was coming.

"They think we're mated."

"But we're not!" she exclaimed, her hands flailing. "We're just having a good time. This wasn't supposed to happen."

"Kari." Jane knelt in front of her. "That's why we want you to run, so that they can't try to take your choice away from you."

"Fuck choice!" Karina pushed her sister away and stood, turning to Tyler. "What do they want from us because if they just want to bind us together I've got no problem with that regardless of how things turn out between us. If that's what they want, someone give me a knife. I'll do it now. If it's something else, I want you to say it." Karina felt her whole body trembling as she faced Tyler. "I need you to say it if it's something else. I have to hear it from you because otherwise I won't believe it. I can't."

"Kari, a binding may not help. They want us, but they also want –" Tyler gulped, unable to finish his sentence.

"You have to say it or it's not real," she repeated in a panic. "Tell me that it's not our child that starts the war that ends the world." Karina couldn't wrap her head around being a mother, little less being saddled with the kind of responsibility that could result in the apocalypse. Her frantic gaze sought out Tyler, appreciating the view while still not sure how she felt about having a child with a man she'd just started getting to know on an intimate level.

Tyler met her gaze determinedly, trying to push some of his strength into her. "They're not forcing us into anything. We're not mating if we don't want to, we're not going anywhere and they're not taking anything that we're not willing to part with. Danalia!" he called loudly, looking up to the ceiling. "Get back here!"

Danalia appeared in front of him. "Are you ready?"

"No. We're not leaving with you. We're not mated. We're not going to be." Tyler took Karina's hand in his. "That means that if you're right and if Karina does have a child then it belongs to this life and this world, not yours. She's not my mate, she's not a goddess and I don't know how we could possibly have created a child without fixing all of that."

"Sex usually works," Danalia replied, examining her manicure.

"No shit. What I'm saying is that the terms of our immortality don't allow us to have children without being mated. I'm pretty sure Karina and I would remember if that had happened."

Danalia sighed. "Do you really think it matters how it happened? Someone working for Apollo could've put an aphrodisiac in your food for all it matters. What matters is that she is pregnant, she will have this baby, you're the father and our family wants it. They're owed it. A life for a life." She glanced over at Jane. "You have to abide by the terms of the agreement. Your child will be a god and must be raised on Olympus. I don't want to do this but you have to come with me. They could've sent someone else but I begged to be allowed to retrieve you myself. Anyone else would have been cruel and we're still family. Karina will survive life on Olympus, you have my word." She paused, fully taking in the fear on both of their faces. "This is not a death sentence. This is good. It is a blessing. You're having a child and it will be a beautiful, wondrous thing. You do not have to fear what comes next. You're giving them what they want, what they've always wanted from you. Traegar, this is what you and Anyasis were created for, to be the perfect children, to mate and continue our line. You're both mated. There is the potential for children from both of you now. The strongest elements of our line will survive in your children. Traegar, your mate, or girlfriend or whatever the two of you want to call yourselves, is a true immortal. Combined with your immortality your child will be strong and protected. It will be raised with full knowledge of who he is in our world and how that

303

relates to the other worlds that you love so much. And it will be loved by your family. Can't that be enough for you?"

"I didn't make the deal. It's not mine to fulfill." Tyler shook his head in denial and gripped Karina's hand almost painfully.

"It doesn't matter. Read the fine print. You know that all deals made with our kind are subject to interpretation. How do you think I was able to make a phoenix out of Karina?"

"I'm okay with it. It's worked out well for me," Karina croaked out in a hollow tone. "I can even forgive the amnesia and the stint in the mental ward. Am I really pregnant?"

"I have no doubt. I am a creator. I know how these things work. I make these things work." At Karina's stunned expression, she waved her hands as if willing away the other woman's worry. "Don't worry, I didn't do this to you. As far as I can tell this was done the old fashioned way and trust me, I had nothing to do with that. Congratulations to the two of you though. I can smell you all over each other. It's kind of nauseating." She wrinkled her delicate nose in disgust.

Tyler shook his head. "I can't let you take her, Danalia, even if I can come with her. I can't give her to them and they can't have my child. That was not my agreement."

Danalia's beautiful face turned furious. "You do understand what you're doing if you refuse their summons and stay here. If that child is a god, it's royalty. And then it does belong to Olympus, not to a group of humans who imagine themselves above our laws. You have until the child is born, perhaps until it is of age, but they will come. And they will take the child from you if you force their hand. You're not mortal anymore, Traegar. You and your family, you're like us now. You can't go back, no matter if it was your choice or not. That child will be born and it won't be human. Your only variable is how much time you might can force from their hands before they bring the fires of hell down on you to claim what is theirs. You know this. Traegar, please, come with me now, while it's still a choice."

"My name is Tyler and you can tell them that they can't have my and Karina's child."

Danalia took a deep breath and crossed the floor to stand in front of her brother, her silk gown almost soundless as it slid across the floor in her wake. "Traegar, please tell me that you know what you're doing. You can see the future now so you know what can happen."

"I know that the future's not set. We can still make our own choices." He met her pleading eyes with a determined stare of his own. "They can't have my child. They can't have my brother's. If they want a god child so badly, you're full-blooded. Give them one."

"Do not mistake my empathy for kindness, Traegar. I've taken a great risk to come here to you rather than sending someone else. If you have no care for me, appreciate my sacrifice and the situation that you've put us all in. I didn't ask for this anymore than you did but you know that our kind must continue and your child is a way to do that. They won't give up, they won't stop hunting you and they will take what is theirs. Resign yourself to it or watch the vision you saw play out and your mate die!" Danalia shouted, her hands balled into fists at her side.

Jared stepped up and laid a hand on his sister's arm. "You know that we're different from them. You won't win any battles for them today," he said gently.

She laid a hand over his, dipping her eyes down to keep them from seeing the fear held there. "Keep them safe, Anyasis. He knows what's coming if things don't go your way in this. I can't take sides but I'll help you in any way that I can. You're my brothers and my family." Danalia stepped back to allow her gaze to encompass the other two women as well. "You may not all be bound but you're tied so that makes you my family too. I will be in touch when I know something.

Keep me informed of the child's progress. You have nothing to fear from me unless my hand is forced." Danalia turned to Karina. "I will not come for you again. If someone else does, your sister is correct. You will need to run and searching this world will not take them long. If you lose your temper, if you use your phoenix powers, you may kill the child. Please nod that you understand what I'm telling you." Karina nodded obediently. "Good, child. Make sure that you know what you've done here today and that you're willing to live with what happens going forward." Danalia stepped back and vanished.

Jane broke the silence that followed hesitantly. "Are you okay?"

Karina nodded in response and turned to Tyler, slowly finding her voice. "What did we just do?"

"Potentially, we just declared war on Olympus."

ABOUT THE AUTHOR

Author, music lover, avid film watcher, and devourer of literature Arianna Swain lives under her own personal rock in the Hollywood Hills. When not writing, rock climbing, gallivanting across the planet, or doing all three at once, she can most likely be found baking under the careful supervision of Angeles, the vampire kitty.

BOOKS ALSO BY THIS AUTHOR:

THE LIVING SHARDS: BOOK 1 IN THE CHILDREN OF APOLLO TRIOLOGY

www.ingramcontent.com/pod-product-compliance
Lightning Source LLC
Chambersburg PA
CBHW070650180626

46817CB00006B/2305